THE HUNTER

THE REALM #2

EVE LANGLAIS

Copyright © 2010, Eve Langlais,

2nd Edition Released 2016

Cover Art by RazzDazz Design ©2016

Produced in Canada

Published by Eve Langlais

http://www.EveLanglais.com

ALL RIGHTS RESERVED

This book is a work of fiction and the characters, events and dialogue found within the story are of the author's imagination and are not to be construed as real. Any resemblance to actual events or persons, either living or deceased, is completely coincidental.

No part of this book may be reproduced or shared in any form or by any means, electronic or mechanical, including but not limited to digital copying, file sharing, audio recording, email and printing without permission in writing from the author.

eBook ISBN: 978-1-988328-06-5

Print ISBN: 978-1530855643

Ingram ISBN: 978 177 384 0529

PROLOGUE

When he strode into the nursery and found it empty, a loud screech of rage burst from him. A primal, venomous sound that shook the plaster and would have made the one who'd angered him wet her pants in fright...if she were here.

The screamer, in the grip of a full-blown tantrum, grabbed the nearby rocking chair and swung it hard against the wall, splintering it into matchsticks.

Not enough.

He tore the soft, white bedding from the crib and ripped it to tatters. But his rage bubbled like a volcanic inferno requiring ever more fuel. He kicked the wall, right through a hand-painted bunny, the momentary pain ignored by his adrenaline-soaked body. He ripped down the mobile hanging on the crib and flung it to crash into the wall, its fluffy little sheep lying in a tangled heap of string and broken plastic. A yellow moon lamp sailed across the room and broke through the window, the sound of tinkling glass raining down on the street below and finally waking him from his destructive tantrum.

It wouldn't do for the authorities to arrive. He didn't have time for their stupid questions, not if he was going to catch them.

Breathing deeply through his nose, he shoved his rage deep down inside, stored for use later when he found what had been taken. He paced the wrecked nursery, the cogs of his cold mind starting to turn.

How dare she leave me! How dare she take my son! To think he'd thought her cowed enough. Never would he have imagined she'd have the nerve to dare to go against him like this. To actually plan her escape behind his back and succeed. That bitter fact made his rage try to rise again, and he tamped it down with promises. When he caught her, for he would find her. *That stupid cow isn't smart enough to escape me forever.* She would regret ever defying him. He'd let her meet the force of his fury, let it sate itself on her fear and pleadings. The thought of her on her knees begging made him smile, a sweet appetizer to tide him over till he made it reality.

But how to find her? He doubted she'd left a forwarding address. Ah, but she would have filled out paperwork when she enrolled. The university office would have an address, a contact in case of emergencies. The cow had a mother back East. Perhaps she'd fled there with the boy.

She would never be able to flee far enough, though. He smoothed his dark hair back and smiled coldly. No, never far enough. He would search the ends of the earth to find his son, his heir. And when he found his son and his cow of a mother, well, he'd finally do the nasty, evil things he'd been dreaming of doing to her. Maybe then would the hunger of his wrath, that living creature inside him, be satisfied.

CHAPTER 1

Three years later...
    As his calf cramped for the third time that night, he wondered, *What, by all the higher powers, am I doing here?* This was, to put it bluntly, degrading. *I am the Hunter—renowned killer, stealthy stalker, and mysterious spy.* Men respected and feared him. His foes trembled at his name, and the ladies... Let's just say the ladies *loved* him. Yet here he crouched, in the dark hour after midnight, hiding behind a rank Dumpster in an alley bordering some burger place. Definitely not something they'd be writing ballads about back home.

And what was the mightiest of hunters using his carefully honed skills for? *Sigh.* Pixies. Yes, his latest mission involved the capture of one of the pesky little critters that had escaped through the thinning boundary separating the magical Realm from the rest of the world. Talk about a waste of his skills. He, who'd fought an ogre barehanded and won, the man who had taken on assassins and beasts of legend, reduced to hunting cute faerie creatures.

When he'd accepted the assignment to work undercover from his feared commander on the other side of the boundary, he'd mistakenly thought he'd be seeing a lot more action. After all, the briefing he'd received had made him believe that he would be saving the Realm from being discovered and seeing their way of life destroyed.

"The boundary is getting thin in spots, and we've had incursions into the Other Side. Completely unacceptable. We cannot afford to be discovered!" barked his commander as he paced his stark office. "The mundanes would never understand. We need someone on the other side. Someone with your skills to hunt down these trespassers and take care of them."

The hunter's shoulders had straightened, and his already lean stomach sucked in. Excitement had filled him at the thought of a mission on the Other Side. His buddies would have, and had, killed for this mission. He'd just done it better.

"This task we are setting before you will be difficult and require the utmost discretion. You will need to blend in with the mundanes around you so begin studying at once that you may blend in without notice. We've located a home for you near the agency offices that guard the portal. You will be given a mundane identity and job. You have one week to prepare." His commander leaned forward on his scarred wooden desk and narrowed his eyes. "The Realm is counting on you, son. Your acceptance is assumed. Dismissed." With a sharp salute, the hunter whirled about and marched out, shoulders straight, the huge smile on his face unseen by his commander.

Back in the barracks, his comrades had whacked him overly hard in congratulations when they found out. He'd strutted around, the envy of all, and as he prepared to move into the Other Side, he'd harbored grandiose visions of his new life. Sadly, while the Other Side had proven to be wonderful with things as incomprehensible as magic itself—like cars, computers, and action movies—the job, unfortunately, had not turned out to be the heroic quest he'd thought it would be.

Take where he hid now. For four nights in a row, he'd been staking out this stinking Dumpster, all because the agency had received reports of a little creature with wings in the area. He, the top of his class, reduced to faerie catcher. He even had a—*sigh*—net.

Hold on a second, though. It seemed his stakeout was finally going to pay off. He heard a faint whirring sound that increased in volume as something approached and came into view. A tiny, winged figure flitted through the air. Pulling his facehood down to hide his face in the shadow of his hood, the hunter watched with predatory eyes, the professional in him taking over, as his prey hovered over the open Dumpster. With a quick look around and blonde curls jiggling, the little mite dove into the giant trashcan for a snack.

Time to earn his keep.

He stood up silently, and the hunter glided forward to peer over the edge of the bin. His prey, oblivious to his presence, nibbled on a discarded French fry with great gusto. With a swoop, the net came down, the low whistle of its flight not enough warning. With a scoop and a flick, he trapped the pixie within its silken threads. The little creature went into panic mode, its little body thrashing and twisting inside the net, its squeaky words coming so fast they were incomprehensible. "Enough!" snapped the hunter, almost immediately feeling contrite. He'd have fought, too, if someone had trapped him like a bug.

The pixie settled down and peered up at him with big, jewel-like eyes, the reproach in them making the hunter uncomfortable.

"Don't look at me like that. You know you're not allowed to cross the border." The pixie's eyes glistened. The hunter felt guilt poking him hard. After all, he happened to love greasy fries and burgers too, and he could understand the temptation.

"Don't do that," he said, sighing. *Why do I feel like such a bully?*

Squashing his guilt, he reminded himself of the job at hand. "You know you've got to go back." Pulling out a small jar with holes in the lid, he lifted the net up and showed it to the pixie. "I don't suppose you'll just get in here, will you?"

The pixie shook its head and crossed toothpick arms over a tiny chest. Wouldn't his comrades be laughing at him now to see him reduced to begging a stupid pixie, which he could squish with two fingers, to obey?

"Tell you what, if you get in the jar nicely for me, I'll buy a bacon cheeseburger and a large fry for you to take back home with you."

The pixie tilted its head for a moment, considering

the offer, then solemnly nodded. The hunter almost chuckled at its response. After all, it didn't really have much choice, but at least the little mite wouldn't go back empty-handed.

Kneeling down on the dirty asphalt of the alley, the hunter set the jar on the ground and popped off the lid. Laying the net beside it, his large, yet nimble fingers spread the net open, taking great care not to snag or tear the pixie's wings. The pixie stood up, and with a hard look at the hunter, sniffed before turning and fluttering into the jar. The hunter popped the cap with the air holes on and tucked it in his pocket, making sure the lid stuck out a bit for ventilation. So considerate of him. Not really, but his little sister thought pixies were cute, and she'd kill him if she ever found out he'd abused one. He might be tough, but his sister played dirty. He still had a scar from the time she'd found out he'd stuck frogs in her bed. And besides, while he'd never, ever, not even under the pain of torture, admit it, he kind of liked pixies too.

He folded up the net and slid it into an inside pocket, one of many—had he mentioned his leather duster had been custom designed for today's modern hunter? Totally badass, as they liked to say out here on the Other Side. A term he still didn't quite understand but had adopted after seeing it in many action-type movies.

Now to find a burger place still open for business so he could keep his promise to the pixie and pick up something for himself as well before his growling stomach got any louder.

Several hours later, having deposited the pixie and a double bacon cheeseburger, two large fries, and an onion ring at the agency's office for transport back to the Realm, he made his way home, balancing a bag of burgers for himself–double patties of course–and an icy milkshake. Not an easy feat considering he rode a Harley while doing it.

But he made it home fine. He'd always had incredible balance. Just ask his mother about the castle ledge incident, a fantastic example of dexterity that she still unfortunately remembered in great detail. He'd never understood how mothers could remember every single mischievous incident that happened in their children's lives. And why did those embarrassing childhood moments always get mentioned at family functions or, even worse, get spoken of in great detail whenever he brought a lady friend home for his mother to meet? He'd put a stop to that! No more family functions and no more bringing women home. The latter was easy because a lot of the women he met weren't the type you brought home to Mother anyways. Marriage and settling down were not high on his list of priorities, no matter how many grandchildren his mother hinted at.

Coasting his bike up his silent street lined with dark houses, he clicked his garage door opener, still amazed at the technology behind it. A pity the Realm remained stuck in its old ways. Hadn't they realized that magic didn't have to be the solution to everything? This side of the boundary might be magicless, but the technology and machines they'd created over the years more than rivaled the finest magic a wizard could perform.

Parking his bike inside the garage, he balanced his late-night snack in one hand as he carefully swung one muscled, leather-clad leg off the bike. *Home at last.* He fought to hold back a yawn. *Damn late nights.* He didn't have any new missions planned for this week, so there would be plenty of time to rest. Clicking his key fob to close the garage door and arming his bike alarm, he strutted from the garage to the front door of his house, his keen eyes taking in everything around him.

The neighborhood he lived in rested quietly at this time of the night—sweet suburbia, as his neighbor Bob liked to call it. The houses gaped darkly as their occupants slept. His gaze flickered to the houses on either side of his own. Always best to be cautious in case the hunter became the hunted, but he found nothing out of place.

No, hold on a moment. Something had changed. The For Sale sign that had adorned the house next door to him for the last three months had disappeared. *Damn, new neighbors.* Hopefully they weren't as annoying as the last ones. Annoying college boys partying all the time. Revving his Harley at six o'clock in the morning after one of the boys' late-nighters and a *friendly* conversation had convinced them to relocate elsewhere.

He'd helped the previous owner clean and repaint the place so she could put it up for sale. Hey, she was sixty-five years old, and she'd said please. He'd kill any man who accused him of going soft. Besides, she'd paid him. Hunting Realm escapees sounded great in theory, but the pay left a lot to be desired.

The smell of his burger made him salivate, so he quickly checked his door for signs of tampering before entering. After a routine check of the house—he still didn't quite trust house alarms—he finally went to sleep, after eating the two double burgers, fries, and milkshake of course.

He awoke to screaming. Instantly, the hunter came alert and rolled off his bed, grabbing his gun—a modern concession—from under his pillow. Crouching, he sidled up to his window, which faced the backyard. Nothing in sight.

The scream came again along with the dreaded words, "Eeeee! Goblins! No! No! Don't hurt me!"

How had the border patrol missed them approaching the boundary?

Without thinking, instinct taking over, the hunter ripped up his window sash and dove into the yard. He ran in a half-crouch to the fence, gun tucked into his waistband. He grabbed the top of the fence and vaulted over it. His body immediately went into a tuck, and he landed with a roll on the dewy grass, springing up, gun in hand, eyes scanning for the troublesome creatures.

No slimy green goblins awaited him. Instead, he stared in shock at three pairs of bright brown, very human eyes. Their expressions were comically identical with their mouths wide open in an O of surprise.

Uh-oh.

CHAPTER 2

Suzie and her kids stared in stunned silence at the stranger who had vaulted into their new yard holding a gun.

What a sight!

A half-dressed, blond Adonis with moves she'd never seen outside of a movie was standing so close she could almost touch the smooth, lightly tanned skin rippling with muscle. Not that she had an urge to. Nope, being single suited her just fine, and she intended to stay that way.

Gathering her two children in her arms, she sat up and stared at the stranger who hastily stuffed his gun in his pants—no pun intended—and backed away with his hands up. His wide eyes had a panicked look to them, and his cheeks flushed.

Oh my God, he's embarrassed. Suzie held in an urge to giggle. Anyone in their right mind should have been scared, but Suzie found herself more intrigued by the man who'd vaulted over her fence. Apparently, she and the kids weren't what he'd expected to find.

"Sorry," he said, his deep baritone making her shiver. A velvety voice, like the kind heard on the radio when you were awake in the wee hours of morning. "I just woke up and heard screaming and . . ."

Trust Jared to be the first to talk. "Loo, Mommy. Da man hath a gun. Ith he a po-wice man?" he lisped adorably.

"Mine!" piped in Jessica, his twin. Did she mean the gun or the man? Knowing Jessica, both.

"What? Um..." The stranger backed up toward the fence he'd flown over, his look of confusion finally making the giggles Suzie had been holding in burst forth. Tempted as she was to let him stutter a little bit more—after all, he'd scared them first—she kind of felt sorry for him, and knowing her two little angels the way she did, they'd make him regret his actions with a million questions. Time to save him.

"Hi, we're your new neighbors," Suzie said cheerily, getting up and brushing the grass and dirt off her scuffed, holey jeans. Nothing like meeting a hunk in your sexiest stay-at-home cleaning clothes. Her always perfectly groomed mother would have been appalled.

Suzie held out her hand, and with a bemused look on his face, her fence vaulter thrust out his to shake it. His large hand engulfed hers—and yes, he had matching big feet. The warmth of his callused skin grasping hers made her tummy turn over and a tingle race through her body. *I must be coming down with something. The flu or some other virus because I am not attracted to him.*

"I'm Suzie, and these two little monsters posing as my children are Jared and Jessica," Suzie said.

"Hi," said the twins in tandem, grinning at the stranger.

"Hello," he said, then seeing their expectant faces, "I'm Hunter."

Suzie almost giggled again. What an apt name though. With a body like his, if he weren't the predator, then hunter would certainly be the next best choice. Okay, so she'd looked. After all, it wasn't every day that a total babe almost landed in her lap wearing low-hipped track pants and no shirt to hide the flattest stomach and most deliciously muscled arms ever. However, that was all she'd be doing—looking. No touching. Definitely no touching. But God, those clear, bright blue eyes and sun-streaked, golden-tousled hair almost made her change her mind.

"Sorry if we bothered you," she said. "We've been cleaning all morning, and the twins needed to let off some steam."

"It is I who must apologize for my irregular behavior. I assure you it will not happen again," he said, shrugging sheepishly.

Jared tugged on her hand so she looked down.

"Is he a po-wice man, Mommy?" he said in a loud whisper that sprayed.

Good question. Suzie looked at the stranger. Good looks aside, why had he dived into their yard with a gun?

"No, I'm not a policeman. Although I do work with them occasionally. I'm a private investigator," he answered.

Wow, a real PI. Suzie's eyes widened, and in spite of her vow to stay celibate, her libido woke up and yawned with interest. *Go back to sleep,* she told her awakening body. *I swore off men, remember?*

"Whassa priva gator?" lisped Jessica, her wide eyes shining as she gazed in—*uh-oh*—adoration at Hunter.

To her surprise, he answered Jessica, crouching down to her eye level. "I find people who are lost and things that are missing," he said seriously.

Jessica cocked her head as if in thought. "Can you fin' ma baby?"

"Oh, sweetheart," said Suzie, crouching down, too, to look her daughter. "I told you she's in one of the boxes. We'll find her soon, I'm sure."

Jessica hung her head and said, "Okay" in her saddest little voice, lower lip trembling. Suzie held back a sigh at Jessica, her natural-born actress and drama queen.

Hunter was new to Jessica's ploys, though. "How about I give you a hand and help you unpack and find her?"

What? Suzie opened her mouth, but it was too late.

Jessica beamed up at Hunter. "Fank you."

"Hey, me too," piped in Jared. With twins, everything went in pairs.

"Did you lose something too?" Hunter asked Jared.

Jared's head bobbed. "Ma dinothaur, an' my car, an' my thord, an . . ."

"Well, why don't you both go choose a box to unpack, and your mother and I will be inside in a moment to help?"

Oh, we will, will we? Suzie thought, annoyed at his assumption.

The children ran off with a squeal, their three-year-old legs pumping. If she could only bottle that energy, she'd be rich.

Suzie waited till they were in the house. "You don't have to stay. We'll find the stuff. It's in there somewhere."

"I'm sorry. I guess your husband must be inside unpacking."

"What? Oh, no husband. Just me and the twins." She shook her head vehemently. No, that rotten bastard, whom she thankfully had never married, was long gone, and good riddance.

"Well then, let me give you some aid. I'm not expected to start any new cases for a few days. You could consider it my welcome gift."

"Okay," said Suzie, still somewhat surprised at the offer. Surely, he had better things to do. *Maybe he's got an ulterior motive,* her paranoid mind retorted. *He could be an axe murderer or rapist or. . . just a nice guy.*

"I will return in a moment after I've changed into more suitable attire."

Suzie felt like saying, *don't bother*. She could stare at those abs all day. *Hey, looking is not touching.* Although she bet he felt good to the touch, too. Suzie chided herself for her naughty thoughts but still watched in fascination as he jogged and vaulted back over the fence. God, the way his muscles rippled when he moved. . . It made her feel a heat she hadn't felt in a long time.

"Mommy," wailed Jessica. "Jari ma'e a mess."

"No' me," yelled Jared.

"Coming," sighed Suzie. Who needed a cold shower when you had two very active three-year-olds?

*W*HAT THE HELL *happened out there?*

Hunter shook his head and pinched himself. Nope, definitely awake. So how, by all the powers, had he found himself volunteering to help a stranger and her two kids unpack? Although, with looks like hers, hopefully they wouldn't be strangers for long. Even with her hair caught in a ponytail, he could tell it was thick, long and dark, the stray wisps framing a creamy complexion, drawing attention to her full lips.

As for her body—nice and curvy with a full bosom. He'd always liked a woman with curves. Full hipped with a nice handful. . .

Whoa. Not a good idea to get involved with the neighbors, even a sexy one. *Think with your head*, he admonished himself, *not with your groin*.

Okay, but he had promised he'd be over to help, and he always kept a promise, no matter what sanity—or drunken—level he'd been at when making it. He changed into a scruffy pair of blue jeans and a well washed T-shirt with a Harley on the front then vaulted back over the fence to get this over with.

WHEN HE TAPPED on the sliding glass door leading to the backyard, Suzie jumped. She hadn't really been sure he'd come back. A part of her wished she'd cleaned herself up a bit, but she'd restrained herself. After all, she didn't care what he thought of her looks. She had no need to impress him since she had no intention of trying to attract his attention. But she still couldn't help the hand that fluttered up and tucked a loose strand of hair back.

"Come in," she shouted, staying on her knees to mop up the rest of the juice that Jared had spilled. Three years old, such a wonderful age—old enough to kind of know how to do things for themselves but still too clumsy to do them neatly. All children should come supplied with a robot maid, one with a vacuum attachment in one hand and a rag in the other.

Hunter had no sooner stepped inside than two whirlwinds materialized and threw themselves at him. Looked like her little angels had themselves a new hero.

"Hunta! Hunta!" screeched Jessica, hugging his leg.

Jared, being a boy, hung back and showed off his Ninja Turtle moves. "Hi-ya," he exclaimed, thrusting out a chubby fist.

Poor Hunter had that dazed look on his face again. Well, he'd volunteered. He'd think twice before he did that again.

"Hey, ankle biters, tone it down. You're going to make him go deaf."

The children, rebuked, calmed down for all of about three seconds.

"See my woom," said Jessica, tugging on Hunter's hand and dragging him through the kitchen while Jared kept up a mostly incomprehensible chatter alongside them.

When he turned to look at her helplessly, Suzie shrugged and smiled. She watched, with way more interest than necessary, the wiggle of his ass in his tight jeans as he walked stiffly into the other room. She'd deemed looking okay. It was the touching she had to stay away from.

Wiping up the last of the mess, she stood and rinsed her rag in the sink. Looking up, she paused to admire the view of her very first backyard from the window over the sink. She'd been so excited when they'd found this place. Well within her budget, a nice neighborhood for the twins, and, best of all, no one knew where she'd disappeared to, so there was no way *he* could find them. With an unlisted phone, a mailbox in town, and no credit cards, she'd done everything she could to ensure they stayed hidden. Hopefully, it would be enough.

It seemed awfully quiet in the other room. As any parent will tell you, that was not a good sign with kids. Silence meant pictures drawn in pen on the walls, several rolls of toilet paper shoved down the toilet with water rising, climbing of furniture in preparation for flight...

Preparing for disaster, Suzie walked into the other room and stopped dead at the scene. The silence hadn't been due to Hunter being duct-taped to a chair by the children. No, it was even more shocking. He'd managed to actually get the children to help him unpack, and they were doing it willingly!

How the hell did he pull that one off?

Hunter had opened one of the boxes on the living room floor. Pulling out objects, he handed items to the twins one at a time with a serious nod. The children solemnly nodded back and then, with a grin, scampered off to various parts of the house to deposit their item.

Hunter flashed her a white smile—with teeth like that he could be a poster child for Colgate. Suzie felt her tummy tingling in response.

"You have very nice children."

"Yes, they can be adorable when they want to," she said, wondering if she'd entered an alternate dimension.

"Looks like the movers just deposited everything into this room. Perhaps you could tell me where you want the boxes, and I'll move them to make it easier to unpack," he said, gesturing to the cardboard towers.

"Are you sure? Some of them are kind of heavy."

He just lifted an eyebrow at her and, with a grin, grabbed two boxes.

Suzie laughed and shook her head. "Okay, smartass. Those two go into the kitchen."

With a strut that had her lower parts tingling again, he took off with the boxes. Under her direction, even with the children underfoot trying to be too helpful, they soon had the boxes divvied up into the rooms they belonged to.

The house had three bedrooms, but the children would be sharing one for now so she could have her own workspace. As a web programmer and graphic design artist, she had the luxury of working from home. Great for her because it meant no daycare expenses, but it sucked at the same time because she could work only early mornings when the kids were sleeping or at night after they went to bed. But it paid the bills, and best of all, she could work in her jammies.

By the time five o'clock hit, the house had begun looking like a home. Most of the twins' toys and books had been unpacked. Jessica had her doll and Jared, all of his various must-have toys.

"Mommy, I hungie," said Jared, her bottomless pit.

"Me too," piped in Jessica.

"I'll take my leave that you may have your dinner," said Hunter, who stood leaning on the kitchen counter.

Suzie felt an irrational urge for him to stay. "Listen, why don't you stay for dinner? It's not much—Kraft Dinner and hot dogs—but you're more than welcome to some."

"I wouldn't want to impose."

"Pwease stay," begged Jessica with her big, pleading eyes. "You can haff my pwincess bowl."

"Well, how can I say no to an offer like that? If it's not too much trouble," he said with a look at Suzie.

"No problem. Come on, kids. You set the table while I get the water boiling."

A half-hour later, with only a few minor skirmishes as they decided where Hunter would sit—between the twins—they all sat down for dinner, or so thought Suzie with a smirk. An educational experience for Hunter, who obviously hadn't spent much time eating with children. No food ever looked the same after you've seen it being spit out, partially chewed so that they could have a drink of juice then—gross—stuffed back in their mouth.

For dessert they made super-duper sundaes—ice cream with bananas, peanut butter, and chocolate sauce. Hunter looked at his portion dubiously but, after a few bites, wolfed it down as quickly as the kids.

"That was delicious," he said, leaning back and patting his tummy. The kids giggled and leaned back, aping him.

Suzie laughed. "I discovered that magical combo when I was pregnant with these two. When you're pregnant, eating takes on a whole new dimension, as did my hips," she said ruefully, eyeing her rounded figure.

"I say your hips look great," drawled Hunter. "Skinny women are way overrated."

Suzie hadn't been fishing for a compliment, but his remark and his admiring gaze made her blush. "Oh, thank you," she said, flustered. She busied herself clearing the table and carried the mess to the sink. Turning around to grab the last of the dishes, she hit a brick wall. Hunter had already grabbed the rest of the dishes and stood right behind her. She bumped into his solid chest and stumbled back. She felt his large, firm hand grasp her around the waist to steady her, and she gasped as a sensual heat flowed through her body. She looked up at him to say sorry, but the words got caught in her throat at the smoky look directed at her. His body, so close to hers, radiated heat, and she felt a matching warmth spreading through her own body.

They stood there, staring at each other, frozen, waiting for the other to move. A thump from the table broke the trance, and he moved back.

Suzie looked over at the kids. Jessica had slumped onto the table, half asleep. Jared drooped, not far behind. Their long day had finally caught up to them. Hunter, seeing their drowsy state, picked up Jessica in one arm and then scooped Jared up in the other. *Wow, those muscles sure are useful*, Suzie thought as she led him upstairs to the kids' bedroom.

Suzie stripped Jessica and dressed her in her nightie then sent her to the bathroom and did the same to Jared. Hunter, who had disappeared, came back with two small cups of water, which he put on each child's nightstand.

"How—" said Suzie.

"The children told me quite a bit about themselves today, including the fact that they need a nightlight and a drink of water for bedtime. And also that Mommy," he said, grinning as he called her that, "gets scared during thunderstorms so they need to crawl into her bed to make sure she's all right."

"What else did they tell you?" she asked. *Oh God, exactly how many secrets had the children revealed?*

"I also know you're scared of spiders, that Jessica hates carrots, and Jared wants to be a cowboy and an astronaut."

"I wanna be a priv gator," said Jared sleepily as he shuffled back into the room.

"Me too," said Jessica, right behind him.

"Well, for now, you both need your sleep," said Suzie, kissing and tucking them each into their own bed.

Jessica held up her arms and puckered her lips. "Wanna kiss, Hunta."

Hunter, with a look at Suzie to see if it was all right, knelt down and gave Jessica a wet, smacking kiss that had her giggling. Jared, being a boy, didn't want a kiss but beamed at the manly handshake Hunter gave him. Suzie, watching all this, felt a pang. If only their father hadn't been such a lying, uncaring bastard. Her children deserved—no, correct that—needed a father. Even just one day spent with Hunter, their first real masculine influence, seemed evidence of that. Perhaps she should revise her no-man policy. For the children, of course.

After closing the door three quarters of the way and blowing kisses through the crack, she and Hunter headed back to the living room.

Okay, now what? Without the children to buffer them, Suzie hesitated, at a loss as to what to say to Hunter. Had she become so socially inept in the three years since the kids had been born? Sure, she could hold her own in a discussion of *Max & Ruby* versus the *Backyardigans*, but she didn't see her hot neighbor being that interested in kids' shows.

"Um, would you like a drink or something?" she offered lamely.

"No, I'm fine, thank you. Do you need help with anything else?"

"Oh no. You've done enough today. I can't thank you enough. If there's any way I can repay you," she said with an inquiring look. Oh yes, she could think of many ways to repay him. Unfortunately, all of them involved him naked. She really needed to get some sleep.

"My pleasure," he said, his deep, baritone sending a shiver through her body. His eyes looked smoky again in the dim living room, and Suzie felt herself leaning toward him, like a plant seeking the light.

He cleared his throat, and the moment passed. "Well, I guess I'll leave you to enjoy your evening. If you need anything, just knock. I work odd hours, but leave me a note if you need any help."

Oh nice, Suzie, scare the nice man off, she chastised herself. *He probably thinks I'm some sex-crazed single mom.*

"Yes, well, thanks again," said Suzie, walking him to the door, the front door this time. He waved as he strode across the front lawn to his place, and watching him, Suzie had an irrational urge to chase him down and drag him back. She'd enjoyed his company today, something that hadn't happened in a long time. He had an easy-going presence about him, and his patience with the children verged on the level of sainthood. But getting involved with a hunky neighbor. . . Suzie shook her head. Bad idea. She'd come here to escape from one man, and if she wanted to give the children a stable home life, she should restrict her dating—if she chose to date again—to men well outside the neighborhood where she wouldn't have to run into them if things went wrong.

But still, it had been a long time since a man had made her feel so attractive, and on that thought, she went to work organizing the little knickknacks that still needed a home. Her thoughts filled with what-if's involving her hot new neighbor.

As soon as Hunter got home, he jumped into a cold shower. He needed one after spending time with the sexy Suzie next door. He'd come so close to kissing her in the living room. She'd looked so perfect with her long brown hair wisping around her face as her ponytail came apart and her full lips, sensual and inviting. He knew what he'd like those lips to be doing!

As they'd worked together, he'd found himself sneaking peeks at her bottom when she bent over, its round fullness begging for a playful slap. Her full breasts, stretching the cotton of her T-shirt, a tempting duo that would fit so nicely in his hands.

By the higher powers! Had he turned into a randy teenager again with a hard-on every time a woman smiled at him?

Come on, think of something different. How about her children? The pair of them proved cute and precocious, he'd quite enjoyed interacting with them. He'd never really been around kids before, and he had to say that the experience with the twins had made the idea of settling down eventually not as scary as he'd once thought it. Something that would please his mother to no end. She'd been subtly hinting for years that he should settle down.

As he imagined his own little troop of children running and playing while he and their mother—who looked an awful lot like Suzie—lounged, he fell asleep.

A FEW KILOMETERS AWAY, while the city slept, a man in a dark cloak pushed through a thin spot in the boundary and emerged in an alleyway, not too far from the burger place Hunter had staked out the night before.

Sniffing the air, he smiled. A cold, calculating smile. The kind of smile that said bad things were about to happen.

Finally, I am free again. Free to finish what I started several years ago. Free to make those who had dared thwart me pay. Free to fulfill my destiny.

Soon now, the man thought as his predatory eyes took in everything around. He would take back what had been stolen from him. And when he did, the whole world would pay.

CHAPTER 3

The next morning, after Suzie had cleared the dishes from breakfast, she heard a knock at the door.

Braless, in a T-shirt, and barefoot with tousled bed head, Suzie answered the door and felt her jaw drop. Her gorgeous neighbor had returned.

Unable to speak—somehow *Hubba Hubba* didn't seem appropriate—she just gaped at him till he lifted a tool box up in front of him and shook it.

"Hey, I figured you'd probably be awake, what with the children and all. I noticed yesterday that you had some things that still needed put together and a couple of things in the house that needed tending. So I thought I'd come over and give you a hand."

He did, did he? Suzie, still speechless, just stepped aside and let him saunter in.

The twins on the floor in the living room turned to look and dropped their blocks to dive on Hunter.

"Hunta! You back!"

Suzie left them talking to Hunter at a mile a minute and went to get another cup of coffee. Maybe a jolt of caffeine would give her back the ability to speak. To say he'd surprised her showing up like he had was an understatement. If someone would have told her that her hunky neighbor would be back to play Mr. Fix-It, she'd have peed her pants laughing. Didn't he have anything better to do? Or did he have some ulterior motive? Maybe he had designs on her body. *Ha!* Nope, there had to be a better reason than that. Could she have found the rarest of specimens? A nice and helpful man? Suzie envied his girlfriend—a guy like him had to have one, maybe even two.

Hunter walked into the kitchen as if he owned the place and set his toolbox on the counter.

"I'll get to work on the stuff I noticed yesterday. If you make a list of things you've seen, then I can repair them for you while you do other stuff."

What, did he think her incapable? Just because she didn't know one end of a hammer from the other didn't mean she couldn't do it. She wanted to be pissed at his high-handed manner, but instead, she leaned back, sipping her coffee, and watched as he turned off the water to her sink and unscrewed the tap to fix the leaky cold water.

Why protest? He seemed determined, and truth was it would cost her more than she could afford to hire a handyman to fix all the little things that needed looking at. If he wanted to waste his day helping out, why not? So long as he didn't think he'd be getting anything out of it because she definitely had no intention of getting involved with any man, no matter how attractive he looked or how much she craved to touch him.

Once he fixed the tap, he re-attached some loose trim and assembled her desk, all while keeping up a running commentary with the kids.

"What dith?" asked Jared, holding up a wrench he'd pilfered from the toolbox.

"A wrench, it's for tightening things."

"What dith?" Jared asked, holding up something Suzie had never seen.

"A level for making sure things aren't at a tilt."

And on it went. He even let the kids help him tighten bolts, guiding their hands to turn the screwdriver, and getting them to hand him tools as he worked. The kids had taken to him like a fish to water, and Suzie watched, amazed. They didn't even squabble once! A miracle on its own.

Suzie knew she should be getting more done but found herself mesmerized into watching him, instead. She studied him like a new breed of animal she'd never seen, trying to understand what made him tick. But she watched him all morning and came no closer to understanding him.

When lunch came, he cheerfully chomped down on grilled cheese sandwiches with the kids and made them laugh at his milk mustache. Still observing him surreptitiously, Suzie wondered if maybe he was a touch unbalanced. She'd never seen someone have so much fun eating such a simple meal.

She couldn't deny his good work ethics. Like a busy

little ant, he went through the house diligently. Suzie made him the list he'd asked for, and by the end of the afternoon, he'd tackled it all and even fixed some things she hadn't even noticed. Like the handle on her dresser drawer—it had to be her underwear one, of course. He'd just casually dumped everything on the bed, her waist-high, granny panties, all in the exciting color of white, pouring out. Okay, so she shopped for comfort instead of sexy. It wasn't as if anyone usually saw them. But talk about embarrassing. After he'd fixed the drawer, she dove onto the bed to put them back herself, the thought of him handling her underwear somehow too intimate for her to handle. He'd, of course, just grinned, a cocky smile that he liked to use a lot and made her insides turn upside down each time he did.

As dinnertime approached, he started packing up his tools, but Suzie didn't want him to go yet. Foolish maybe, but she didn't want the day's camaraderie to end just yet.

"Would you like to stay for dinner?" she asked. "We're having fish and chips. Frozen variety. You're more than welcome." She didn't expect him to accept. Hell, she didn't really like the stuff, herself, but the kids ate it, and it fit in the budget.

"Oh, I don't want to be any trouble," he said, his gorgeous blue eyes smiling at her.

"No trouble," she said a tad breathlessly. Staring into those eyes felt like swimming in an ocean, and she had to remind herself to breathe.

"Well, in that case then, I'd be much obliged."

Obliged—who the hell said that anymore? Someone's mother had raised him right.

Suzie bustled around the kitchen while the kids regaled Hunter with important facts. Like, did he know Jessica's baby didn't like to wear clothes? And Jared hated peas, and Mommy liked to sing in the shower? Yes, a guilty pleasure of hers, usually hits from the eighties, back when they had real music.

Hunter talked and joked with them as if it was the most natural thing in the world, and Suzie, taking in this oh-so domestic scene, felt an urge to cry. *This is what it should be like everyday. A family sitting down to dinner with a father and a mother and . . . But this isn't real*, she thought sadly, and that made her want to scream and sob and rail at the fates. If only *he* had been a different man, a better man, then maybe she wouldn't have had to run, and the twins could have been raised with their father. She'd made her choice, though, the right one, and crying over it now wouldn't change it. But still, the pang of what could have been made her sad, although she put on a cheerful face for her crew.

"Food's ready," she announced, serving them.

Dinner, a chaotic affair with ketchup flying and milk cups getting spilled, was perfect, as it kept her mind away from more melancholy thoughts. She saw Hunter throw questioning looks at her every so often, as if he could see beneath her mask of cheerfulness. Surely he didn't know her well enough to read her, but apparently, he did.

After they'd put the kids to bed, together again, he touched her on the arm and signaled they should go out back.

Suzie followed him to the back deck and sat down, the cool evening air making her arms pimple. She wrapped her arms around herself tight to keep warm, but that did little to chase the coldness of her spirit.

Hunter sat down beside her, almost close enough for his thigh to brush hers. "What's wrong? You look sad."

"Me? No, just thinking about stuff. I really appreciate all the help you gave me yesterday and today. Thank your girlfriend for me. I'm sure she's missed having you." Okay, so she wanted to know if he had a significant other. *Shoot me*.

"No girlfriend, I'm single. But you're trying to change the subject. Something at dinner made your eyes go all sad. What's wrong?"

Damn, figured he'd be perceptive and worse than a terrier with a chew toy. He just wouldn't leave it alone. "You want the truth?"

"That would be nice," he said, his blue eyes boring into hers, inviting her to spill her guts. So, what should she tell him that would get him off her back? Suzie had some secrets that were just too dangerous and painful to share.

"Seeing you with the kids, all happy and stuff, made me wish things were different. It made me realize how isolated the kids and I have been." *Not to mention lonely*, she thought.

"Don't you have any family around, or friends?"

Funny, how he never asked about their dad. Probably assuming a messy divorce.

"The only family I have left is my mother, and she's not a person I want or need in my life. As for friends, once I got pregnant, they kind of drifted away, and I didn't follow. Being a mom changes a lot, including your priorities." *Not to mention fear. Hard to let someone close when you're constantly afraid.*

"That's got to be lonely."

"Oh, I'm never alone," she said quickly. She didn't want him to pity her. "I've got the kids, and they're plenty company." Yes, the conversation with them was so stimulating.

"I know you have the children, and they're wonderful, but everybody needs someone to talk to. Someone to call when the world is against you. Someone to brag to when things are good."

"Yeah, well, I haven't exactly had the time," Suzie said defensively. Why the hell did he care? "Who do you have?"

"I've got childhood friends back home, and my mom and sister. I don't get to see them that much now, they live kind of far away, but I write to them when I can."

Write? Who the hell wrote letters any more? Why not send a text or email? Heck, although not as common anymore, why not pick up a phone and call? Not that his life was any of her business. And this topic was getting uncomfortable. Time to change the subject.

"I know you're a PI, but where do you work?"

"I've got an office downtown, but I work all over the place, depending on the case. I go out of town every so often, but I try to keep my work local as much as possible."

"What kind of cases do you handle?" she asked.

"A lot of missing persons, actually. I seem to have a knack for finding those who want to stay hidden."

Suzie shivered. That comment struck a little too close to her own situation.

He noticed her tremor and slid closer, the heat from his body radiating out toward her. "What about you? Do you work?" he asked when she didn't reply.

"Yeah, I'm a web programmer."

To her surprise, he perked right up. "Really? I love computers, but I am so inept when it comes to them. Owen, a friend of mine, says I need to get with the times and get online, but to be honest, I'm still clueless when it comes to surfing the net, as they say."

"So how do you do your work? Isn't everything done with computers nowadays?"

"Owen helps me out with that. He's a whiz when it comes to finding out stuff. I tell him what I need, and he does his magic."

"How do people find you? Yellow pages, Internet, newspaper?" she asked, trying to keep him talking.

"I get a lot of referrals."

Surely that couldn't be how he got all his business? "Doesn't your agency have a Web site?"

For a moment, he looked startled, as if she'd said something startling. "Oh, you mean my PI agency."

Uh yeah, what the hell else had he thought she meant?

"No, I haven't gotten around to getting a Web site for it yet. Business is pretty good, so I haven't really felt a need to," he said, shrugging sheepishly.

"Well, if you're ever looking, give me a shout. I'll give you the neighborly discount." She might even do a quick one up for free. In this day and age, when it came to marketing your services for prospective clients, a person had to be on the net. She couldn't believe he'd survived this long on word of mouth alone.

"Sounds good," he said, smiling.

Suzie smiled back, her tummy swirling again as his eyes held her. She could see his face moving closer and felt herself moving in, narrowing the gap. Her lips parted and . . .

A cold drop hit her nose. The first of many as the heavens opened up and started to pour. Suzie jumped up and ran to the house while Hunter, with a grin, waved at her and then vaulted over the fence into his own yard.

Suzie stood there in the window, staring at nothing for a moment. The almost-kiss stunned her. If it hadn't rained, would he have kissed her? Would she have let him? Despite all her good intentions about not getting involved, her body seemed to have other plans. Treacherous bodily reactions! Didn't her body understand that, while it might feel good at the time, the emotional pain she'd suffer later would last forever?

Apparently, her hormones didn't care if the ache between her thighs was any indication. Maybe she should go back outside and stand in the cold rain for a minute. Make that several minutes. Hunter had an ability to ignite a fire in her body that nothing short of a deluge would put out.

Suzie sighed and went upstairs to get ready for bed. Slipping into an oversized T-shirt, she settled down with a book she'd been meaning to read but couldn't get into it. Distracted by thoughts of him, like a lovesick teenager mooning over a boy, her thoughts caught in a re-run of the almost-kiss. She wondered what his arms would have felt like, crushing her to his broad chest. How his lips would have felt, pressed hard against hers. *What an idiot I am for having the hots for a man I barely know.* She really hadn't learned anything from her past. Just thinking about *him* made her shiver. Someone was surely walking over her grave.

Suzie snuggled down in her blankets, the gentle sound of the rain sounding so ominous now, the black night an encroaching beast that would devour her in its dark arms. Huddled in her fear, she fell into a jerky sleep. One with lots of running, chasing, and pain, lots of pain.

CHAPTER 4

The growling sound of a motorcycle woke Suzie up. Rolling sleepily out of bed, she peeked out the window in time to see Hunter on a big, black Harley, gliding away down the street. Did the man not have an un-sexy bone in his body? Why couldn't he drive a Vespa? And where was he off to so early? Not that she cared, of course.

Suzie stretched, rubbing her bleary eyes, and looked at the clock. Gasp! Eight o'clock. How the hell had she managed to sleep in? *Oh God, the children.*

She raced out of her room and right into the kids' room. Rumpled beds, but no kids. Flying again down the stairs, she skidded into the living room and sighed with relief as two little heads swiveled around from the television they were watching.

"Morning, Mommy," they sang.

"Morning, angels. How long have you been up? You

should have woke Mommy." *Like you usually do at the crack of dawn everyday*, she thought.

"You were sleeping. We ma'e breafass," said Jessica, holding up a sloppy bowl of cereal.

"Me too." Jared grinned as he held up his own overflowing bowl.

They sure had. The trail of Corn Bran led from the living room right into the kitchen pantry while the milk they'd spilled lay in a puddle on the floor. Maybe she should get a dog. At least then her floors would be food free. She perked some coffee, needing her morning caffeine, while she cleaned up the mess, the first of several disasters the twins would surely make that day. Another thing no one had warned her about. Once you had kids you either lived in a borderline pigsty or you spent your time cleaning the same messes, over and over and over. . .

As she sipped her hot java, the bitter warmth waking her up, she wondered what to do today. With Hunter's help, they'd managed to get almost everything organized yesterday, so today was looking good for groceries and other stuff. She wanted to pick up some cookie-making ingredients. It occurred to her that the kids would really enjoy making some cookies for Hunter as a thank-you. They could take them over to him later when he got home from work. Not that she was looking for excuses to see him. No, this was just the polite, neighborly thing to do.

An hour later and with only a minor clothing skirmish—Jessica didn't want the pink T-shirt and Jared had to have his Spiderman one—she had the kids dressed and ready to go shopping. Stores beware!

They piled into the car, and with her GPS programmed, they headed off to the off-key singing of "Old McDonald," and for a little while, she managed not to think of her new sexy neighbor. Well, at least not as much.

Hunter rode his purring machine to his downtown office and parked in his spot. By all the gods, did he love his motorcycle. The speed, the exhilaration, the totally warrior look. Back in the Realm, if you weren't a wizard who could teleport, then horses were the way to go. Which wouldn't be so bad if it wasn't for the poop everywhere they went. Maybe when he'd completed his mission over here, he could convince the council to let him bring his Harley back. He'd love to see the look on his fellow hunters' faces when he rode up on his lean machine.

Setting his alarm on his bike, he pulled off his helmet and strode into the building that housed his office. He hadn't planned on coming in today, but he needed some distraction. He couldn't get Suzie and her kids out of his head. Well, mostly Suzie. He'd woken early with a throbbing erection and realized he needed to do something to get her off his mind.

He tried working out at the gym first, but pumping iron and sweating had made the urge only worse as he wondered what she'd look like covered in sweat while his body pumped hers. A tad distracting. Where these randy thoughts kept coming from he didn't know. So he'd decided to come into the office and see if anything had come in to occupy his mind.

In order to keep his business legitimate-looking to authorities and the government, he made sure to take enough regular PI cases to justify his expenses and salary. His real job, hunting those crossing the boundary, while a lot more stimulating, really sucked money wise.

The mailbox had only bills, something this world seemed way too fond of. His answering machine blinked at him spastically. After pressing the play button, he listened to the one message.

"The Dragon has escaped."

Uh-oh. That spelled trouble. Good, he needed a challenge.

Hanging his leathers on a hook, he locked his office door before moving a filing cabinet at the back of this office that hid a narrow door. When opened, it looked like a utility closet, but pressing a hidden switch swiveled the rack at the back and revealed an opening that led into the upper floor of the store next door. Hunter had gadgets and secrets, just like in one of those spy movies he loved to watch. Or like the people in this world loved to say, *so cool.*

The room he entered resembled a hacker's wet dream—or so Owen assured him. Hunter wasn't quite sure what that meant but felt sure it had something to do with the state-of-the-art computer systems, some not legal on the private market, that hummed throughout the office. Cables ran all over the place as well, connecting the massive network to the Internet and more. What would have been a logistic nightmare back in the Realm was the height of efficiency here. Need a name, address, looking for strange happenings? With a few keystrokes, the information highway had it all.

"Hey, Hunter," said a slender young man with long hair held back in a ponytail sitting at one of the terminals. "I thought you were taking a few days off."

That was Owen, also from the Realm. Resident computer geek—aka information gatherer—and Hunter's friend.

Hunter shrugged at him. "I was bored so I thought I'd come in and see what was shaking. So what have we got going, Owen?"

Owen typed away for a second on his keyboard, his fingers flashing faster than light—Hunter, a hunt-and-pecker, himself, envied that skill. Owen then scooted his chair across the floor several feet to a printer spitting out paper.

"A couple of possible faerie sightings. One definite troll, but that one was in Devon's half of the country, so he got it."

Shoot, thought Hunter. He could have used the exercise.

"The Bermuda Triangle has gotten even more unstable. Sasha says the boundary is just about gone in that area. We've got a team of wizards on that one. They think they can patch it."

"Any more missing ships and planes?"

"One cruise ship went through the boundary in the Triangle area and ended up in Mermaid Bay," said

Owen, chuckling.

"What's so funny about that?" Mermaids could be nasty, especially when it was that time of the month. Definitely not a laughing matter.

"It was a cruise ship of old folk. The poor mermaids were quite miffed when their singing didn't work on the men. And then the men's wives started calling them hussies and screaming at them to put their clothes back on."

Hunter chuckled. He'd have liked to have seen that. A pissed-off siren wasn't something you got to see often. "How did they cover that one up?"

"Pretended it was a movie set. Amazing what people will swallow sometimes," said Owen, shaking his head.

Actually, having seen a lot of the movies on this side of the boundary, he could see how easy it would be to convince people. Hell, a dragon could fly down the main street of town and people would be looking for projectors. This side of the boundary truly didn't believe in magic. Everything had to be special effects. Made it easy for them to do their job and cover it up. But back to business, there were more pressing matters at hand. "What's this about the Dragon escaping?"

"Yeah, we just heard about the Dragon's escape this morning. Word on the vine is the whole prison over there is in for a reaming from the commander."

Hunter winced. He'd been reamed out by the commander quite a few times—it made hand-o-hand combat with an ogre seem like a day in the park.

"Bob said for you to go see him when you showed up. He's got the full details."

"Okay. Is he in his office?"

"He should be soon. It was his turn to mind the shop," said Owen with a snicker.

"Oh-oh, what did you guys do to him this time?" asked Hunter.

"Oh, nothing except book a *Harry Potter* birthday party."

"You didn't," said Hunter, trying not to laugh. Although it was kind of funny, especially if you knew Bob. He hated *Harry Potter* with a vengeance. Said it made light of a very serious profession—wizardry. Bob lacked innate magical ability to be a wizard, himself, but magic and wizardry were his passion, and he could go on for hours about it.

What Bob lacked in magical talent, though, he more than made up for in brains. His smarts and organizational skills had made him an ideal choice for the head of the new department called Realm Incursions. A new agency created a few years ago to deal with the growing problem created by the thinning of the boundary—the magical barrier that separated the Realm, where magic still existed, from the rest of the world. The main agency office hid in plain sight above a mundane store while the portal itself lay below ground, well hidden, of course, not that the guardians would let any pass without proper authorization first. There were various other offices scattered around the world, mostly in areas where the boundary had been showing signs of decay. A phenomenon that had the Realm's brightest wizards baffled.

The boundary had held magic and its denizens at bay

for hundreds of years. Why it had suddenly started to thin out was a mystery, one he'd leave to the scholars. His job, and that of the other hunters, was to find those who kept slipping over the boundary. He tracked them, trapped them, and then brought them back to the portal for transport back to the Realm. But the incursions were increasing, and the media kept reporting more and more strange happenings. It wouldn't be long before something caused the mundane world to sit up and take notice.

As to how a portal—a magical doorway to the Realm—ended up being below a mundane store? Simple—when initially created, the portal in this area lay surrounded by wilderness, no signs of habitation anywhere. Unfortunately, civilization came along, and to protect the Realm, a building was established around the portal area. To cover its use, it started out as a bordello—easy to sneak people in and out in muffled cloaks back then. But then bordellos became frowned upon—damn prissy womenfolk didn't like knowing their men were straying—so, for a short while, it changed venues and became a book store. Boring! And then, about thirty to forty years ago, right around the time *Star Wars* came out, and cults collecting plastic figurines were born, somebody in management with a sense of humor came up with the perfect cover. The store became The Magic Emporium, a collectors store for the arcane and weird. If someone wanted pewter dragons, wizards, or unicorns, the Emporium had it. *Dungeons and Dragons* cards, *Star Wars* and *Star Trek* collectibles, real swords and crystal balls, the Emporium carried it all along with costumes, magic books, Ouija boards. . . Well, you get the idea. Turned out the idea was also financially sound. The store not only supported itself it also made enough for them to afford all the high-tech gadgets and gizmos they required in a world where magic was considered a children's fairy tale.

Given the store's odd merchandise and even odder clientele, this switch to the arcane, which many still found ironic considering their ancestry, made it easy to stay open twenty-four hours a day and served as great camouflage for the sometimes strange visitors that came through here. Take the giant bunny that had hopped over last March. Being close to Easter, nobody on the street had said a word when he'd brought the giant pink bunny hopping up the street and into the store. Yes, another one of his less-than-stellar moments.

A loud cursing was heard from the far end of the room where the stairs to the store below were. In lumbered a heavyset man with jowly cheeks wearing a ridiculous pointed, black felt hat covered in stars and a black, flapping robe shimmering with pasted-on moons.

"Stupid bloody *Harry Potter*. I swear, when I find out which of you rotten scoundrels booked that party, I'm gonna kill you!"

Hunter winced, but Owen just grinned. "Aw, come on, Bob, weren't the kiddies just adorable?"

"Kiddies!" roared Bob. "The youngest one was sixty-two, and they all wanted to sit in my lap."

Flinging the hat one way while tearing the robe off with his other hand, Hunter's boss, Bob, jerked his head at Hunter and indicated he follow him into his office.

Once the door shut and Bob had safely ensconced himself in his leather chair, he sighed.

"That Owen. I am going to get him one of these days," Bob said with a scowl. Then he let out a big belly laugh. Good thing Bob had a great sense of humor for all his gruffness. "Silly kids. Well, Hunter, I knew you couldn't stay away. Good thing, too. We got a worrying report about the Dragon."

"He's escaped?" asked Hunter, leaning against the wall.

"Yes. Seems they allowed some rookie inside the prison to bring him his meal. The commander is on a rampage. Apparently, nobody thought to tell the rookie never to look in the Dragon's eyes. He got mesmerized by the Dragon and let him loose. Poor kid didn't even know what had happened till they found him sleeping like a baby in the cell."

"What about the rest of the guards? Didn't anybody notice?" Hunter's brows were raised high in astonishment. Sounded like the prison guards deserved a good reaming. That was just plain lax on their part.

"Nobody even knew the Dragon was gone till they went to bring him his next meal and found the rookie in his cell. By then it had been about four hours. Needless to say, heads are now currently rolling."

Yes, the commander would definitely not be happy about a screw-up like that. *I'm glad I'm not there*, he thought. Although, if he had been, it probably never would have happened. "So, what's the Dragon got to do with us?"

"Well, you heard about his capture on the West Coast, this side of the boundary, three years or so ago?"

"Yeah. I heard about it, but that was before I came to work for the agency. So?"

"Well, our trackers say he's heading toward our portal this time. And while I know he's not stupid enough to try and go through the actual portal with the guardians, the boundary has been getting thin enough in spots in this area that someone with his powers could probably get through."

"Shit!" Even without his magical powers, the Dragon remained someone you did not want loose, anywhere. The higher powers only knew what kind of deadly mischief he'd get into.

"Shit is right."

"But," said Hunter pensively, "what is there for him in this world? Even if he escapes through the boundary, his powers then become neutralized. The thinning of the boundary hasn't changed the lack of magic on this side."

"We think he's coming to finish what he started three years ago. We only wish we knew what that was."

"Were you able to trace his movements back then?" asked Hunter.

"We did our best after the fact, but we'd just gotten the agency offices set up, and well, we were still learning our way around computers back then."

"So, what do we know?"

"We know he pretended to be a professor at a West Coast university, his subject— don't laugh—Fairy Tales and Other Myths. We're not quite sure what he was attempting. We checked the archived news records for unusual occurrences and deaths, but nothing came up. We'll keep digging, though." Knowing Bob, he'd do more than dig—the man was very thorough. Give him a few days and he'd probably know what brand of detergent the Dragon used to wash his clothes.

"Maybe he wanted to try and turn over a new leaf. Live a new life free of the magic that had tainted him." Hunter didn't really believe it, but hey, stranger things had happened. Look at the ogre a few years ago that had decided to become vegetarian. He'd been unfortunately eaten by his comrades, but at least he'd tried. And then that oddball unicorn that decided it preferred courtesans to virgins—claimed they knew how to rub his fur better.

"Not likely. Our intelligence says he was making plans to come back to the Realm when he got captured three years ago. He claimed that he'd accomplished what he'd set out to do, and when he escaped, we would all rue the day we'd imprisoned him."

"Hmm, that doesn't sound too promising," said Hunter pensively. What the hell had the Dragon been up to? "Keep me posted. Any pictures of this guy in case he does show up on our turf?"

"How's tall, dark, and handsome?" said Bob sarcastically. "We couldn't get anyone to paint him in the Realm safely—you know those artsy types are too fragile for his type of magic. And, well, once caught, no one bothered to get a photo of him, and the university that hired him as a professor missed him when they took staff photos. About all we know is he's about six foot with raven-black hair and gray eyes. Handsome according to the ladies. He tends to prefer black for his clothing. Oh, and while living this side of the border, he used the name Damian Draco."

Hunter raised an eyebrow and laughed. "You've got to be kidding. Damian Draco. What kind of stupid name is that?"

"Yeah, well, I guess he didn't think Phineas Porter went with his image."

"Ouch," winced Hunter. "I'd change names too if I got stuck with that."

Bob leaned back in his chair, which groaned alarmingly at the weight. "I think the clue to his current whereabouts might lie in his past, so we'll be sure to dig deep and hard. Find out who his friends were back then. If someone was crazy enough to date him."

"Sounds good. Let me know if you find anything. If he's in my turf, I'll find him," said Hunter. Yes, he could use a good hunt. And this Phineas, or Damian, whatever the hell he liked to call himself, sounded like the perfect thing to get his mind off of other soft and luscious things.

With a farewell wave to Owen, who diligently tapped away, Hunter went back to his office to putter for a while.

What did the Dragon want? Crossing the boundary made him magicless, so what had he accomplished during his time here? Did he have accomplices? Lots of questions rolled through his mind, but without further info, his hands were tied for the moment.

A knock on the door had him calling, "Come in."

An elderly, hunched-over woman stepped in. "Excuse me, young man, but you're a private eye, aren't you? I need help finding my cat. She's missing."

Swallowing a sigh, Hunter stepped into his role of mundane investigator. Another not-so-exciting day awaited, but once the Dragon was found, the real fun would begin.

CHAPTER 5

God, Suzie hated shopping with kids. It had been much easier when they were babies. Strap them into a stroller and off they went. But they were too big for strollers now, and unfortunately, their new grocery store had only the single-seater carts, so she spent a good portion of her time chasing down giggling monsters. The rest of the time she spent pulling out groceries she hadn't put in the cart—Lucky Charms, double fudge cookies, chips. All the healthy stuff, of course. The kids whined when she put them back and replaced their choices with Corn Bran, rice crackers, and —shudder—yogurt. Yucky, slimy stuff. She wouldn't touch it, but all the kids books and magazines swore by it.

Finally, the groceries and other errands done, they piled in the car with their purchases to head back home. They were pulling out of the parking lot when Jared said, "Mommy, why is da man wooking at uth?"

"Hmm," she said, only half listening. "What man?"

"Over dere," he said, pointing.

Suzie tried to look in the direction Jared waved one pudgy finger in and caught a glimpse of a man in black walking rapidly away.

"I think you were mistaken, honey. Looks like the man was just running his own errands."

"He was wooking at uth!" stated Jared stubbornly.

Jessica started crying. "I don wan' him to wook at me!"

Thankfully, Suzie's hands were on the wheel, or she would have yanked her hair out. "There is no man watching us." But her claim did little to reduce the rising decibels in the backseat. A chorus of fear that showed no signs of stopping and it was all her fault. She couldn't deny she'd spent a lot of the past few years looking over her shoulder, watching constantly for danger.

"Hey, how about we get some McDonalds?" Okay, call it cheating, bribing, whatever you want to call it, but guess what? The wailing stopped.

"I wanna booger!" said Jared.

"Burger," Suzie corrected.

"I wan' noogies," said the now-beaming Jessica.

Suzie didn't bother trying to correct her. The kids had stopped crying, so who cared about a few dropped consonants?

Pulling into the drive-thru, Suzie made a mental vow to give them extra veggies for dinner to compensate for their lunch. Then had to amend her vow to include some extra veggies for herself when she ordered a Big Mac with extra sauce. Hey, she needed to eat, too!

They finally got home with no further meltdowns

THE HUNTER

and stranger sightings. She settled them in front of the television to watch something with cartoon mermaids while they munched on their Happy Meals. Okay, so shoot her for being a lazy mother. But the half-hour respite she'd get while they boob-tubed and ate was well worth it. Besides, she'd grown up with television and McDonalds, and she'd turned out all right for the most part. Her mother might have been strict, but when she worked, she often took the lazy way out too.

Once she'd finished eating her sin for the day, she put away the groceries and prepared the ingredients for the kids to make cookies. And thinking of the cookies made her thoughts turn, once again, to her handsome neighbor.

He'd claimed to be single last night. A hot guy like him, he probably had women chasing him constantly, though, and she had no intention of joining the crowd. And besides, she highly doubted slightly chubby, single mothers fell into his usual type. Sure, she had a nice complexion, all pale, unblemished skin. Her hair lacked pizzazz, though, just a thick mass of brown. Not golden highlighted or layered, just straight, hanging brown to match her normal brown eyes. Her body since the twins wasn't exactly the kind that made men drool. How sexy can you be with several extra pounds around the ass and hips, not to mention the stretch marks and not-so-perky boobs? Breastfeeding might be the healthier choice for babies, but they should have mentioned the effect gravity would have on her boobs. Thank God for super support bras!

Having seen her children interact with Hunter yesterday, though, had made her realize how selfish her decision had been to wall herself completely off from men. The children needed some kind of father figure in their life. But this time, if she did get involved with someone, it would be for the right reasons—mutual respect and affection. Not infatuation, and definitely not lust. Look where that combination had gotten her last time—pregnant with twins and alone. Not that she ever regretted having the twins, she loved them way too much, but a better choice for a father would have helped.

She still couldn't believe she'd been so stupid and naive. There were no excuses. So what if she'd gone from an all-girls school and a strict mother to university, eager to learn and live life? She'd learned, all right. She learned that sometimes life sucked!

A sharp pain broke through her trip to the past. Damn, she'd squeezed the plastic tray she held so tightly she had cut her finger. Running her hand under cold water, she washed away the blood and bandaged the cut. Pity she couldn't heal her wounds from the past so easily.

But enough of the past. She'd escaped that jerk and made a new life for herself and her precious angels. And besides, he'd been good for one, make that two, things—Jessica and Jared. The twins were her life, and she would protect them from anyone who ever dared to hurt them, even their so-called father.

Arranging the last of the ingredients needed for the cookies, she braced herself and called in the twins to help her create chaos in the kitchen. Whoever said cooking with kids was fun was either lying or insane. She had flour on her ceiling and dough on the walls to prove it!

THE HUNTER

~

THEY'D JUST finished dinner and were doing a big puzzle on the floor when they heard the sound of Hunter's motorcycle. The twins flew to the window, squealing.

"Mom! Mom! Bike!" screamed Jared.

"Yes, yes, I know." Jeez, the whole neighborhood probably knew. Jared definitely had good lungs.

"Can we—can we—can—" he stuttered in his excitement.

"Yes, you can go see him, but mind your manners and *do not touch!*" said Suzie in a stern, no-nonsense Mommy voice. At this age you had to remind them at least a dozen time, and even then, it was hit or miss whether they listened.

With an energy that only the young have, they went flying out the front door screaming, "Hunta! Hunta!"

Suzie followed more slowly, grabbing the plate of cookies first. When she walked out the front door, her first thought was, *Oh my God, he's gotten even sexier*.

Picture one hot man in black leather chaps, leather jacket, big black boots, and aviator glasses—talk about every girl's bad-boy dream come true. Suzie felt herself getting aroused just watching him swing his muscled leg off the bike. Maybe she should invest in some personal pleasure toys. Apparently, her body had suddenly discovered it had needs, and they needed to be taken care of *now!*

Taking a deep breath, and telling her raging

hormones to settle down, she sauntered over to her excited munchkins and their new hero.

"Can we go for a wide?" asked Jared, whose eyes were so big they were liable to fall out of his head.

"Maybe when you get a little bigger, buddy."

Jessica didn't say a thing. She just hugged a leather-clad leg with a smile. *Lucky girl*, thought Suzie wistfully, wishing she could wrap herself around that hot bod too.

She needed to change the direction of her thoughts. "Um, here," Suzie said, thrusting the plate of cookies forward. "The kids made these for you as a thank-you for your help yesterday."

"They're chocolate," whispered Jessica.

"Thank you," said Hunter, crouching down and giving Jessica a hug. "Chocolate cookies are my favorite."

Jessica beamed in his arms, and Suzie felt a pang. *Great, now I'm jealous of my own daughter.*

Hunter whipped off his sunglasses and, to Jared's delight, put the glasses on him. Jared crowed in glee and strutted around in them, pretending to be cool. Picking Jessica up with one arm, he finally smiled at Suzie, whose tummy immediately went into a flip-flop routine.

"Hi," he said.

"Right back at you," said Suzie. Oh God, she really needed lessons in casual conversation because she sounded like a moron again. "Nice bike." *Ooh, so smooth, gonna tell him it's shiny next?* She really needed to get out and talk to grownups more.

"She's a beauty, all right. Ever since I discovered motorcycles a few years ago, Harleys are my favorite. Ever ride?"

"What? Me? Oh no," she said, shaking her head vehemently. "Too scary!"

"Scary? No, more like thrilling," he said with a grin, his eyes twinkling with mirth. "All that power between your legs."

Mmm, that sounded way dirtier than it should have.

"Maybe I'll take you for a ride sometime," he said huskily.

Yes, a ride sounds reallllllly good. Oh God, she really needed to get her hormones back under control.

"I'll think about it," she said. "Anyway, hope you like the cookies and, again, thanks. Come on, kids. Time for your bath."

To the chorus of "Aw, Mom," Suzie and the twins walked back over to their house. Unable to resist, she peeked back over her shoulder and saw Hunter watching her. At her look, his lips curved into a cocky, cream-your-panties grin, which, to her chagrin, worked just like a charm, shooting a hot, wet warmth through her suddenly wakened lower parts. And judging by his grin, he knew it too! Shoot, now he'd start thinking she liked him. Which she did, even if he was so definitely wrong for her.

Ushering the kids inside, she ignored her body's pleading and, instead, prepared for the tsunami also known as bath time. As she washed behind ears and scrubbed little heads, she tried to forget that smile, which ended up being a lot harder than it should have been. Although the wet washcloth thrown at her face did banish it for a moment.

When Suzie turned and looked back at him, Hunter felt a stirring in his groin. By the higher powers, he needed to get laid. His sexy new neighbor went beyond distracting, but getting involved with her was such a bad idea. Not to mention the fact that he had to be careful about not blowing his cover.

The agency didn't care if he slept with women, but he had strict orders not to become involved with any who were not in on the secret. You know, Realm security and all. So when the itch hit, he usually just found a bar in town and, well, not to be too conceited, with his looks, basically had his pick. He rarely saw the same woman twice, and he never, ever brought them home or told them where he worked. He liked sex. He just didn't want any of the emotional baggage that came with a relationship. The women he slept with knew this, though. Hell, they were looking for the same thing—no-commitment sex. It wasn't as if he didn't intend to settle down one day —a long, long time from now. But till he found the right girl—or dear old Dad chose one for him—he planned on having lots and lots of fun.

Suzie, however, not only lived too close to home she just wasn't the type of girl to engage in one-night stands. Pity! Her effect on his body, though—a constant ache in his groin—made him realize he was past due for some "relaxation." Maybe then he'd be able to stop thinking about that luscious ass of hers and how he wanted to smother his face between her...

By the higher powers! It was definitely time to get some action. Too bad he needed to do some laundry first. He'd run out of underpants, and he couldn't go without them. It just wasn't comfortable in jeans. Not to mention his manly parts and his zipper had already had one accident, and he wasn't keen on another. The pain still made him shudder.

Nope, laundry first, but tomorrow, though, he'd definitely take care of his overdue libido. Maybe twice just to be sure it didn't start poking its head again whenever he saw Suzie.

CHAPTER 6

Suzie resisted an urge to pull her hair out. The bank had called and needed her to go in and sign some paperwork. No big deal unless you had a pair of three-year-olds who were stubbornly refusing to go.

"No wanna go," said Jessica, arms crossed over her chest.

"Me too," said Jared, aping his sister.

"It won't take too long, guys. Mommy's gotta go sign papers. Then we'll come back." But the twins were adamant. Why? Who knew! It wasn't as if they had anything exciting planned to do at home, unless you counted cleaning. She couldn't even bribe them with food. They'd just eaten. But last time she'd looked, her job description said Mommy, so, too bad. That meant they didn't have a choice. Ha, apparently someone need to explain that to them.

Suzie wrestled them into some clothes, emerging victorious but sweaty. She struggled to hold on to her temper. She really hated yelling, but this was getting ridiculous.

Whoever had coined the phrase terrible twos had forgotten to mention the stubborn threes. By picking one up under each arm, she finally got them outside where they were still kicking up a fuss.

"Enough!" Suzie finally shouted. The kids both looked up at her, and then their lower lips trembled. A symphony of wailing started that, to her tired ears, had the same effect as nails on chalkboard. *Duct tape anyone?*

A tap on her shoulder had her turning to see Hunter looking as sexy as ever. Not that she cared. Nope. And that tingling she felt from head to toe? Just her imagination.

"Why are the children crying?" he asked, his brows raised at their loud, impromptu concert.

"I need to go to the bank, but they refuse to go. The last time we went, even with my appointment, I was there about two hours, and well, it wasn't a lot of fun for them, shall we say?" Now there was an understatement. Last time, she'd exhausted every creative bone in her body trying to entertain two active kids in a tiny cubicle.

"I'll watch them while you're gone."

Suzie almost burst out laughing. The idea of Hunter playing nanny for an hour or two was just too incongruous.

Unfortunately, the kids heard him.

"Yay, Hunta play with us," said Jessica, her eyes glowing with hero worship.

"Bye, Mommy," said Jared, not even waiting for her reply.

Outvoted by two master manipulators. But Suzie barely knew Hunter. How could she trust her kids with him? Sure, he didn't seem like a perv, but what did he know about minding kids?

As if he read her mind, he said, "We'll be fine. I am sure I can manage to entertain two kids for a few hours. How bad could it be?"

At his boast, Suzie made up her mind. She wouldn't be gone long, and a teensy tiny part of her—her naughty side—wanted to see how he'd cope. She hoped only that the house would stay intact. As for Hunter's sanity, well, he had volunteered.

"Fine, you guys can stay here with Hunter. But you'd better behave," she said sternly at her smiling cherubic-looking children. Or, should she say, imps in disguise?

With a kiss for each and another firm admonishment to behave, she smiled at Hunter and left.

Let's see how the big, hunky PI likes babysitting. Suzie giggled all the way to the bank.

HUNTER ALMOST SHOOK HIS HEAD, bemused by what had just transpired. He'd volunteered to babysit! How the hell had that happened? Maybe he'd caught something. Some kind of fever of the brain that hit whenever he got close to Suzie. Every time he saw her, he found himself offering to do things that he'd never agree to do for anyone else. If he didn't know this side of the boundary was magicless, he'd wonder if she had some kind of magical power over him. No, he had only his stupid self to blame. That and a lack of blood to his brain whenever she showed up.

But he couldn't run away, not with two pair of identical brown eyes staring at him, waiting. Waiting for what, though? First things first, he ushered them inside into the living room.

"Um, so what would you like to do?" he asked. *What do children do all day?*

"Pway pwincess!" squealed Jessica.

"Piwates!" exclaimed Jared.

Hunter had no idea how to play either. They quickly showed him how. Jessica dragged him by the hand upstairs and put on a play princess dress with a string of beads and a tiara. Then she proceeded to dress Hunter in a red cape with a second tiara. Hunter mentally groaned. If this ever got out, he'd be a laughingstock.

Jared, meanwhile, dressed in a pirate skullcap with a sword harness and play sword. Then he added a pirate patch, which—yay—he had two of. Guess who got to wear the other one?

So Hunter ended up transformed into a princess—er prince—slash pirate. He then went around grunting "Arrr!" with Jared while waving his sword and shouting, "Off with his head." Jessica's favorite line seemed to be, "Bow peasant. I'm a pwincess."

To Hunter's surprise, he rather enjoyed himself, not that he would ever admit it under torture to anyone over the age of three.

He also quickly learned that, no matter how much fun a game was, it never lasted longer than ten or fifteen minutes. The pirate-princess game was followed by blocks, then coloring, then cars, then a tea party, then hide and seek, then . . .

When Suzie arrived home just over two hours later, Hunter was exhausted. But good news, so were the kids. Lying on the couch, completely relaxed, he had a child nestled under the crook of each arm, fast asleep.

The look on Suzie's face when she walked in? Priceless. Her jaw literally dropped at the sight of her children napping.

"How did you manage to get them to sleep? I haven't been able to get them to nap since they were two."

"We played hard," said Hunter with a satisfied grin. He wouldn't tell her he'd nodded off, too, and woken only when she opened the door. Some things a man had to keep to himself.

"I hope they weren't too much trouble."

"Nope, it was fun," he said, and truthfully, it had been. Jared and Jessica were energetic, sure, but discovering the world through their eyes had been, well, fantastic. Hunter had never really had a chance to play as a youngster. His father had been big on lessons—sword lessons, reading and writing, hand-to-hand combat, tracking. . . There hadn't been much time for play with his strict schedule. Although, now that he thought about it, his mother had usually managed to squeeze in something special every other day, whether it was a story for pure fun or a walk in the woods to pick flowers or a swim in the creek. He'd have to remember to thank his mother. *Funny, the things you take for granted as a child.*

Hunter eased himself off the couch, rolling the

outside twin farther onto the cushion so he wouldn't fall on the floor.

"Sorry it took so long. The previous appointment ran late, and then their printer wouldn't work. What a pain!"

"No problem." He decided not to tell her about the paint incident on the carpet. He'd scrubbed it pretty good, so maybe she wouldn't notice.

"Well, I really appreciate it. If you ever need a favor, just let me know."

Oh, I can think of a few things, Hunter thought, his lips curving into a mischievous smile. He knew a way she could pay him back. He squashed the interest rising from below. *That's it. Time to go out and take care of my needs tonight.*

With a big grin at Suzie and a last look at the sleeping twins, Hunter went home. He needed a nap so he could go prowling that night.

When he woke a few hours later, he had another raging erection. He'd been caught up in a naughty dream that featured Suzie as a princess being kidnapped by him, the randy pirate. And let him just say that the princess really enjoyed the dirty things the pirate did to her.

By the higher powers! He hadn't been this horny since his teens. He needed a woman, any woman, to take care of the ache in his groin.

And he did try later that night. He showered and dressed in tight, black jeans with an open-neck white shirt, sleeves partially rolled up to show his muscular arms—the ladies really enjoyed that look. Dressed in his leathers, he rode his bike into town and hit his favorite bar. A sure place for those looking for unattached fun.

Walking in, he knew he looked good, really good, and the women were flirting with him left and right. Problem was none of them did anything for him. *What the hell is wrong with me?*

Take the gorgeous blonde in front of him. She had her hand high up on his thigh— any higher and it would have been illegal in public—and she kept leaning forward, showing off her deep décolletage, but he felt nothing. Not even a little stir of interest. Determined not to give up, Hunter grabbed the blonde by the hand and they went outside, where he pushed her up against the wall of the bar and kissed her. He ground his hips against hers while her overly red lips devoured his. She even rubbed her curvy body in all the right ways against him, but nothing. All lay dormant down below.

Shit! What the hell is going on? A few hours ago, he'd awakened harder than hell from a naughty dream featuring his hot neighbor, and now he couldn't even muster up a little enthusiasm. Although, at the thought of Suzie, something finally did start to stir, and Hunter pulled away from the blonde with a groan.

"What's wrong?" she asked huskily with heavy-lidded eyes.

"Sorry, I just remembered. I've got an early-morning meeting. We'll have to get together another time." And before she could protest, he took off.

Riding his bike, the cool evening air streaming over his body, he thought, *What is it about Suzie that has me so bewitched? She's attractive, but then again, so was the blonde I just tried to pick up.* Never had a woman filled his thoughts like she had from the moment he'd met her.

So what made her special? Sure, he liked the twins, but that still didn't explain his attraction to Suzie. The urge he had to talk to her, be with her, touch her...

Hunter wished his mother were here. She'd always been great at listening and giving him advice. He wondered what she'd think of Suzie. That is after she got over her initial shock because the women he usually went after weren't the type you brought home to mother. Just the fact that he wanted his mom to meet her said a whole lot more than Hunter felt ready to admit. He knew his father would hate her on principle.

"She's a mundane," he could hear the commander saying now. Yes, had he mentioned that his commander was also dear old Daddy? Not that he'd called him anything other than Sir since, well, forever. He'd always been Daddy's little soldier and had always been treated as such.

Hunter had never understood how his parents got together. His mother had such a free spirit, caring and giving, while his father was, well, the commander. He'd asked his mother once what she saw in him, and she'd replied, "I love him," as if that was the only answer he needed.

Did he love Suzie? He didn't think so. He barely knew her, but for the first time in his life, he couldn't stop thinking about a woman. And he hadn't even slept with her!

Is this what this is all about? My ego? Could his interest simply be the thrill of the chase? In that case, then having sex with her should take care of it. But, somehow, he didn't think that was the only problem. For some reason, Suzie and her kids scared him. Not the "ooh I'm shaking in my boots" type of fear. This one came from deeper inside, more of a man fear. A part of him found himself attracted to the comfort and family life she represented, but his wild, testosterone-filled side screamed, *run for the hills before she puts a bridle on you!*

And now he came to the root of the matter—commitment or, the dreaded word, marriage. Did his subconscious somehow fear that he'd suddenly stop being him, the hunter, if he found himself a family and settled down? Or was he scared he'd be like his father—a cold, unfeeling man who treated his children like soldiers instead of his own flesh and blood?

Well, that wouldn't do. After all, he'd trained to be a hunter, and hunters weren't scared of anything. He'd prove it. Tomorrow morning, he'd take Suzie and the twins out for a day at the park. Right after a long, really long, workout. Maybe if his body was tired, he'd have a chance of resisting the urge to kiss her. Maybe.

CHAPTER 7

Suzie didn't mean to spy on him. She'd happened to look out the window of her room while making her bed, and there he shone. A half-naked, golden god in the early morning light.

Hunter stood in his backyard wearing only a low-hanging pair of track pants. His muscles rippled as he took his body through a series of exercises that had him stretching and bending. *And lord help me, it is so sexy.*

Finished with his stretching, he picked up a wooden cane, and with it in one hand, he began moving again. Pirouetting and slashing with the cane as he spun his body first in one direction then the other, the exertion made his body shine so temptingly. Lunging and twirling, he circled his yard, his wooden cane striking at imaginary foes. A whirlwind of action, his body moved sinuously like an ancient warrior engaged in a killing dance. Suzie watched him, enthralled at the raw power and energy he exuded. She held her breath when he began to rapidly spin and slash, a cyclonic whirlwind of motion. He finished up his routine with a tumble and upward jab.

Suzie couldn't help the heat that coursed through her loins. Her breasts felt heavy, her kitty throbbed, and she had an insane urge to run downstairs and fling herself on him so she could lick the sweat off his chest.

She really needed to get laid.

Dashing into the bathroom down the hall, she stripped and jumped into the shower with only the cold water on. Shivering and teeth chattering, she tried to get the image of his body out of her mind. She needed to control this. She had promised herself three years ago that she would never let her hormones make her choices again. And that was all it was. Hormones. Lust. And lust wasn't the foundation to build a relationship from. She wanted more this time.

But, said a nagging little voice in her head, *he's also nice, polite, great with the kids...*

And he happened to also be a private eye who had to leave town on business, who rode a Harley, and could have his pick of just about any woman he wanted. Especially ones who didn't come with a past, emotional baggage, or a built-in family like her.

Suzie sighed. A good dose of reality, while not always welcome, was sometimes needed. Feeling more in control, Suzie stepped out of her cold shower and toweled off. Only halfway through her drying, the doorbell, of course, rang.

Shoot! "Don't answer that," she hollered. Suzie rubbed at herself frantically, trying to dry off marginally before trying to pull up her jeans over still-too-damp legs. And everyone knows how well that works.

She had them wedged halfway up her legs when she heard the children squealing and a low voice rumble back at them, a familiar rumble she might add. So much for them not answering, then again, once they knew who rang, nothing short of strait jackets would have stopped them. Of more concern...

Hunter is here. Oh damn, did he see me spying on him?

Yanking roughly on her jeans, she hopped and squirmed till she managed to finally wiggle them up over her hips. Her bra was nowhere in sight so she threw her T-shirt on, which, of course, rolled up around her boobs. Tugging it down while cursing under her breath, she scurried out of the bathroom, wet hair dripping down her back, and flew down the stairs.

Hunter had pulled on a shirt before coming over, she noticed. A shame.

He smiled when he saw her, and his eyes grew smoky as he stared at a point below her chin. Looking down, Suzie wanted to sink into the ground and die. Her wet hair and still-damp body made the T-shirt cling to her full breasts. Her nipples, prominent already through the thin fabric, hardened into little nubs. Cheeks pink in mortification, she crossed her arms over her chest and glared at him.

The jerk just chuckled. She took back every thought she'd had about him being nice. Nice guys didn't stare at women's boobs. *And nice girls didn't spy on their neighbors exercising*, her snide inner voice replied.

"Hi, I was wondering if maybe you and the children would like to go to the park today? There's nothing at the office for me to do, and I thought these little goblins might enjoy a change of scenery. We could bring a picnic for lunch. They've got tables and stuff set up there. There's even a small pond we could hunt frogs in."

"I, uh, don't know. . ." *Bad idea, bad idea*, her mind chanted.

"Pwease," begged Jessica, looking up at her with her big doe eyes.

"Yes, Mommy, can we go?" said Jared, his eyes just as pleading.

Faced with such cuteness, what was a mother to do?

"Okay, we'll go, but first I want you to tidy up your room and get dressed." The kids were gone in a flash, screaming in glee as they raced up the stairs.

"I've got some sandwiches already made. Peanut butter and jelly all right?" said Hunter, an amused quirk still twisting his lips.

"Pretty sure of yourself, were you?" she asked, a little miffed.

"Hoping," he said, unabashed.

"I'll get the kids ready and pack some snacks and juice. When do you want to leave? And how are we getting there?"

"I'll wait for you out front. We can walk, I think. It's about a ten- or fifteen-minute walk from here. Can the children handle that?"

"We should be all right, but I'll bring the wagon just in case. Okay, we'll see you out front in a few."

Suzie closed the door and leaned on it for a minute.

Well, the attraction looked as if it might be mutual. Too bad it wasn't going anywhere.

So why the hell had she agreed to go on a picnic with him? *For the children, of course. Yeah right*, her mind snickered back.

Speaking of which. . .Suzie jogged up the stairs and checked in on the twins. Miracle of all miracles, their room appeared to be actually tidy, and they'd even attempted to make their beds by pulling up the covers. They were both sitting on the floor pulling on socks and grinned up at her when they saw her checking.

"Awmost weady," they sang.

I'd better get ready too. Shrugging off her damp T-shirt, she towel dried her hair vigorously before cinching it back into a tight ponytail. She pulled out an old sports bra that smashed her boobs flat and then put on a baggy T-shirt. *Ha—nothing to ogle now*.

Herding her dressed—if mismatched—children in front of her, they went back downstairs. She left them putting on their shoes while she went into the kitchen and pulled out juice boxes, grapes, and watermelon. She also grabbed some cold cuts and cheese. She'd never been a huge fan of peanut butter and jelly, made her gums stick together—yeck!

Now, where had she put the cooler? The garage. Grabbing her keys and sunglasses, along with her bag of food, Suzie and the kids left the house, locking it behind them.

The twins, squealing, raced over to Hunter, who lounged outside waiting for them with his own plastic bag of food. Opening the garage door, she spied the fabric cooler bag and wagon amid the pile of boxes. Shoving everything in it, she pulled it out and met up with her excited kids and Hunter, who listened attentively to their babble.

"So, which way?" she asked, looking at him from behind her sunglasses.

"Straight up the street, actually. It's only a couple of blocks."

With a firm admonition to watch for cars and to stop at the corner, the twins raced off down the sidewalk, Suzie and Hunter following behind with the wagon. Hunter insisted on pulling the wagon, and Suzie let him. It was man's work, after all. Sound sexist? So what? It wasn't as if she often had the chance to have a man do any work for her, so she decided to enjoy it while it lasted.

"How you liking the new house?" he asked.

"Love it. Our last few places were apartments and kind of cramped, so we're really liking having a yard and so much room. I've got to say I'm surprised to see a single guy living in the burbs."

"Yeah, well, I'm not really into the whole big-city thing myself. Too noisy. Parking's a lot easier in the suburbs, and I like the space and privacy. Apartments just seem too—" He struggled to find the word.

"Crammed. Packed in like sardines."

"Yeah. Anyways, a friend of my mine helped me find this place, and, well, the rest, as they say, is history. So, what made you move here? Where are you from?"

"I needed a change. I used to live out on the West Coast, and after the twins were born, I couldn't stay."

"Couldn't stay because?" he prompted.

"Personal reasons," she said. How to explain that she'd run away from the twins' father? Hunter would surely think she was a class-one bitch. *He wouldn't if you told him why*, said her niggling inner voice. She really needed to get that voice gagged.

Hunter went silent for a moment. "Tell me it's none of my business if you want, but what happened to the twins' dad? I take it he's the main reason you left."

Ooh, perceptive man. She'd forgotten about his living as a private eye. How much should she tell?

"Their father wasn't a very nice man, as it turns out." Now there was an understatement.

"Did he hurt you?" Hunter asked in an oddly tight voice.

Suzie turned her head to look at him and saw him clenching his jaw. "Not too much physically, but the mental abuse and his plans for the children were pretty bad."

"Do me a favor, will you?"

"What?" she asked.

"If he ever shows up on your doorstep, call me."

"Why? What can you do?" Suzie asked.

"Lots of things," he said, his voice low and menacing.

Suzie got a shiver, not of fear, more like excitement. She'd never had someone want to come to her rescue before. And, to be honest, she'd love to see her ex getting one right in the kisser. He so deserved it.

"Well, I highly doubt he could find us now. He'd need magical powers or something to be able to follow the muddy trail I left behind."

The kids had stopped at the corner and were tapping their little feet impatiently as they waited for Hunter and her to catch up.

With each of them holding a child's hand tightly, they crossed. The park came in sight up ahead, and the twins' enthusiasm at its sight was contagious. With a laugh at Hunter stuck dragging the wagon, Suzie sprinted with the twins toward the swings.

When he finally arrived, the twins were soaring on the swings, powered by Mommy pushes.

"Hunta!" screamed Jared. "Wook at me!"

"Me too!" squealed Jessica. "I go high!"

To the twins' vast amusement, Hunter stood in front of them and pretended to be hit by their flying feet. Falling to the ground in theatrical fashion, Hunter would then spring to his feet with a mock growl. The children howled and kicked their legs at him. He pretended to lunge at them and, when their little feet hit his chest, went rolling backward in the grass. Suzie laughed. She'd never seen a grown man go through such antics to amuse children.

As is the case with all young children, though, this game lasted only for about fifteen minutes before they were off the swings and racing for the slides.

Suzie and Hunter wandered over to a bench in the shade and watched them play.

"You've got really nice children."

"Yup," replied Suzie smugly. Hey, when it came to kids, hers were the best!

"It's funny. I'd never really hung out with little ones

and stuff before. Never realized how much fun it could be."

"It's great most of the time. Scary sometimes, though, too. Like when they run high fevers in the middle of the night or when they decide to play hide and seek but don't tell you first. And then there are the times they drive you mad whining and bickering. But all in all, I have to say, being a parent is hugely rewarding. Nothing beats hearing that first word. Or the first time they walk." Suzie looked at him sideways. "You planning to have kids some day?"

"Hadn't really thought about it before, but now, having met yours, I have to say I'd like at least a half-dozen."

Suzie looked at him with her jaw hanging open. "Are you insane? Six kids!" Suzie started howling with laughter.

"What's wrong with six kids?" Hunter asked defensively.

"Well, first of all, you need to find a woman crazy enough to go through childbirth that many times. Let me tell you, pregnancy is not a bed of roses. Then there's the cost of raising that many kids. Not to mention your sanity."

"Okay, so maybe just a couple to start with," he said with that endearingly cocky grin of his, eyes dark with some emotion she couldn't identify. Once again, as if he were the sun and she a flower, she found herself leaning toward him and . . .

"Hunta, where the fwogs?"

They pulled apart guiltily as Jared came flying up to them.

"Ready to catch some frogs, little buddy?" Hunter asked.

Jared bobbed his head eagerly. A hilarious, but successful, frog hunt ensued with the handsome Hunter wading in murky pond water, jeans rolled up to mid-calf. Watching him with the twins, crouched down to their level, holding a slimy frog for them to pet, Suzie felt her heart bursting. *Is this what it would feel like to be a real family with a daddy?* Maybe she shouldn't dismiss Hunter as a possibility. But what if he turned out to be a jerk? Could she afford to allow her children's hearts to be broken? *And what about my own heart?*

She had no time to ponder this thought further, as her hungry frog catchers came running up to her, demanding food. Laying out the lunch items and watching the twins' tousled hair and animated faces, she knew she had a lot more thinking to do.

Hunter and the kids tore into their peanut butter and jelly sandwiches with relish. Suzie stuck to her ham and cheese. *Grownup food*, she thought with a grin. Watching Hunter and the kids fool around, trying to talk with peanut butter tongues, she wondered how a man who'd never been around children could get down to their level so easily. He acted like an overgrown kid, himself. And the kids loved it!

After their picnic lunch, Jessica wanted to be pushed on the swings again while Jared wanted to play in the sandbox. Hunter went with Jared and started helping him build some roads with trees and bridges while Suzie pushed Jessica on the swing and exhorted her to pump her legs. To no avail, apparently only Mommy pushes would do.

A tinny song erupted from the vicinity of Hunter's pants, some catchy salsa number that had her raising her brow in amusement. Hunter pulled out his cell phone with a sheepish grin.

"I changed the ringer by accident and can't change it back." Hunter looked at the number on his cell phone's display. "I have to take this. Are you all right with the children for a few minutes?"

Um, hello, who does he think has been watching the twins for the last three years? "Take the call. We'll be fine."

Hunter wandered off with his phone, and Suzie kept pushing Jessica while Jared played in the sand.

"Down, Mommy," said Jessica, tired of swinging.

"Okay, sweetheart, hold on. Let me slow you down." Moving around to face Jessica and grab the swing's ropes, she turned her back for a moment on Jared. She brought the swing to a standstill and helped Jessica off the swing. Jessica took two steps, and legs wobbly from swinging, fell on her knees in the pea gravel.

"Ow!" Jessica wailed.

"Let me see," said Suzie, crouching down to sit Jessica on her bent leg. Jessica raised the gravely injured knee—a little white scratch, oh my—and Suzie, as was her habit, kissed it.

"All better," sang Jessica, jumping off Suzie's lap and racing off to the sandbox behind Suzie to join Jared.

Suzie turned to watch her go and then felt her heart stop.

Where's Jared?

Suzie didn't panic yet, although her pulse sped up. "Jared!" she called. Maybe he'd wandered back to the slides while she'd been tending his sister. She scanned the playground but couldn't spot him on the slides or anywhere in the playground area. *Where the hell is he? Oh God, did he fall in the pond?*

Running to the edge of the play area, she looked around and finally spotted him talking to someone with a cap pulled down low. Jared backed away from the man, who reached out a hand. Jared, though, slid sideways, out of reach.

"Jared!" she hollered and started running. "Jared!" The man speaking to Jared ducked his head, turned, and started walking away quickly.

Hunter ran by her, heading for Jared while asking over his shoulder, "What happened?"

"I was helping Jessica," she panted, running. "I just turned my back for a second and, when I turned to look again, Jared was almost out of the park talking to that man who took off."

The man in question had jumped into a car parked on the road bordering the playground and drove away.

Jared came running to Suzie, who hugged him tight, then scolded him.

"Jared, what has Mommy told you about talking to strangers?"

"Mommy," he said, tears starting to fill his eyes at her angry tone. "Dat man thay he my daddy. He thay he mith me an' he gonna take me home. But I don wanna go, Mommy. I wanna thtay with you."

Suzie's face froze.

No, no, no, went the screaming in her head. This couldn't be happening. The man had to have been lying. There was no way *he* could have found them.

"I no like dat man, Mommy. He thcary," said Jared in a tiny voice clogged with tears.

"Did he say anything else?" asked Hunter as Suzie crouched there, paralyzed with fear.

"He thay tell Mommy hi an' dat he come back to take me 'way."

"Never, baby, never. That man was lying. Mommy would never let anybody take you." Suzie crushed Jared to her chest and held in the wail that threatened to burst out of her. *This can't be happening. I've been so careful. There was no way he could have found us!*

Jared squirmed out of her arms, her tight embrace scaring him. Suzie felt her mind swirling in a panicky mess, her only coherent thought—grab the children and run. They needed to hide. *Oh God*.

Hunter, sensing her fragile state, took charge.

"Come on, Jared and Jessica. I think your mother's tired. Let's take her home."

It was a much quieter group that dragged its feet home. The kids huddled in the wagon, arms wrapped around each other while Hunter pulled them. Suzie walked in a zombie-like trance. Her thoughts whirled in her head.

She'd have to move. She needed to hide the children.

This couldn't be happening. She'd been so careful. *Why did this have to happen?* her mind cried.

When they got home, Hunter settled the kids in front of the television and took her into the kitchen.

"Listen. I got a partial on the plate that stranger was driving. I'll run it through my contacts, see what they come up with. You know it may have just been a random perv, which isn't to say that it's better, but could mean it was just a random occurrence. Did you get a good enough look to see if it was the twins' father?"

"No, he had a cap pulled down over this face. I didn't really see anything. It could have been anyone, I guess. God, this can't be happening!" Suzie slammed her fist onto the counter then immediately winced as pain shot through her.

Hunter came close and put his arms around her, hugging her tightly. Suzie stood frozen for a second in the circle of his arms then relaxed, leaning into his strength. This time, while she felt heat, it wasn't the sexual kind. Instead, she absorbed the cocooning warmth of his body as she would a favorite blanket, the one she wrapped up in when the whole world seemed to be against her. And it felt nice. *I am so tired of being scared and alone.*

"You need to calm down. You can't let the twins see you like this. What have you told them about their father?"

Suzie squirmed in his arms. She didn't want to say. She knew Hunter would disapprove. In a low whisper, she said, "I told them their daddy was dead."

Hunter winced. "Okay, I'm sure you had a good reason for that. You'll need to have a talk with them about strangers again. If I were you, I wouldn't leave them alone, even in the yard for the next little while, just in case. I'll make some calls and find out if you have anything to worry about. I don't suppose you'll tell me their father's name? If I can locate him, and he's nowhere near here, then we can easily clear this up."

Suzie couldn't tell him. What if, by saying his name, she conjured him up somehow? *Do names have power?* Could she take that chance? Slowly, she shook her head.

Hunter didn't press her. "I'm going to leave for a little while. I want to take this information to the office and see if Owen can find anything out. Will you be all right for a little bit?"

Would she? All she wanted to do was crawl into a corner and cry. But that wouldn't solve anything, and her babies needed her. Suzie took a deep breath. "I'll be fine. I'll lock the doors after you leave."

"I'll be back in a few hours," Hunter said. He tilted her chin up and looked her in the eyes. The blue of his eyes reflected back like a calm lake, soothing and gentle. "I'll do everything I can to keep you and the kids safe," he said, and she believed him.

For just once, she wanted someone else to take on the burden she'd shouldered for the last three years. Fear could be a heavy weight to carry all alone. It would be nice to finally share that load. To not live constantly looking over her shoulder.

He kissed her lightly on the forehead, a comforting kiss like the one you'd give a child who is hurt, and left.

Suzie stayed in the kitchen a few moments more to collect herself. She needed to put on a brave face for the children. She couldn't let her paranoia affect them. It was bad enough she trembled in fear. The last thing she needed was a chorus to go along with the screaming in her head.

She took a deep, calming breath and walked into the living room. "Who's ready to play 'I Spy'?" she said with false cheer.

HUNTER SIMMERED, his anger a pot ready to boil over. He wanted to kill the bastard who'd put such a scare into Suzie, but he was even more pissed with himself. This was supposed to have been a nice day. Should have been a nice day. And even though he'd been there, something bad had happened, and he'd been unable to prevent it. He'd failed them. It didn't matter that no one could have predicted this. There was no excuse. He should have been more watchful, had his guard up. But how could he have known they'd need protecting?

No excuse! And just where had this protective, guard-dog attitude he had toward Suzie and her children come from? When had he decided to become their champion? Hell, he couldn't even blame this on sex. The comforting hug and kiss on the forehead he'd given her was the closest they'd gotten yet. But right now, he wanted to squeeze the neck of not only the perv from the park that had so frightened her but also the jerk of an ex-boyfriend who had her so terrified. The look of absolute terror on her face was not something he ever wanted to see again. Not on hers or anybody else's face. He needed to fix this. He wanted her to smile again. *Damn it, I am turning into a pansy.*

No, his sly inner voice said, *you finally found someone to care about.* Several someones.

He stormed into the agency office with only the barest grip on his rage.

"Owen!" he bellowed.

"What?" said Owen, startled from his computer screen.

"I need a favor. I need you to look up the ownership of a dark blue, four-door sedan, partial plate ending in O8M."

"Sure. What's this about?"

"Neighbor of mine's child got accosted in the park by some man. She's afraid it's her ex coming to take the children. I told her I'd look into it."

"That's not good. No problem. I'll get right on it," said Owen, his fingers already skipping over his keyboard. "So, tell me, is this neighbor hot? I don't mind if she's got a couple of kids, so long as she's hot."

"She's not available!" Hunter growled. Why he lied, he didn't know. But he knew the thought of her with another man made him want to punch something. Hard.

"Sorry, Hunter. Just asking. Anyways, I think I found the car."

"Who's it belong to?"

"Not your suspect. The car was stolen last night. Sounds like your neighborhood has itself a problem. I'll check the sex offender registry to see if there's anybody on their list in your area. But my advice is keep the children close till the cops catch the stranger or he moves on."

"Damn! Well, thanks, Owen. I owe you one. Oh, and any word yet on the Dragon?"

"Still working on it. We managed to get somewhere with his past. Apparently he set up house with some girl back when he was teaching. Even got her pregnant. We're still trying to find out her name so we can locate her and see if he's contacted her."

"Let me know when you hear anything. I'm going to do some poking around of my own before heading out."

Hunter called in some favors—the cops had appreciated his help on a couple of "bizarre" incidents— but no one had anything to add to Owen's report. The stolen car had been recovered. No prints. The thief had wiped the car down before ditching it. They promised to step up the neighborhood patrols, though.

With nothing left to do, and concerned about Suzie and the twins, he headed back home on his bike. His mind was full of the dark things he'd do to the man who'd made Suzie and Jared look so scared.

CHAPTER 8

Suzie heard Hunter's bike pull in next door around supper time and stupidly felt relieved. For some reason, having Hunter nearby made her feel safer, which made her kind of mad. What was she now, some weeping damsel in distress needing a man to save her? *No, I'm a scared mother who's got no one else to turn to for help, and for once, it feels nice to know that someone else just might be looking out for me and the kids.*

As she readied the kids for bed, she pasted on a smile for them. They'd already forgotten all about the afternoon's drama at the park and were chattering away. If only Suzie could forget as easily.

The kids tucked in for the night, Suzie double-checked the locks on her doors and windows before she grabbed her baby monitor and went out back on her rear deck to sit down. Looking up at the sky, she tried to not let her paranoia and terror overwhelm her. Not an easy feat, though. Her fear crept in like a spider, binding her tight in its cocooning thread, and it seemed the more she tried to fight it, the tighter she became caught.

A thud startled her, and she looked up to see Hunter had come over the fence and, in some feat of dexterity she'd missed, managed to bring two open beers with him.

"Here," he said, handing her a sweating brown bottle. "Figured you could use one."

Suzie tipped the bottle and chugged half of it before saying, "Thanks."

He just arched a brow at her and then, as if not to be outdone, chugged his entire bottle.

Men! Always have to one-up a girl. But he did manage to make her smile.

"Feeling better?" he asked.

"Not really. I guess it's stupid to be so scared, but dammit, you don't know what their father was like."

"Are you sure it was him?"

"No." She sighed. "And the chances are that it was just some stranger looking to lure Jared, which is just as bad. What kind of world do we live in nowadays that we can't even go to the park without fear?"

"The world has become a scary place," agreed Hunter. "But you know, you can't always run from what you fear. Sometimes you need to stand your ground and face it down."

"What do you know about fear?" she scoffed. "You're big and strong. Who the hell is going to tell you what to do, or threaten you?"

"Only someone with a death wish," he joked. Suzie

almost smiled again. "And for your information, I know a lot about fear. I just don't show it. In my line of work, I face things sometimes that best belong in nightmares. But I learned a long time ago that giving into my fear didn't accomplish anything. And running never works."

"Worked so far," muttered Suzie, taking a swig from her beer.

"No it hasn't, or you wouldn't be so terrified. I know your ex did some bad things to you, and I don't expect you to tell me. But to always be running . . ." He sighed. "It's not a life, Suzie, for you or the children. Maybe it's time to stop hiding and face him, once and for all."

"I can't," she whispered dejectedly. She'd need to be courageous and strong to do that, something she'd never been around him.

"You can, and if you need a friend to be the rock at your back, I'm available."

"Why would you offer that?" she said, turning to look at him, puzzled at his offer. "You've only known me for a couple of days."

"Long enough to know you're a good mother and person. I also know that your children are very sweet and don't deserve to be hurt. We might have only met a few days ago, but that doesn't mean I don't consider you to be my friend."

"We're friends now, are we?" said Suzie. What an odd concept. Friends with a man that she wanted to jump so badly it made her kitty hurt.

"Yes," he said with a grin. "Whether you like it or not. So get used to me coming over."

Suzie laughed. A friend. God, it had been so long since she'd had one. She'd spent so much time running and surviving, and just being a mom, that she hadn't had the time.

"Does this mean you're going to start borrowing sugar and stuff?" she asked teasingly.

"Yes, and probably milk too. I always forget to buy some."

"And you'll babysit for me when I start dating?"

"Dating?" Hunter sat up straight, brows arched high. "Who are you going to date?"

"I don't know. But I think it's time I started again. The kids could use a little masculine influence in their life, and I'm tired of being alone. Know any decent single guys?" *Someone just like you*, she thought.

"Nope. None of the guys I know are good enough for you and the twins."

Suzie almost laughed. If she didn't know better, she'd have said he sounded jealous. Which was silly, wasn't it?

"Pity. So, where do you find your dates?" she asked.

Hunter squirmed on the deck, and even in the faint light coming through the back sliding door, she could see the heightened color in his cheeks.

"I—um. I don't really date much," he finally stammered.

Suzie just arched a brow at him and smirked. Just like she'd thought. Women threw themselves at him. Bloody guy probably didn't even have to try.

"Maybe I should buy a book about dating first. It's been so long I'm not sure what I'm supposed to do anymore."

"Let me help you refresh your memory," Hunter murmured, and then to Suzie's shock, he turned and, cupping her face in his hands, pulled her in close for a kiss.

Actually, it was less a kiss and more like a shockwave. As soon as his lips touched hers, Suzie felt a wave of heat rocket through her body. His lips slid across hers, coaxing them open, and Suzie felt heat blossom in her body. She trembled and leaned into him, wrapping her arms around his solid waist. The warmth of his body and the subtle scent of his aftershave was like an aphrodisiac, and she groaned against his mouth as wet heat pooled in between her thighs. *God, he feels and tastes so good.* Suzie drank him in, his essence and warmth, like a sponge immersed in water.

His fingers left her cheeks and slid into her hair so he could kiss her more intently. His tongue delved deep inside her mouth to dance with hers. A sinuous dance that had her panting and aching. She pressed herself tightly against him, enjoying the feel of his hard body against hers, wanting to get closer... To feel his—

A cry from the baby monitor beside her had her pulling away from Hunter, her dazed senses still reeling from the scorching fire his kiss had ignited.

"I've got to go," Suzie mumbled, and stumbling slightly—her legs weak and wobbly—she went into the house to take care of her children, leaving Hunter alone.

OUT ON THE DECK, Hunter leaned back and groaned.

Oh, by the higher powers, she tastes so sweet. He'd thought there was no way she'd feel or taste as good as she looked. *I was wrong.* His entire body felt consumed with lust, his erection a flaming rod that threatened to burn through his jeans. If it hadn't been for the cry of the child, he'd have probably taken her right there on the deck. So much for being her friend. When she'd mentioned dating, his mind had screamed, *No, you're mine!* and he'd felt an urge to punch the non-existent man she was talking about dating.

Hunter had never felt jealousy before, and he didn't like it one bit. He wanted her with a passion and urgency that was almost frightening in its intensity. *Why her and why now? Have I finally fallen in love? Am I ready for marriage?* He knew Suzie wasn't the casual type, and the twins deserved better than someone who would use their mother and leave. *But am I capable of being the man she and the children deserve?* Or did his father's genes run too strongly in him? Would he turn into a cold, unfeeling man who made her miserable? *Mother isn't miserable,* said that stupid inner voice. *And I am not my father.*

Damn, he wished his mother were here. Perhaps she'd be able to tell him if what he felt was just a bad case of lust or—gulp—love.

Damian Draco, also known as Phineas Porter and the Dragon, watched with soulless eyes from across the street. So this was where his little brood mare had thought to hide herself. Suburbia, as the mundanes called it. Stupid cow. Did she really think she could hide from him? His magic, while perhaps non-existent on this side of the boundary, didn't mean he'd lost his dangerous edge. After all, he hadn't stayed alive this long due to magic alone. Cunning and ruthlessness required no magic. This new neighbor of hers might be a bit of a hassle, though. The man looked as if he could take care of himself, and he seemed to have appointed himself their guardian. No matter. He couldn't stand guard over her night and day.

First, he'd try the direct approach. Maybe now that she had a new suitor she could be persuaded to give him the children, or at least the boy. His heir. The girl child he didn't really care about. Females were stupid, vapid creatures whose only use was to serve the needs of men. But while in prison, it had occurred to him that a daughter might be useful. Alliances through marriage were still common and a great way of increasing one's power base. His first objective, though, remained the boy.

Rage twisted inside him like a demonic beast that kept burrowing deeper and deeper into his body, darkening his heart and clouding his mind. He'd finally achieved what he'd been trying so long to do. Create an heir. Someone he could teach, who would stand by his side when he set out to conquer the Realm first then the world. Someone to carry on his legacy once he died, although that hopefully would not happen for a long time. And that bitch, that stupid cow that had birthed his children, had stolen his son, his most valuable treasure. No one stole from the Dragon!

The time had come for him and his brood mare to

have a talk. Once her suitor was gone, of course. He'd make her see reason, his reason. And if she refused, well then he'd just have to do things the hard way, which he preferred anyway. How evil! How dastardly, you say. Why that was what he did best. They didn't call him the Dragon for nothing.

CHAPTER 9

Suzie woke the next morning feeling lethargic—gee, could it have been because she only got about three hours of sleep? Jessica had gone back to sleep after a drink of water and a cuddle, but sleep had eluded Suzie for quite some time. Between the kiss Hunter had given her—she could still feel the heat—and the fright she'd gotten from the stranger in the park yesterday, she'd tossed and turned all night.

Her mind spun in circles thinking about Hunter, unable to decide. Her body wanted him, no question about that. The kids loved him. She really enjoyed his company, and while she appreciated his offer of friendship, could they be friends considering their attraction for each other? And as for being romantically involved, he didn't seem ready yet for the kind of commitment hooking up with a single mom would entail.

And what about the stranger from the park? Was it the twins' father?

Sure, she'd taken precautions each time she'd moved—not leaving forwarding addresses, ensuring everything was unlisted, and the utilities that were in her name used her initials only. Even her mother didn't have her new address.

Anybody would be paranoid, too, if they'd been through what she had, but had she done enough?

God, it all seemed so long ago now. A lifetime ago, when life had seemed so full of promise and when she'd still naively believed the best of people. How stupid she'd been.

She'd started university later than most kids, at twenty, having had to work to save for tuition first because her mother, as promised, refused to help. What did she need an education for? her mother would say. A good girl should get married and have babies like God intended. Kind of ironic considering her mother's youthful marriage ended up in her husband—Suzie's dad—leaving when Suzie was only two. Needless to say, her mother never remarried, and Suzie ended up an only child. Made her wonder, though, if her mother had always been a bitch and made her husband leave or if her husband leaving became the catalyst to bitchdom. Dear old Mom, a bitter, tight-fisted, religious woman who'd made Suzie's life hell.

Suzie had always been made to feel she could never do anything right, and according to Suzie's mother, she never did. According to her, Suzie was a stupid, lazy slut who was easily swayed by the Devil. Never mind the fact she'd always been a straight-A student who never drank, didn't do drugs, and didn't lose her virginity till well after she'd left home. Nice childhood, huh? Forget having friends over, and God forbid Suzie should date. When she'd come home in her senior year all excited over being asked to the prom, her mother quickly made her regret it. She spent that whole weekend on her knees with her mother, praying. Of course, she didn't attend the prom. Although, in retrospect, Suzie wondered how the hell her mother expected her to find a husband if dating was such a no-no. She stopped speaking to her mother once she left home.

The day she'd gotten accepted by university the farthest away she could find from her mother, she'd walked on clouds. Nothing her mother could say burst her bubble. Finally, she would escape!

She still remembered the elation she'd felt when she walked onto that campus the first time, the sense of freedom quickly followed by the intimidation of seeing all those busy scholars bustling to and from class, the large campus always in motion.

But she'd adapted. Unlike many girls, she didn't go boy and party wild. Her strict upbringing still had a hold of her in many respects. She made herself some friends—finally—and studied hard. Her third year, she finally narrowed her career path—computers—and she selected courses on that subject—programming, graphics, animation. But on a whim, she'd added something completely off the wall—Fairy Tales and Other Myths. As a child, she'd always been fascinated by the Grimm brothers' tales and anything to do with magic and fantasy, especially the happy endings.

The first day of her fairy tale course still remained

vivid in her mind. It was the day that changed the rest of her life. Arriving to her new class early, she'd sat at the back and watched the other students come in, talking and laughing as they took seats of their own. When *he* arrived, the buzz of dozens of voices died off, stunned into silence. Apparently, many of them, Suzie included, had preconceived notions of what a man teaching children's stories would look like—short, geeky, probably bald with glasses. That was not what they got, though.

Their professor was striking, not a classically gorgeous man but attractive in a dark, dangerous way. He had thick, black hair that hung in waves to his shoulders with a high widow's peak. The angular face of a poet, all hard planes and shadows, his lips surprisingly full, and his gray eyes like mirrors of the soul. The girls in his class all, to a certain extent, fell in love, Suzie included. He had a presence about him, a dark radiance that fascinated Suzie. Kind of like the forbidden apple, the bad-boy your mother warned you about. In other words, every girl's fantasy.

Suzie sat there, entranced, the whole class. The timbre of his voice and the somber intensity of his face attracted her like no one else ever had.

She had his class twice a week, and as the weeks passed, she inched her way down in the seating till she sat in the front row, head propped on her hand, watching him as he analyzed the fairy tales of her youth.

It was just before the Christmas break that he first asked her to see him in his office after classes were done for the day. She'd knocked on his office door nervously, wondering what he wanted. Was she flunking his course? She thought she'd done well on her term paper.

His smooth, tummy-tingling voice told her to enter, and she drifted in to stand in front of his desk, chin down.

"Suzanne, thank you so much for coming."

"No problem, Professor Draco." Even his name sounded dark and mysterious.

"Please, when it's just us, call me Damian. Professor Draco sounds so old and stodgy. You don't think I'm old, do you?" he'd asked, his mesmerizing gray eyes boring into hers as if the answer was of the utmost importance. Unable to hold his gaze, Suzie dropped her head.

"What? No, of course not Pro—Damian." Despite his years, mid-thirties to her bare twenty-three, he definitely couldn't be considered an old man. On the contrary, his entire being exuded strength and virility. Standing across from him, Suzie felt drawn to him like metal to a magnet.

"I'm sure you're wondering what this is all about."

"I failed my exam, didn't I?" she replied in a little voice, still looking at her toes.

His rich laughter filled the room. "Failed? By no means. You passed with flying colors, my dear Suzanne. That's why I called you in here. See, I've selected you to be my assistant in a project I'm doing."

"Really?" she exclaimed, her tone quite incredulous.

"Yes. It will have to be done after school hours, of course, as this is an extra project. Will that pose any problems with your boyfriend or family?"

"I don't have a boyfriend, and my mom lives back east. I've got plenty of time to help you. What's the project about, and when do we start?"

"Why don't I tell you over dinner?"

That became the first of many dinners—first, out in public places, where he fed her a web of lies on this supposed project. Then, the dinners and meetings started happening at his condo.

In retrospect, she realized he'd been grooming her, easing her into the relationship. Cutting her off from her few friends, consuming all her time till her only focus became him.

The first time they had sex, a painful experience due to her virgin state, he'd put on a great act afterward.

"Oh, Suzanne, how I love thee. Alas, our love is doomed. I shall be cast from my job at the university. Will you still love me when I am penniless and shamed before my peers?"

Rushing to reassure him she'd said, like an idiot, "No one has to know. I'll never tell. In another year, I'll graduate, and we can be together then. I don't mind hiding our love for now."

The next few months, they snuck around like star-crossed lovers. He gave her a key to his place so she could come over whenever she had free time. She'd cook dinner and wait for him, like a good little wife would, not that they ever talked about marriage. In fact, he never talked about a future with her at all. But he had said he loved her. Surely he wouldn't lie about that? And she had loved him with every inch of her being.

The budding trees signaling spring was when she started feeling ill.

After throwing up for the third morning in a row, she had to face the truth. She either had the flu, or she'd become pregnant. After buying the test from a pharmacy, she smuggled it back to his place in her purse and peed on the little stick. She spent an agonizing three minutes waiting.

Double cross. Oh-oh, definitely pregnant.

She skipped all her classes that day, huddled in a ball in his apartment, dreading telling him. How would he react? Would he make her get an abortion? Would he still love her? Would they marry? The parade of questions seemed endless, the fear of losing him overwhelming.

His reaction was not what she expected.

"That's fantastic!" he exclaimed when he finally came home and heard the news.

"Really?" Suzie said, stunned.

"I'm finally going to be a father. This is fabulous!" he said, wrapping his arms around her in an exuberant hug. "You'll move in with me once the semester is done."

Suzie should have asked more questions. Such as, what about marriage? And how would she manage school with a baby? But it was hard not to get caught up in his excitement, so she just assumed everything would all work out. Naive? No, blindly in love.

When they found out at her first ultrasound she was pregnant with twins, she thought he'd jump up and dance a jig in the doctor's office.

"My beautiful fecund Suzanne," he'd exclaimed, hugging her.

Suzie, though, found the idea of twins terrifying. She had no idea how to take care of one baby. How on earth would she take care of two? But Damian seemed so happy, which made her happy, too, most of the time.

At his urging, Suzie didn't register at the university for her return in the fall.

"There'll be plenty of time to finish your degree later. You wouldn't want the stress of exams to harm the babies, would you? And besides," he'd said in a masterful stroke of manipulation, "think of the questions that might arise once it's known you're pregnant. If you're a student still, and they find out I'm the father, I'll be out of a job. Then how could I support my favorite girl and our children?"

He played on her guilt like a finely tuned violin. Suzie would have done anything for him. What he asked for wasn't that bad, and she could always go back to school once the babies were old enough. And, at that point in time, he still treated her like a fragile princess, bringing her treats and delicacies for the babies, healthy ones, of course. He put her on a strict, very healthy diet. One with lots of red meat and protein. She didn't care. It happened to be what she craved. Mmm, medium rare steak, baked potato smothered in sour cream, and Caesar salad. When you're pregnant, food tastes soooo good!

The one thing Damian stopped once she got pregnant was making love to her. When she asked him why, he claimed it might hurt the babies. Her doctor had told her sex was okay, but if it made Damian feel better, then that was fine. Truth be told, she hadn't enjoyed lovemaking all that much. It tended to be kind of quick and painful. Nor did she feel especially sexy with her rapidly increasing girth. So they stopped being intimate, but even without the lovemaking, he remained solicitous in other ways.

When she hit thirty-four weeks, though, things

changed. While he still brought her home things to eat, he stopped being nice to her. Oh, he didn't start calling her names or hitting her. No, he just stopped talking to her. Gone were the sweet compliments, the cuddling, the thoughtful flowers. Instead, all of his focus and attention turned to the babies, *his* babies, as he liked to call them. His legacy. He began to talk about taking the babies home with him.

"Oh, where do you come from?" she'd asked. "I can't wait to meet your family."

He never did answer her, just changed the subject, and she forgot about it for a time. She should have paid more attention, as it turned out.

At thirty-seven weeks and a whopping seventy-five pounds gained, her gynecologist booked her for inducement. Damian paced, even more nervous than Suzie, badgering the nurses and doctors on the status of the babies.

Jared and Jessica were born at three o'clock on a chilly autumn afternoon, weighing in at five pound two ounces for Jared, the first born, and four pounds eleven ounces for her baby girl, Jessica.

Exhausted but happy, Suzie held her two little bundles of love and beamed up at Damian, only to be taken aback by the possessive and cold look in his eyes.

"Aren't they just perfect?" she'd said, nuzzling them one at a time.

"Yes, he is," said Damian, scooping Jared up and crowing over him. Suzie, who held Jessica, looked at him in askance. Surely, he meant both babies? Right?

It soon became clear once they got home with their

bundles of joy which one he cared about most. Jared was Damian's pride and joy. He held him and rocked him to sleep. Told him stories. Would have fed him, too, if he'd had boobs of his own, Suzie used to think nastily. Poor Jessica, he ignored. Damian had the son he'd always dreamed of, and he had no room in his heart or mind for his daughter.

Nor for Suzie.

Nope, she became his unpaid maid and nanny. He left her a list of chores to be done each day, all of them directed toward making him and Jared comfortable. Suzie, who slept alone in the room with the crib, cried herself almost nightly to sleep. She quickly learned he had no patience for tears—her first black eye taught her that. Meek as a mouse, submissive to his whims or face punishment, she almost wished she'd gone back to her mother and her strict household rules.

Where had his love for her gone? What had she done? She'd been so sure it had to be her. She must have done something to change his love for her. It never occurred to her at the time to place any of the blame on him. Desperate thoughts plagued her. Was it because she'd blossomed in weight? Her body never did regain its pre-pregnancy shape. Maybe she wasn't interesting enough. Or maybe, said that damned little voice in her head, he'd never loved her at all. No, she couldn't have been so wrong, so blind, so stupidly naïve . . .

When the twins were three months old, Damian started preparing for a trip.

"Where are we going?" she'd asked. Not that she

really cared, but maybe if they went elsewhere, the Damian she had fallen in love with would come back.

"Jared and I are going home."

"What about Jessica and me?" she'd asked, her whining tone grating even to her ear.

"Frankly, my dear, you and Jessica can do whatever you like. I have no further use for either of you," he'd said with disdain, the coldness in his eyes making her shiver.

Appalled, Suzie tried to talk to him. She cried, pleaded, trying to understand, but Damian slapped her and told her to shut up and stop her whining. She cowered and swallowed her tongue and watched as he continued with his plans. It began to dawn on her that this was the real Damian. Not the silver-tongued devil who had seduced her but this cold, calculating man who treated her like the basest of creatures. He'd never loved her. She'd just been a means to an end.

As he continued his plans to take her son away, she realized no one was going to come to her rescue, and if she didn't do something, he'd leave, disappear into the vast world, taking Jared with him. Finally, a spark of anger ignited. Fuck that, and fuck him! He'd lost his mind if he thought she'd let him take off with her precious baby boy. Damian obviously wasn't the man she'd believed him to be, and bemoaning her fate wouldn't change it. He'd used her—impregnated her like some prize mare—and now planned to take off with his prize colt.

Over her dead fucking body.

Suzie, the anger finally clearing the blinders from her eyes, made plans of her own. She called a distant aunt who'd always been friendly to her growing up. Together they made plans for Suzie to come and stay for a while with the twins till she found a place of her own.

Suzie packed in secret. She bought second-hand luggage and hid it in the storage locker that Damian never used. She began squirreling away the household money he left her.

Finally, the day arrived. Damian told her he'd be gone most of the day finalizing his plans for Jared and him to leave.

"The lease is paid till the end of the month. Stay or leave, I don't care, but don't expect any help from me for you and the girl child."

He left her on those cold words, and as she watched his lanky form going up the street for the last time, she had to hold back an urge to scream what she really thought of him, although she thought it hard and venomously—Goddamn, lying son-of-a-bitch! But better than words were action.

Calling a cab company, she lugged her packed suitcases out of hiding and, with two used car seats she'd picked up at a garage sale, made her way to the train station. What a nightmare! Imagine being alone and trying to cart around not just one but two three-month-old babies. Absolutely helpless in their innocence, wrapped in their car seats, a pitifully small pile of luggage beside them. Thank God for the ticket seller. Her kind eyes had taken one look at her, so young and helpless-looking, and had ordered one of the security guards to help her.

Heart pumping, she boarded the train with the most precious of cargoes, expecting at any minute that Damian

THE HUNTER

would come flying out of nowhere to steal her little boy. She could see it so vividly in her mind—he'd swoop down upon her out of nowhere, an ominous black vulture with widespread arms flying toward her, freezing her with the cold, gray iciness of his eyes. His long fingers, like claws, would rip Jared out of her arms, and he would laugh that cynical chuckle that hurt more than any words. A discordant, denigrating sound that had the ability to make her feel less than two inches tall.

But the train—surprise!—left without disruption, and she arrived at her aunt's house safely. She spent that first week huddled in the house, peering through the drapes while her aunt looked on with soft, pitying eyes.

As the days, and then the weeks, passed, she gradually relaxed. He hadn't followed them. Maybe she'd escaped. If only that little voice inside would stop saying, "What if..."

But she couldn't live in fear forever. Life went on, and babies had needs. And so did Suzie. She bucked up and started living again. The first few months after she escaped were spent mostly caring for her two time-consuming babies. But that wasn't all she did. She went back to school. Her aunt, a blessed saint of a woman, talked her into going to some classes and volunteered to watch the twins, whom she adored.

The months passed. The twins turned one and got their first taste of chocolate, a momentous event that Suzie had well documented with dozens of pictures. Suzie studied hard and got her credits to graduate and began doing freelance work at home creating small business Web sites. Life, she realized one day, was actually good. She'd stopped freezing every time she saw a tall, dark man when she went out, and she finally realized she felt happy again.

Suzie and her aunt got on famously. Widowed and childless, she'd taken Suzie and the twins in and treated them better than her own mother ever had. When she died in a random street accident, Suzie cried for days. It didn't help that her mother showed up for the funeral—although Suzie had quite enjoyed the look on her face when she'd seen Suzie and her out-of-wedlock grandchildren. The "I knew you'd turn out to be a whore" was a bit of a slap in the face, though, that Suzie could have done without.

The only good thing that came out of that tragedy was money. Suzie's aunt had some money put away, and she left all of it to Suzie and the twins. Not trusting her mother, and unable to live with the memories in the house, Suzie sold her aunt's home and moved and moved again. Each time farther and farther east. For some reason, she had a feeling, almost as if she knew that one day Damian would come back. Something in his eyes, his look, his voice, told her that he would never let them go.

But now, the time had come to stop running. Hunter was right. She needed to stand her ground. She'd grown up over the last couple of years, become wiser, and after all, Damian was just a man. There were laws that would protect her and the children.

Speaking of which, her little Tasmanian devils came flying into her room and dove onto her bed. Suzie pushed away the painful memories of her past and set herself to the task of tickling her sweet angels breathless.

Damian might have been a conniving, cold bastard, but he'd sure created sweet kids.

ONE MESSY PANCAKE BREAKFAST LATER, Suzie decided to attempt her first lawn mowing. The previous owner had left the gas mower behind, so with an avid audience of two, she wheeled the rusty, red machine out from the garage and into the backyard. She'd done her research on the net on how to work one of these suckers and felt pretty confident she could handle this new household chore. She grabbed the pull cord and yanked while holding the gas handle. The engine made a whirring sound that immediately stopped.

The twins giggled from the back deck.

"Hey, you two!" Suzie mock-growled at them. "No laughing in the peanut gallery." The twins giggled louder.

Suzie bent over the mower again and pulled hard. Again, a little whir then nothing. Stupid thing! She grabbed the cord and yanked it really hard and fast. Too hard! She lost her balance and fell flat on her butt to the howls of her children. A shadow covered her, and she looked up to see Hunter shaking his head at her.

"Need a hand?" he said, offering her one to help her stand up.

"Stupid mower won't start!" she said, glaring at the offensive red machine.

Hunter winked at the kids and said, "Watch this!"

With one fast and fluid pull, he yanked the cord, and the mower started with a rumble.

Suzie stood there, fuming. *Show off.*

Hunter grinned at her and then started to mow the lawn. Suzie opened her mouth to protest, but shut it when her new lawn boy pulled off his shirt and tossed it on the deck beside the kids.

Talk about hot! His muscled upper body looked golden in the morning light, his skin smooth and begging for a hand to stroke it. Suddenly, Suzie remembered in vivid detail the evening's previous kiss. That searing, panty-wetting kiss. A tingling started in her groin and moved up her body, and as she watched, she wondered what it would feel like to be kissed by Hunter shirtless, skin-to-skin, her breasts rubbing against his hot bod, her hands...

She must have been drooling or something because Jessica asked, "Mommy, why you loo so funny?"

Crap, caught by my kids lusting after the lawn boy. Dammit! Needing some distraction, Suzie went inside and made up a pitcher of Kool-Aid. What she really needed was a really cold shower, but she settled for sucking on an ice cube, trying to not think of how it would feel if she rubbed that cold piece of ice across Hunter's skin, licking up the water after it.

A while later, after she'd pinched herself hard a few times to get her libido under control, she came out with the frosty glasses and pitcher. She stopped in the middle of the deck and smiled, both amused and touched to see that Jared was helping Hunter mow the lawn. *Aw, how cute!*

Hunter had Jared holding the crossbar while he held the handle and actually pushed the mower.

Jared beamed at her. "Loo, mommy, I mow da grath."

"Good job, big boy," she praised him. *God, is there anything Hunter does that isn't cute and heart melting?* Jessica watched them avidly or, should she say, watched Hunter with hero worship again. Turned out everybody in the family liked Hunter.

Suzie poured a tall glass of Kool-Aid and handed it to her daughter. "Here, baby, why don't you take Hunter a drink?" Jessica took the glass in her two hands and, with a careful walk that spilled only a little juice, carried it to Hunter, who stopped the mower when he saw her coming.

"Thank you, precious," he said with a smile, taking the glass from her. Jessica beamed at him.

Suzie poured out more Kool-Aid in two plastic cups for the kids, who came tearing at her when they saw them.

How domestic! Suzie again felt that pang, seeing how life would be with a husband around. Father mowing the lawn, teaching his son. Daughter hanging out while Mom's in the kitchen cooking. Everyone happy. Sigh. Reality could be such a bitch.

Hunter came striding over the freshly mown lawn, his tight abs glistening with sweat. Yes, she could definitely wake up to that bod every day! And go to sleep with it and lick it and . . . all kinds of nasty things that would appall even Mrs. Robinson.

"Thanks," he said, tipping the glass, his throat working as he swallowed the last of the juice. *Betcha he tastes nice and sweet right about now*, thought Suzie lustfully, watching his tongue lick the last drop from his bottom lip.

The kids, high on sugar, raced around the yard chasing each other. Hunter watched them, smiling, then turned to her, his eyes smoky.

"I was thinking," he said. "Um, you know how I told you last night we were friends."

Suzie nodded. *Oh-oh, is this where he tells me he doesn't think it's a good idea?* That would suck. She'd gotten kind of used to having him around.

"And you said you were thinking of dating. Well, I was thinking that most relationships start out as friendships and . . ." Suzie started to feel hope and wanted to shake him to hurry up and spit it out.

"I think we should go on a date," he said nervously.

"Yes." No hesitation. She wanted to date Hunter. *I know he's all wrong for me, and I shouldn't, but I want to be with him.* Now she sounded like Jessica—*Mine!*

"Really?" He looked relieved, as if he'd been unsure of her answer. "Great! Um, so where would you like to go?"

"Well, first I need to figure out what to do with the kids. I don't really know anybody around here yet, and I don't let strangers mind my kids."

"Oh, I think I can finagle something there," he said with a grin. "My mother's been dying to visit. I was thinking of telling her to come out. Knowing her, she'd be more than happy to mind the twins so we could go on a date."

His mother! Talk about getting serious real quick. Maybe too quick.

He must have seen her uncertainty but misconstrued its cause. "It's okay. Mother's great with children."

"Oh, I'm sure she is. Are you sure about dating and stuff, though?" she asked. "I'm not into casual affairs. I can't, not with the kids to think about."

His eyes were serious when he answered. "I know you're not into casual dating, and I've given this a lot of thought. Believe me. The truth is I—" He hesitated, and to Suzie's amusement, his cheeks turned pink. "I can't stop thinking about you. I can't make any promises, but I do know I want to get to know you better."

That had to be one of the nicest, most sincere things anybody had ever said to her and, on impulse, Suzie leaned up and gave him a kiss. Hunter's eyes widened then crinkled as he kissed her back. Immediately, the fire in her body that had been simmering on low heat flared to life.

"Eew!" exclaimed Jared from behind them.

"Mommy, why you kiss Hunta?" asked Jessica, looking at them quizzically.

It was Suzie's turn to blush as she stepped back. "Um, well, Hunter and I have decided to go on a date."

"Whatha date?" asked Jared.

"He's gonna be our new daddy," whispered Jessica loudly, beaming from ear to ear.

Oh dear, thought Suzie frantically. What had she done? Maybe dating wasn't such a good idea.

Hunter, to his credit, didn't panic and run. Instead, he crouched down. "I like your mother a lot, and I think she likes me," he said with a wink up at Suzie. "A date is when two adults who like each other go out and have dinner and see a movie and stuff to see if they like spending time together. That won't make me your daddy, but no matter what, I am your friend. Is that all right?"

Jessica bobbed her head hard enough to get whiplash. Jared, though, gave him a little scowl. "Are you gonna kith my mommy 'gain?"

"I might if she lets me," said Hunter with a grin up at Suzie, who watched this interplay with her children with fascination. He'd handled that a lot better than she would have.

"Okay," said Jared. Then, leaning in closer. "She wikes wet kitheth," he whispered conspiratorially.

Suzie just about dissolved in giggles, and judging by Hunter's clenched jaw, he had to fight hard to hold his laughter in too. "I'll remember that, little buddy. Anyways, I'm going to finish back here and then go mow your front lawn now, if it's okay. Then I have to go to work for a little bit. Will you take care of your mom for me while I'm gone?" Two little heads bobbed, and Jared puffed up his chest with importance. "How about I come by and see you all later?"

"How about you stay for dinner? The kids make a mean hamburger."

"That sounds delicious," Hunter said, staring at Suzie's lips. She blushed again. *What am I, sixteen?*

"Okay, so we'll see you later then," said Suzie, trying to act nonchalant, a hard thing to do when her panties were wet enough to wring. What exactly did her body plan to do with Hunter tonight?

"See you guys later," he said with a cocky grin at Suzie as he started up the mower again. She and the kids sat out back, watching him finish the little patch that was left. Once done, he waved before he took the mower to the front of the house.

Suzie, bemused by the whole episode, floated into the house to make some lunch. She and Hunter were going on a date. She felt like dancing. And he'd be coming over later for dinner. Oh God, she'd have to shave. *Wait a second, I'm not planning on sleeping with him yet. Of course not.* Okay, so no shaving her kitty, just her legs. But maybe she'd give her kitty a trim, just in case.

An hour or so later, she heard the sound of Hunter's Harley. Off he went to the office like he'd told them. God, could he be any sweeter, mowing the lawn for them and doing, well, man stuff? Was it too soon to dream of the what-if's? She wondered if he'd stay for a while after dinner so they could talk again. She'd love to know more about him—his family, his interests, maybe another kiss. Not a quick kiss like out back earlier. Oh no. She wanted a hot, tummy-tingling, scorcher of a kiss like last night's. Even the thought of it was enough to make her body get all hot and aroused. She wondered how soon he could get his mom to visit so they could go on that date. Which made her wonder what his mom was like. What if she didn't like Suzie? Time enough to cross that bridge when they got to it.

Deciding that standing around mooning after a man wasn't going to get much done—fun as those daydreams were—Suzie went to work setting up her workstation while the kids colored. Her new Web project would be starting in a week, and she wanted to be sure everything was ready to go.

About mid-afternoon, the doorbell rang.

Odd. Couldn't be Hunter. She hadn't heard the bike coming back, not that she'd been listening for him, of course. The doorbell rang again, and Suzie frowned with annoyance. Probably a stupid door-to-door salesman. Well, she'd take care of him.

Suzie swung open the door and then just about slammed it shut. *Oh my God, no*, she thought as she stared at him standing there, looking the same as he had three years ago. On second impulse, she swung the door shut, but a leather-clad foot slid between the door and the jamb, stopping it. Suzie backed up, the urge to run so strong, but she couldn't. She had to protect the children who were, thankfully, still up in their room playing.

"Go away, Damian," she said as he opened the door and walked in. *Gee, make yourself at home*, she thought, trying to calm the rapid beating of her heart.

"Is that the way to greet an ex-lover and the father of your children?" Damian said. His voice, the voice that once she'd loved to listen to, now grated on her ears and caused her flesh to prickle.

"Donating sperm doesn't make you a father. Go away before I call the cops." *And before the children see you*, she thought. Suzie snuck a quick look at the stairs and was relieved to see the children hadn't come down to see who had come to call. *Please let them stay up there a few minutes while I take care of the bastard who abused me.*

"And whose fault is it that I didn't have a chance to be a father? Hmm, Suzanne?" he said, stretching her name. Damian and her mother were the only two people who ever used her full name. She'd always preferred Suzie. "It wasn't me who left and kidnapped my children."

Suzie felt a pang of guilt. What she had done was wrong, maybe. . . .Wait—he was doing it already. Trying to get inside her head and twist things. No, this time she'd make damn sure she didn't let him get under her skin. Gone was that naive girl he'd manipulated three years ago. Being a grown woman now, she could see the game he played, and no way would she be falling back into that trap. She'd had every reason and right to leave him. Abuse in any form was unacceptable! *Yeah*, said her little inner voice, *stick to your guns!*

"If you wanted to be a father, then you shouldn't have mistreated me and the children." Ha, she'd told him, and her voice hadn't even shaken when she said it.

"Cry me a river," he said sarcastically. "You were free to leave with the girl child. Not my fault you chose to stay."

Nope, he hadn't changed. "You bastard!" Suzie spat. "Get out!"

"Not without my boy, Suzanne."

"Never. You leave Jared alone, or I'll call the cops." And she would. No way was she letting him bully her this time round.

"And what will you tell them, you stupid slut? That you're refusing a poor father the right to see his children? Will you tell them how you kidnapped them?"

Suzie glared at Damian. "Get off my property. You can't prove the children are yours. It'll be my word against yours. It was your decision not to put your name on the birth certificate. Guess you're regretting that now." Another odd thing she'd explained away at the time. God, the clues had been there all along, but she'd just been too blind to see them.

"Now, Suzanne," he said condescendingly, talking to her as if she were a simple-minded child. "A simple DNA test will prove my claim. You can't win. Hand the boy over."

"Over my dead body."

"That can be arranged if you like," he said, his cold eyes like an arctic breeze freezing her into stunned silence. He couldn't be serious. Could he?

"You're really sick, you know that? I will not hand Jared over to you. He deserves better than you."

"Better, like your new suitor?" At Suzie's stunned look, he laughed. "I know all about you and your neighbor. Just can't keep your pants on, can you? Easy back in college and easy now. Your mother was so right about you."

Suzie couldn't help herself. She slapped Damian, and God help her, it felt good.

Damian's face snapped to the side with the force of her blow. He turned back to regard her, one hand rubbing his jaw as he worked it. *Oops, that might have been a mistake*, she thought, judging by the way his whole being seemed to harden. The sharp planes of his face sucked in, giving him a cadaverous look. How had she ever thought him handsome?

"Now you've made me angry, Suzanne," was the only warning she got before he lunged at her. Suzie didn't even have a chance to scream. His hands were around her throat, choking her. Suzie clawed at his hands, but they were like steel bands around her throat, squeezing and cutting off her air. She felt herself going faint, black spots dancing in front of her eyes, her knees buckling as her body grew weak from lack of oxygen.

Suddenly, the pressure was gone, and Suzie crouched on her hands and knees, gasping, her throat raw with pain.

Dear God, no! Jared had come downstairs and attacked Damian, his little fists pummeling to no effect.

"You leave my mommy alone!" he screamed. "Go away! Go away!"

"Hello, son," said Damian, grabbing Jared's hands and holding him immobile. "Aren't you glad to see your daddy?"

"You're not my daddy!" Jared cried, struggling.

Suzie wanted to cry too. This couldn't be happening.

Suzie struggled to her feet, wheezing as she attempted to breathe. The sight of Damian holding her son, his claw-like hands, hands she'd once thought graceful, digging into Jared's flesh was too much. Suzie saw red. How dare that bastard touch her son! If anger could have killed, Damian would have keeled over then and there. She should be so lucky.

"Let him go, you bastard," she said, the words coming out raspy. She grabbed Damian's arm, trying to pull Jared free.

Damian let go of one of Jared's hands, only to swing it at Suzie and punch her in the face. Suzie held on through the dazing pain and kept tugging. But a second fist came flying and smashed her even harder. Down she went, hitting the floor hard, the whole left side of her face throbbing. Her left eye swelled shut from the force of the blow, and she could only squint through it blearily, trying to see what was happening.

A new wail pierced the room, and Suzie looked up in horror as Jessica came flying down the stairs and threw herself on Damian, pummeling him with her little fists.

"No! No! No!" screamed Jessica, her face tear-streaked.

Suzie tried to cry out "stop," but her voice was just a low whisper that Jessica never heard above her wailing. Suzie watched in horror as Damian backhanded her baby girl and sent her flying to land in a crumpled heap on the floor. Oh God, had he killed her?

Suzie wanted to scream. How could this be happening? It was her worst nightmare realized. She struggled to her knees. She needed to get Jared.

Damian watched her struggling with a cool smile, his flat eyes glittering in satisfaction.

"I told you to give him to me, but you just had to do this the hard way. You always were a stupid slut. One can only hope my son got my brains instead of yours."

Jared was crying, wet streaks making his still chubby cheeks glisten. Suzie wanted to tell him it would be okay, but before she could say a word, Damian dragged Jared outside.

Suzie crawled to the door, tears running down her face, and peered out. Jared was screaming as Damian dragged him off the front porch, his little body twisting as he tried to escape his father's iron grasp, but one little boy was no match for the strength of a grown man.

Suzie prayed a neighbor would come out and stop this. *Anybody. Please.*

But the street remained silent. Suzie, using the door, pulled herself up and staggered out onto the front porch.

"Bring him back," she pleaded. "Please. We can set something up. Visitation? Anything? Just don't take him. Can't you see how scared he is?"

Damian just grinned evilly. "He's mine, bitch. Say good-bye because you'll never see him again."

"I'll tell the cops. They'll make you give him back," she said desperately.

"Good luck with that. Where we're going, none of you mundanes can follow."

What the hell did he mean? Where was he taking Jared?

Suzie lunged out the door and tried to grab Damian. He just sidestepped and laughed as she fell to the ground at his feet.

She could hear Jared screaming, "Mommy!" But a couple of hard kicks in the head by the world's biggest bastard knocked her out cold.

CHAPTER 10

*H*unter walked into the agency with a whistle. Suzie had agreed to go out with him. He had no idea why this made him so happy, but it did. And she'd said yes, even after the pathetic little speech he'd given about liking her. Okay, so it was true, but talking about your feelings like that, out loud, well, that just wasn't manly. He'd just have to remember not to tell anyone. Oh, and he'd have to hit the gym and sweat a little maybe, too. Anything to bring his testosterone levels back up so he stopped spouting sappy shit whenever he saw her. Since when did the hunter talk about his feelings? The boys back home would just be howling if they'd heard him. Hell, he'd have howled, too, if it was one of them.

No one sat at the computer desks, and Bob's office lay empty, so Hunter made himself comfortable at one of the desks. Grabbing a piece of paper and a pen, he started writing a letter to his mother. What to tell her?

Dear Mother, he started writing.

I hope you and the rest of the family are doing well. I know it's been a while since I wrote, but I've got good news. I've met someone I really like, and I think you'll like her too.

Hunter paused. Oh by the higher powers, that sounded so lame, so not him!

He crumpled up the sheet and started over.

Dear Mother, I miss you, and was hoping you could come for a visit. Love, Hunter.

PS. I think I've found the one.

Ha! That would get her going. Hunter grinned as he sealed the short note into an envelope addressed to his mother for transport back to the Realm. He wondered how soon he should expect her. Knowing her, she'd be here by tomorrow.

Owen's lanky form came striding into the room.

"Hey, Hunter, you're looking like the cat that ate the bird. What's got you so smug?"

"Nothing. Just inviting my mother for a visit." So he could go on a hot date with Suzie.

"Here give me the letter. I've got a dispatch of them going out within the hour."

Hunter handed over the missive. "So, anything new? Got any more info on the Dragon?"

"Actually," said Owen, sitting down at his desk. "I just finished typing up the report on some stuff that just came in. We think we found out why the Dragon came back."

"Really?" said Hunter, leaning forward in his chair with interest. "Hidden treasure? A cult? Burger King?"

Hunter sure wished the Realm had one of those. Whoppers with cheese had become an addiction of his.

"Nope, something even better. Well, at least where the Dragon is concerned. Children. Twins, actually."

Hunter froze at the word twins. Surely a coincidence. Although, as his mother always liked to say, there was no such thing as coincidence in the Realm.

"Yeah, seems he played house with one of his students back west. Got her pregnant with twins. They'd be about three years old now."

Hunter felt a sinking sensation. No way, this had to be the world's biggest coincidence. "What's her name?"

"Funny thing," said Owen. "She apparently took off with the kids. Guess she figured out he was a jerk. Pity no one told her about him being incarcerated. She ended up moving quite a bit. I guess she was trying to stay away from him. Had a bit of a time trying to follow her, but if I do say so myself, I am good."

"Owen, her name," said Hunter through clenched teeth, resisting an urge to shake the information loose from him.

"Oh, Suzanne Clarke. You've probably met her, actually, since she lives in the house next door to yours."

"Damn!" said Hunter, slamming his fist down hard on the desk he'd sat at, toppling the cup that held pens and pencils. For the first time in his life, Hunter felt dread. He'd left Suzie and the kids all alone with the Dragon on the loose looking for them. The park incident hadn't been a random act by a stranger. It had been the Dragon. He needed to get back now.

"The Dragon's already made contact once.

Remember that incident in the park I told you about?" Owen nodded, eyes widening in realization. "He's after the boy. I've got to get back and make sure they're protected."

"Oh damn, Hunter. I hope they're okay. Did you want some backup?"

"No," said Hunter with a cold smile. "I'll take care of the Dragon myself." *Permanently.*

Hunter tore out of the office and jumped on his bike. His pulse raced. Surely, they'd be all right. He hadn't been gone that long. The Dragon wouldn't be brazen enough to try something in the middle of the afternoon with the whole neighborhood watching. Right?

Hunter prayed to the higher powers like he'd never prayed before.

Please, just let them be safe.

He drove like a bat out of hell, weaving in and out of traffic, the usually short fifteen-minute commute cut in half but still seeming like an eternity.

But he arrived too late. His worst fears were realized when he arrived to see Suzie collapsed on the front porch.

Hunter jumped off his bike and ran to Suzie, his heart pumping madly in his chest.

How could he have failed her like this? *Please, don't let her be dead.*

Dropping to his knees, his eyes scanned her for injuries. And he stifled a groan at the extent of them. Her face was a bloody mess. In between the streaks of blood, her skin blossomed into a rainbow of colors, and she had one eye swollen so much that, even were she conscious, it would have stayed shut. And then there was her throat. Hunter swallowed his anger hard else he would have howled at the bruises ringing her neck. The bastard had tried to choke her. He could hear her breathing though, a whistling, rattly sound, but it meant she still lived. After scooping her up, he carried her limp body into the house and then stopped dead and finally let loose the pent-up bellow of rage and pain when he saw Jessica, that sweet little angel, lying in a boneless heap on the floor.

He laid Suzie carefully on the couch and went over to Jessica, knelt beside her, tears pricking his eyes as he checked over her delicate little frame for injury before picking her up. Apart from a goose egg on the back of her head, she appeared fine. But what if she had internal injuries? What if they both did?

He scooped his precious little girl up and cradled her featherweight in his arms. To his chagrin, he felt tears rolling down his cheeks. Men didn't cry. But the sight of this child, almost a baby, hurt, was more than he could bear. He laid her with her mother and then checked the rest of the house.

Of Jared, there was no sign. Hunter hadn't expected to find him, but he had to look just in case.

"Damn!" he screamed, his rage a living thing that needed outlet. He whipped out his cell phone and punched in the number for the agency. Bob answered almost immediately.

"Magic Emporium, how may we help you?"

"It's Hunter. The Dragon was here."

"Owen filled me in. Have you apprehended the Dragon?"

Hunter took a deep, calming breath before answering. "He took the boy and injured the mother and daughter. I need a pickup for transport to the Realm immediately."

"Now wait a second, Hunter," said Bob. "We can't just haul two mundanes into the Realm like that."

"This is not negotiable, Bob," said Hunter coldly. "They're hurt, and it's our fault. We let the Dragon loose, and because of us, they're hurt, bad. They need healing quick, and the best healer I know is my mother. Don't make me go over your head." Hunter was in no mood to argue, and it must have been apparent in his tone.

Hunter heard Bob sigh in his ear. "The commander won't like it."

"I don't give a damn what the commander likes or not. I'll deal with him. Now get me a team out here now for pickup and send notice to the portal guardian that we're coming through."

"We'll be there in fifteen minutes."

"Make it ten," Hunter growled before flipping his cell phone shut. The girls both still lay on the couch, their skin waxy white. Damn, he hated feeling helpless.

Hunter raced up the stairs and started throwing clothes into a suitcase he found in Suzie's closet. When he went into the twins' room, he felt a pang of dread staring at their little beds and toys. Would they ever see them again? He grabbed some of the kids' clothes and stuffed it into the suitcase before walking out of the room, only to walk back in and grab Jessica's doll. *Shut up, my precious angel is going to need her dolly when she wakes up, and I'll punch the first person that makes a comment about it.*

He heard doors slamming outside and hurried down with the suitcase and doll. Hunter flung open the door before Bob, who had come in person, could knock. He'd brought Owen with him, along with the Magical Emporium van. Scanning for passersby—the street gaped clear of traffic and prying eyes—they opened the back of the van that had been cleared of seats.

Hunter first grabbed Suzie and carried her out to the van. He lay her down carefully in the back. Then, he went back in and scooped Jessica, her frightful stillness scaring him more than any ogre or assassin could. He climbed into the back of the van with her cradled in his lap. Owen shut the van door and climbed into the front. Bob had the wheel and, with a squeal of the tires, took off like a bat out of hell. Hunter hoped they wouldn't get pulled over because they'd have an awful hard time explaining themselves to any cops.

But they made it back to the agency without incident and parked in the back of the shop. Hunter ended up letting Bob carry Jessica so he could carry Suzie while Owen brought up the rear with the suitcase and one little girl's dolly.

It took precious minutes to unlock the several locks on the door that led to the basement, but once opened, they hurried down the stairs, emerging in a dimly lit storage area. Boxes were strewn all over the floor and stacked up against the cinder-block walls. Only one section of wall had been left partially clear, and Owen went over to it. By pressing on the cinder blocks in a complex pattern, a doorway appeared with more steps leading down. A musty smell wafted up, along with a tingle of power—an alien feeling this side of the border. The stairs were hewn out of rough rock and went down about fifty steps, where they emerged into a large stone cavern.

The torches were already lit and cast eerie shadows on the rough stone walls. Hunter strode to the portal, Suzie cradled in his arms, followed by Bob holding Jessica and Owen with the luggage, the dolly tucked under his arm. The portal stood like a shimmering mirror except nothing ever reflected on its glassy surface. This close, the hum of magic could be felt—a buzzing along the skin that awakened the magic dormant in Hunter this side of the boundary.

Hunter spoke the traditional words. "Guardian of the portal, I seek passage."

A heavy feeling descended over them—a presence that could be felt but not seen. A low, rumbling voice came from nowhere, yet everywhere at once. "I see thee, Hunter, Bob, and Owen. I sense you bring others though. A girl child, daughter to the Dragon. One that has never been to the Realm but within whom the magic is strong. I also sense a mundane female, the mother of the one whom the Dragon calls son. What cause have thee to bring them here to seek passage to the Realm?"

"They have been injured by the Dragon, who recently escaped from the Realm. They require healing. We also seek to find the son whom the Dragon has stolen."

"The Dragon already moves within the Realm, his

son an unwilling passenger at his side. He dares to weaken the boundaries that hold the Realm safe. I will grant thee and your party passage, but on one condition. Thou cannot pass back through the portal again till the Dragon has been caught. Do ye accept my charge?"

"I gladly accept," said the Hunter without hesitation. He'd not rest till he'd found Jared and destroyed the Dragon. Although, he had to admit, this was the oddest conversation he'd ever had with a portal guardian. It would seem even powers as old as the boundary itself worried about the Dragon being left loose.

A boom sounded. "The charge has been accepted, the conditions understood. I grant thee passage. Good luck in your hunt for the Dragon."

"I thank thee, guardian."

The heavy feeling left as the guardian returned to his slumber, or whatever it was that they did between portal calls. Their magic was an old one, lost from the time of the boundary's creation, but who cared so long as it worked?

The three men approached the portal and, one by one, stepped through. It felt like stepping into a cold shower, yet they remained dry. They emerged in a room, an exact mirror of the one they'd just left except for the desk where a wizard in robes, who'd been napping, jumped up.

"Halt and state your business," said the dumpy-looking wizard, tugging on his robe, looking down his nose at them imperiously.

"Stuff if, Norbert," said Hunter, in no mood to deal with him.

"I'm just doing my job," stated Norbert huffily. "You don't make the rules. The commander does. And those rules state I have to ask your business, starting with who those two strangers are," he said, fluttering his hands toward Suzie and Jessica.

"They're with me," said Hunter flatly.

"And they are?"

"None of your business," growled Hunter. "I need a teleport to my family home now."

"Now, Hunter, these two aren't Realm citizens. You can't just . . ." The words froze in the wizard's mouth, and he gulped hard at the dangerous look Hunter gave him.

"They're hurt, just like you're going to be in a minute if you don't teleport us to my house in the next five seconds," said Hunter with a menacing scowl.

"But the commander. . ."

"I'll deal with the commander. Now just do it!" Hunter roared. There would be consequences to his actions later, but right now, he didn't care.

Norbert swallowed, his Adam's apple bobbing in nervousness, but he wisely decided to do as Hunter asked. Too bad, Hunter was in the mood to hit something.

Norbert grabbed Hunter's sleeve in one hand and Bob's in the other. "I'll have to come back for Owen," he said almost apologetically. The wizard closed his eyes. "Teleportus!"

With a wrenching sensation, the cavern with the portal disappeared, and they found themselves in the front hall of Hunter's home. Norbert immediately let go of Hunter and flashed out of sight, reappearing moments later with Owen.

"Mother!" bellowed Hunter.

The bald head of the butler popped into view from an archway off the front hall, only to duck back into the room he'd peeked out of at the thunderous look on Hunter's face.

"Mother!" yelled Hunter again. Where the hell was she? Didn't she know he needed her? Now!

"Goodness, dear," came his mother's voice as she floated down the stairs. "There's no reason to—" She stopped halfway down the stairs and took in the odd group in her front hall.

"Please, Mother," Hunter said, holding Suzie up, his eyes full of anguish. "Help them."

Without any questions, his mother took charge.

"Benson!" she called, her bellow almost as formidable as her son's.

"Yes, my lady," said the bald butler, coming out of hiding.

"Get my things and bring them to the pink room. Quickly, Benson."

"Yes, my lady," Benson said, bowing before quickly walking away, his long stork legs giving him an awkward gait as he scuttled off to do her bidding.

"Come on, Hunter, and you too, Bob. Bring them upstairs so I may examine them."

"I'll just leave then," said Norbert before popping out of sight.

Coward, sneered the little voice in Hunter's mind. Hunter carried Suzie carefully up the stairs, walking lightly so as to not jostle her. He looked back to ensure Bob was taking the same care with Jessica and gave a grunt of approval when he saw him carrying his sweet little girl just as gently. Owen, the doll still tucked under his arm, followed them, as well.

His mother cast a few curious looks back at them but held her tongue, leading them to the pink room on the second floor that had an enormous bed. Once Hunter and Bob had settled the girls carefully side by side on the pink comforter of the bed, though, she took charge.

His mother eyed them both, calculating, then put her hands on Jessica first.

Hunter could feel a hum in the air, almost an electrical tingle, as his mother called up her healing magic.

Benson came bustling in, arms full of linen, followed by a housemaid holding a basin of steaming water and another with his mother's healing basket.

"I need the purple bottle, Benson," said his mother, holding out her hand without looking.

Benson reached into the basket and withdrew a small, purple vial. He unstoppered it and placed it in Hunter's mother's open palm. She opened Jessica's mouth and let three drops fall in then placed her hands on Jessica again. The hum came back, and slowly, the pallor leached away from Jessica's face. Her breathing came deeper, and her cheeks began to turn pink.

With a gasp, Jessica opened her eyes.

Hunter was immediately by her side, cradling her in his arms.

"Mommy. Jari," Jessica cried softly in his shirt.

"Shhh, baby girl," Hunter whispered into her hair.

"Mommy's going to be just fine. I'm here. I'll find Jared and bring him back. I promise."

Hunter's mother stood staring at Hunter, a bemused look on her face. "I'll be damned," she said, her voice full of wonder.

Owen approached the bed and held out the dolly to Jessica.

"My baby," she whispered, hugging her doll tight.

Jessica, clinging to Hunter, turned to look around and saw her mother beside her on the bed, her face a grotesque, bloody, swollen mask. She let out a wail.

"It's okay, baby girl," said Hunter, rocking her in his arms. "Watch. My mommy is going to make your mommy feel better."

His mother approached Suzie and, using a clean, damp cloth, first wiped the blood from her face. Even clean of blood, Suzie's face looked horrible, swollen and discolored, while her breath rasped through her damaged throat. His mother placed her hands on Suzie, and Jessica's eyes went wide as she felt the hum of magic.

"What dat? It tick-les," she said, looking up at Hunter.

"That, my little angel, is magic. Look," he whispered, pointing.

Intrigued now, Jessica watched as Hunter's mother poured some more of the purple vial into Suzie's mouth. Then, his mother laid her hands on Suzie again. The hum of magic vibrated stronger this time, the injury obviously more severe. The tingle of magic grew in intensity till it made his teeth vibrate while Jessica's hair floated lightly around her head.

Hunter's mother's face scrunched up as she fed the healing magic into Suzie's body. Slowly, the bruising faded from Suzie's face and neck. Going from purple to green to yellow then gone. The horrible whistling when Suzie breathed eased until it became whisper quiet again, her chest rising and falling smoothly. By the time Hunter's mother was done, all Suzie's physical injuries were gone. But Suzie didn't wake.

"Why isn't she waking up?" Hunter demanded, placing Jessica on the bed so she could snuggle up to her mother.

"Her injuries were not just external but mental, as well. She should awaken shortly on her own. It's a good thing you brought them when you did. Both of them had bleeding in their brains and would have probably died. Who are they, Hunter?" asked his mother, her piercing blue eyes, the mirror image of his own, full of questions.

"I'll tell you in a bit."

"You'll tell us now!" barked the voice of the commander, also known as his father, from the doorway.

"Not now," said his mother, going over to her husband and placing a delicate hand on his arm.

"But," blustered the commander. Hunter's mother gave him a stern look and took him by the hand as she led him out of the room.

"I'll be back to check on them in a bit," he heard his mother say from the hall.

Owen shuffled to his feet. "So, um, I guess, if you don't need me anymore, I should get going. I'll keep any eye on your house, hers too, while you're here. Let me know if I can do anything," he said before leaving.

Bob cleared his throat. "I guess I'll be going now too. I take it you'll take care of the Dragon from here."

"Oh, I'll take care of him all right," said Hunter in a menacing tone. "Don't you worry. He'll be made to pay for this." Bob left Hunter alone with the girls.

My girls. No use denying it. He felt a bond with Suzie and Jessica that defied all logic. Was it love? He didn't know, but he did know that he would do anything to keep them safe. But there was one thing missing. Jared.

Jared needed to be found, but Hunter didn't want to leave till he knew Suzie would be all right.

He went and kneeled beside the bed, taking Suzie's limp hand in his own.

"Why she no wake up, Hunta?" asked Jessica, her little face mirroring his own anxiety.

"I think she's real scared."

"Da bad man has Jari. You find him for me?" she asked, her sweet, trusting eyes sending a pang of guilt right through him. Jared should never have been taken. Hunter should have been there to protect them. The fact that he hadn't known the Dragon was their father was no excuse. He still felt responsible, and he needed to fix this.

He leaned forward and lightly kissed Suzie on the lips, murmuring, "I'll find Jared and bring him back. I promise. Please wake up."

And, like a princess in a fairy tale, Suzie's eyes opened. She smiled at Hunter when she saw him leaning over her, but he knew when the memory of what happened washed over her because her eyes widened with horror and a high keening came out of her.

"Noooooooooo!" Suzie wailed. "Jared! Jessica!"

"Mommy, I here," said Jessica, her eyes wide with fright at her mother's cries.

Suzie wrapped her arms around Jessica, her eyes scanning the room, looking for Jared. Her eyes found Hunter's, the hopefulness in them almost breaking his heart and control in half. Hunter, with great regret, shook his head.

Suzie screamed. And screamed. The pain over losing one of her children too much to bear. Her anguished cries cut through him like a knife. His fault. All his fault. He should have been there to protect them. Hunter wrapped his arms around her, trying to rock her like he had Jessica, who now also wailed in concert with her mother.

But nothing could calm Suzie. And he couldn't really blame her. The worst part was she still didn't even know the full truth of what the Dragon was.

Suzie continued to scream heartrending sounds that made him want to howl, and Jessica, her cheeks tearstained, cried along with her.

Hunter's mother hurried into the room. "What happened? What's wrong with her? Didn't the healing work?" she asked worriedly.

"The Dragon has her son," Hunter stated flatly.

"Oh dear," his mother replied. Hunter could see the shock on his usually unflappable mother's face. She approached Suzie and laid her hands on her. "Sleep," she commanded with a push of magic, and Suzie, thankfully, stopped screaming and went back to sleep.

Jessica hiccupped, her teary little face all blotchy and red.

Hunter scooped her up. "It's all right, baby girl.

Mommy just went to sleep again for a little bit. She'll feel better when she wakes up. Why don't you come with me and see if we can't find a cookie for you to eat? I know Cook likes to keep some hidden in her special cookie jar."

"Baby wants one, too," Jessica said softly against his chest.

"Baby can have one, too." Hunter carried Jessica out of the room, his mother following him.

Hunter left Jessica with the rotund cook, who took one look at little Jessica's face and immediately took her under her ample wing. He followed his mother into the den, where his father paced, his florid face even more red than usual.

"What is the meaning of this?" his father barked. "You brought not one but two mundanes into the Realm. What the hell were you thinking?"

Hunter was not in the mood for his father's bluster. "I was thinking of saving their lives," he shouted back. "Seeing as how it was your crew of incompetents at the prison who let the Dragon loose in the first place!"

For the first time ever, Hunter had rendered his father speechless.

"I—Ah. Well, that was an accident. And what the hell do you mean the Dragon injured them? What the hell does the Dragon want with a bunch of mundanes?" Figured, his father was looking to shift the blame.

"Remember when you all lost him a couple of years back? Well, turns out he was busy seducing and then impregnating an innocent. That innocent is upstairs right now."

His father sat down heavily in the chair behind his

desk. "Tell me the whole story," he said with a sigh, rubbing his florid face.

Hunter did—he told them about the Dragon impersonating a professor and seducing Suzie. How she had twins and left right around the time the Dragon had been re-apprehended. Then, how the Dragon had come back into her life and taken Jared.

"I don't know all the details yet. Suzie was unconscious when I found her. He beat the living daylights out of her, hurt Jessica, his daughter, and then took off with Jared, his son."

"But why go through all that trouble?" said his father. "Why use a mundane?"

"I think I can answer that," said his mother. "The Dragon is one of a kind among shape-shifters. I'd heard stories through the grapevine of other women in the Realm who had the misfortune of becoming pregnant by him. None of them survived. Leaving the Realm for the magicless side of the world nullified his powers, so even if the child inherited his powers, they were inactive in the womb. So the pregnancy could progress to term."

Hunter, appalled, finished her thought. "He finally created an heir."

"So the Dragon kidnapped his son," said his father. "But that still doesn't explain why you brought the mundanes here."

Hunter's mother rounded on her husband in a fury. "How dare you speak of them like that, Adrian! After all that poor woman and child have been through and are still going through. They would have died if Hunter hadn't brought them. This is our fault, and he was right.

We should bear some responsibility for what happened. The better question now, though, is, what next? We can't allow that monster to keep that child."

"I'm going after them," said Hunter, and when he caught up to the Dragon, he'd make sure that he never, ever hurt Suzie or the twins again!

"Now, wait just a second," said the commander. "You can't just go haring off, chasing the Dragon. You have respons—"

"Like hell! I'm the best tracker you have, and you know it. If anyone can find that bastard and save Jared, it's me." And if his father, oh excuse him, the commander didn't like it, too bloody bad!

"Listen here, boy!" roared his father. "I've had quite enough lip from you. I'm your commander and your father, and you will do as I say."

Hunter leaned forward on his father's desk, his nose only inches from the commander's face. "No, you listen to me," Hunter said in a quiet, deadly tone. "I'm going, and I really don't give a damn whether you like it or not. Suzie needs her son back, and I am going to bring him back for her. And..." He continued before his father could interject. "You are going to make Suzie and Jessica welcome here while I'm gone. You will not ship her back home to sit terrified and worried. I want her here where she can be kept abreast of how the rescue is going. This is nonnegotiable."

"Or else what?" said his father sarcastically.

"Or you'll answer to me," said his mother coming to Hunter's rescue. "Hunter is that boy's best chance, the best tracker you have, and you know it, Adrian. Stop acting like an ass and open your eyes. Can't you see our son cares for this woman and her children? I shouldn't have to tell you it's the right thing to do. Don't you feel any responsibility or compassion over what has happened to them? I may put up with a lot, Adrian, but I will not stand by and watch you turn into as great a monster as the Dragon. You know it's the right thing to do."

To Hunter's amazement, his father hung his head, unable to meet her eyes. What, the great commander humbled? Mark it on the calendar. This was not something that happened too often.

His mother lay her hand on Hunter's arm and said to him, "Don't you worry, dear. I'll make sure they're taken care of. You do what you have to do. They'll be safe here. I'll put a call in to your sister. She can take some leave and come back home for a while and fill the role of bodyguard for your Suzie and Jessica."

His sister, yes. If he couldn't be here to protect Suzie and Jessica, then she was the next best thing. He nodded. Thank the higher powers his mother was here. He could trust her to make sure his father didn't screw things up while he tracked down Jared.

"Now why don't you get ready? Adrian, you need to get to work, too. Call in your scouts and other sources. Find out where the Dragon's been. We need to find his trail so that little boy can be saved. We'll also need supplies and a wizard for transport to the last known location."

Hunter hugged his mother and strode out of his father's office without looking at him. He needed to get ready.

Hunter could feel his blood starting to pump. His senses were coming alive. Coming back to the Realm meant his magical senses were awake again. The world was, once again, a multi-dimensional place of sound, smell, and sight. It felt good to be home. Too bad the reason had to be such a horrible one. He couldn't help the shiver of excitement that ran through him, though.

Time to hunt.

CHAPTER 11

Suzie fluttered her eyes open and stared at the strange ceiling—a painted fresco of flowers that, while quite pretty, she'd never seen before. *Where the hell am I?* But right on the tail end of that thought came the memories.

Oh God, my baby boy is gone. Suzie felt like wailing again but held it in, afraid that woman would come back and put her to sleep again. She needed to find out what was going on, so she swallowed back the tears and sat up, looking around.

Where's Jessica? She remembered her little body pressed against hers when she'd awoken last time before that woman had made her pass out. *Where is she now?* Had she been taken too? No, that wouldn't have happened because Hunter...she remembered seeing Hunter. He'd make sure Jessica stayed safe. Where did this certainty come from? Deep down in her gut, she just knew. If anyone could protect them, it was Hunter. If only he'd arrived before Damian had.

Suzie swung her legs off the bed, only to suddenly remember her injuries. But to her amazement, nothing hurt. She touched her face gingerly. No pain. Had they given her painkillers? She sure as hell didn't remember any. She got off of the bed and wandered to an antique, silver-framed mirror on the wall. Suzie stared at her reflection and blinked to make sure it wasn't a mirage or her imagination. Her face stared back at her, unblemished. Not a bruise, scratch, lump—nothing. She tilted her chin up. Her neck appeared unmarked, as well. Had she dreamed the whole thing, or had she been unconscious long enough for her wounds to heal? *And what the hell am I wearing?* Suzie frowned down at what she wore. Someone had obviously undressed her and put her in a white chemise that hit about mid-thigh. Almost like a slip she'd wear under a dress.

Looking around, she wondered again just where she'd been taken. This not knowing anything had passed the point of annoying. She prowled the huge, absolutely gorgeous room—definitely expensive. This place didn't look cheap. She hoped only that nobody would be expecting her to pay for her stay because she knew she couldn't afford these digs. The walls of the room seemed to be gray stone covered in embroidered tapestries. It reminded her of a medieval castle. Plush pink carpets covered the stone floors and matched the pink of the coverlet on the bed, a huge, four-poster monstrosity that belonged in the Middle Ages. There were two doors in the room. The first, when she opened it, led into an antiquated bathroom with a claw-foot tub and what she assumed—hoped—was a toilet but definitely not of the porcelain variety she'd come to know judging by the box with the dangling chain above the wooden seat.

She finished her perusal of the bathroom and returned to the bedroom in time to see the second door open. The petite woman she'd seen before came bustling in, holding a dress over one arm. *She'd better not be coming back to put me to sleep*, thought Suzie fiercely. No way, not without a fight anyway. Suzie wanted some answers.

The woman first looked at the bed and, not seeing Suzie, turned till she saw her framed in the bathroom doorway.

"There you are, dear," she said with a soft smile. "I was just coming to check on you. How are you feeling?"

"Who the hell are you? Where am I? And where the hell are my children?" asked Suzie rudely, her questions running into each other.

The woman seemed unfazed by her outburst. "I'm Hunter's mother, Beverly. You're in our home. Jessica is downstairs playing 'I Spy' with Molly, the maid."

Hunter's house and mother? What the hell had happened while she slept? And just how rich were Hunter's folks to afford a maid? Just goes to show how little she actually knew about the man she was thinking of dating. Not that they'd be going out now with Jared missing. Or had he—*please*—been found already?

"What about Jared?" She crossed her fingers behind her back, praying the answer would be good.

Hunter's mother's eyes, so similar to Hunter's in their

blueness, looked sad. "I'm afraid the Dragon still has him." Suzie felt her heart plummet. "But don't worry. Hunter is prepping to leave as we speak. If anyone can find your son, it's him. He's the best we've got."

Suzie felt confused. Had she stepped through a mirror or something? 'Cause either she had completely lost her marbles or something really strange was going on. *Like who the hell is this Dragon they keep referring to, and why do they think he has Jared?*

Beverly came toward Suzie and handed her the gown draped over her arm. And what a gown! Suzie went back in the bathroom to pull it over her head and then shook her head in bemusement. Welcome to the eighteenth century. The gown glistened, a pale blue with a snug bodice that laced up the front and a long, loose skirt that went down to her ankles. Kind of like the dress Hunter's mother wore, actually. But Suzie had never seen women wearing these types of gowns outside of movies. Another oddity that made no sense.

Suzie, feeling better armed now that she at least had clothes on, wandered back out into the room and sat down in an overstuffed pink chair, resisting an urge to rub her head. She had a sneaky suspicion she'd want to be sitting for the discussion ahead.

Beverly still stood in the room, hands clasped demurely in front of her, her face placid, a small, sad smile on her lips.

Suzie felt like screaming at her but resisted, and said, "I don't understand any of this. Damian took Jared, not a dragon. And I know Hunter's a private eye and all, but shouldn't we be calling the cops and reporting Jared as kidnapped? You know, get an Amber Alert set up or something? And even curioser, what the hell happened to my injuries? How long have I been here?"

"Oh dear. You really don't know about any of this, do you? Goodness, where to start?"

"How about with the truth?" said Suzie with a sarcastic edge.

Beverly laughed. "Dear, I think this is one instance where the truth will seem stranger than fiction. Let me ask you something. Do you believe in magic?"

Suzie frowned. *Is this lady nuts?* "No, of course I don't believe in magic. I'm a grownup. I know fact from fantasy. Magic is something for stories and fairy tales. And what does that have to with anything?"

"Yes, well, given your upbringing, I could see why you'd think that. You see"—Beverly paused as if gathering her thoughts—"magic is real. Not in your world, of course, but here in the Realm, it is very much a part of everyone's life."

"Okay, you lost me already. What do you mean, my world? Are you trying to tell me we're not on Earth anymore? And again, what does this have to with my son?" Suzie felt her frustration rising. She'd asked for answers and, instead, seemed to be receiving the runaround.

"Oh no, we're still on Earth, and this has everything to do with your son and why his father took him. I'm not explaining this right. See, a very long time ago, magic used to be everywhere, as well as all beings magical like fairies, pixies, wizards, ogres, and even dragons."

Suzie arched a brow—*Hunter's mom is coo-coo.*

Beverly saw her look and pulled her little frame up indignantly. "I am not crazy. Listen, I know this will be hard to believe, but I promise it's the truth, and you need to hear this so you can understand what's happened to your son. So, where was I? Oh yes. A long time ago the world was full of magic, some good and some evil. Now, creatures can't help themselves. After all, is it evil to kill to eat and protect one's home? No, but there were some who pursued evil for personal gain. Men and women who lacked empathy but craved power. They used their magic for nefarious purposes. They killed, maimed, destroyed. The world was turning into a very horrid, violent place due to their greed. Finally, there came a time when the world said, enough. Humans have always been a populous species, and while some had magical abilities, the majority didn't, and they got tired of seeing their hard work destroyed by those who abused their magical gifts. So, a spell was created. Thirteen of the world's most powerful wizards gave their lives to this spell."

"And what, they destroyed all the magic in the world?" Funny how the Grimm brothers had never told this tale, this supposedly true tale. Poor Hunter. Must have been hard growing up with a crazy mother. And again, what did this have to do with Damian kidnapping Jared? Suzie wondered if she could make it past Hunter's mother out the door. She needed to find someone sane to talk to. Preferably Hunter. He'd tell her the truth. Of course, he might not be too happy with her if she was mean to his mother. Crap. Guess she'd listen a little more and hope his mother got to the point.

"The thirteen didn't destroy the magic. They contained it. They created a boundary around one continent and some other areas of magical importance. On the one side of the boundary, the side where you lived, all magic was drained. On our side of the boundary, known as the Realm, the magic remained, including all the beasts and creatures of legend that you thought only myth."

"Oh please," said Suzie, rolling her eyes. "Are you kidding me? So what, next you're going to tell me I'm now on the magical side of this so-called boundary?"

Beverly blinked. "Well, of course. How else do you think we healed you and your daughter? You were both injured quite severely when Hunter brought you."

"Ha, that's good. Magic for healing. Please. I know you believe magic healed me, but come on. I'm an adult. My guess is the hospital put me in some kind of a coma so I could heal? How long was I out? A week? Two weeks?"

"How about a few hours?"

Suzie felt like saying impossible, but really, it didn't feel as if she'd been out long enough for her injuries to heal. And shouldn't some of her injuries, especially the kick in the face, have left scars? But the alternative was impossible. *Right?*

"No." Suzie shook her head. "You tell a neat story, but I'm sorry. I'm not that gullible."

"Oh, then how do you explain this?"

Suzie looked at Beverly and stifled a gasp. Beverly's body hovered in the air. Suzie looked at the floor and saw a definite space between Beverly's feet and the floor.

Suzie looked up but already knew she wouldn't see any wires.

"That still doesn't make your story true," said Suzie stubbornly. "It could still be a trick. I don't know. Maybe there are mirrors or something. I know there's a guy on television who can do the same trick."

Hunter's mother sighed as she floated back to the floor. "Dear, you know I'm telling the truth. Magic is real, at least in the Realm it is."

"Okay, let's say for a minute that magic is real. What the hell does that have to do with me and the twins? Or Damian kidnapping Jared?" *Ha, explain that.*

"Damian is from the Realm. He's a shape-shifter."

Suzie burst out laughing. This just kept getting better and better. "So what, he's a werewolf who changes on the full moon?" *Oh yeah, and I'm a mermaid when I hit the water. Like, hello, where is Hunter? Someone needs to lock his mother back up in the loony bin.*

"Werewolf? Goodness, no. He's a weredragon. An extremely rare type of shape-shifter. Rumor has it that his mother was a sorceress, his father a dragon. From what we've learned, it was only because of the sorceress's magic that both she and the baby survived the pregnancy. The man you know as Damian was the result."

"What? Do you mean you're trying to tell me that Damian's a dragon? Um, don't you think I would have noticed?" Suzie had once known every inch of his body. She'd have remembered scales and a tail.

"There was nothing to see when he was on your side of the boundary. Keep in mind that, once he entered the magicless side of the boundary, his powers disappeared, making him just as human as you are."

"Let's say for a minute I believe you, that Damian's a dragon thing. Then why on earth would he come into my world and be a professor? Why get me pregnant and steal my son? Why not just stay here where he has his magic?"

"Because his very essence made it impossible for him to sire a child here. I have it on good authority that he's been trying for a long time to create a son. Unfortunately, they all ended in tragedy, both for the unborn child and their mothers. The babies, while developing, shifted in the womb and tore their mothers apart, killing both themselves and their mothers."

Suzie swallowed hard. Were her babies shape-shifters too? Would she have died if she had been in the Realm while pregnant? Not that she believed any of this. Jessica and Jared were normal, active, very *human* children.

"Your very lack of magic made it possible for him to sire a son and a daughter. I don't know about your son, but I do know when I healed your daughter that I felt something. I'm not entirely familiar with shape-shifters, they tend to keep to themselves, but I'd say the chances are good that both your children are part dragon like their father."

"No, my kids are normal. Not lizard things. I think I would have noticed. I'm their mother. And mothers always know."

"Not in your world, you wouldn't have. Now that we are in the Realm, do not be surprised if you see them displaying gifts you've never seen before. My own son and daughter, while not full shape-shifters, have some of the blood. It's what makes them such good hunters and trackers. Their eyesight is much keener. They can both see in the dark, as well as smell things that normal human noses can't. They both have special extra senses that make them more than human. Special, like your children."

Oh, come on, thought Suzie, *just how much crap am I expected to believe?* "So what, Hunter is part dog?"

"No, according to the family tree, we believe his abilities stem from his great-grandfather who was a werepanther." A panther. Yes, if she'd had to choose an animal, that would be it. Feline grace, sleek power—Suzie shook her head. *Wake up*, she scolded herself, *do not get drawn into the delusion.*

"This is nuts! You're telling me Damian purposely impregnated me so he could have a kid that he could steal and do what with?"

"The Dragon wanted an heir, so he created one. Now who knows what he plans? The last time he got loose, he caused great havoc. More than likely, he will start again."

"Why didn't you guys stop him?" Yeah, like before, he'd ruined Suzie's life.

"We did catch up to him three years ago and had him placed in a very special prison. Unfortunately, he escaped."

"This is your fault then—you and all this Realm place—that my son is gone! If this Dragon was so dangerous, why the hell didn't you kill him? Or do you not believe in the death penalty?" Suzie asked, her temper simmering.

"Usually, someone with his crimes would have been put to death, but because of his uniqueness, the fact he was one of a kind, and the closest anyone has ever been able to get to a dragon, even a partial one, he was kept alive for study."

"That's great. So your bloody science experiment escapes, and now my children and I get to pay the price. Tell me, what the hell are you going to do to find my son? I want him back," said Suzie, close to tears.

"Like I said before, Hunter is preparing to hunt him down and bring your son back. It's too late today for him to leave. We're still waiting on some field reports to try and help us track what direction the Dragon is going in. But he leaves at first light, and I promise you, he will find them. Hunter always catches his prey," Beverly said, the pride in her son clear in her voice.

"I want to go with him. Jared will need me when he's found."

"Sorry, dear, but you would only slow Hunter down. And besides, your daughter needs you. Don't worry, when Hunter finds them, he'll keep Jared safe and bring him back to you."

"I still don't understand or like this," said Suzie. "I want Jessica. I need to see her."

"Of course you do. Think about what I've told you. If you have any questions, I'm available to you. I'll have your daughter sent up right away."

Beverly left the room, and Suzie paced, overwhelmed with all the fantastical info she'd had thrown at her.

Real magic. Could it be possible? Look around me. I am definitely not in Kansas anymore, but still. . .

"Mommy!" squealed Jessica as she hurled herself across the room into her mother's arms.

Suzie caught her in a tight hug, burying her face in her little girl's soft hair. To think her baby had almost died. Hell, Suzie had almost died. But Hunter had saved them. Would he be able to save Jared too?

"Mommy, we in a castle. And I eat cookies and saw a fairy," Jessica babbled.

"Are you okay, baby? You're not hurt anymore?"

"No, Hunta's mommy fix me. She fix you, too. She nice. And Hunta say we can stay. He gonna find Jari. He pwomise me."

"Indeed, I did," said Hunter, coming into the room and dragging in with him a vibrant energy that she could almost reach out and touch. Suzie caught her breath looking at him. He seemed different somehow. Larger, more alive, and, with that look in his eyes, definitely more dangerous. Suzie felt a shiver, and it pissed her off that her body could be so easily be aroused at a time like this. With her baby boy still missing, now was not the time for naughty thoughts.

"What the hell is going on, Hunter?" Suzie snapped. Jessica whimpered at her sharp tone and burrowed her face in Suzie's chest. *Great, now I've scared Jessica. Nice mother.*

"How about we talk after Jessica goes to bed? It's been a long day, and I think she could use a good sleep."

Dammit! Where did he get off acting like Jessica's daddy? Never mind that he was right about Jessica being tired. Suzie hadn't carried the twins for nine months to have someone usurp her spot. She'd earned the right to be the one who got to make those decisions, not him.

"I think it's bedtime, sweetie. Why don't I tuck you

into this big, pink princess bed? Mommy's going to talk to Hunter, and then I'll be right back and I'll sleep with you. Like a sleepover, okay?"

"Okay," mumbled Jessica, stifling a yawn.

Suzie tucked Jessica and her dolly under the heavy pink covers and kissed her.

"Wuv you, Mommy."

"I love you too, baby."

"Hunta, I wanna kiss," Jessica said, puckering her lips.

Hunter leaned over the bed and gave her a resounding smack on the lips that had Jessica giggling. Then, he kissed dolly too.

"'Night, precious angel," he murmured.

"'Night, Mommy. 'Night, Hunta."

Suzie followed Hunter out into the hall, leaving the door open a crack. A man dressed medieval-ly in a tunic and leggings with a sword across his knees—yes, a sword—sat in a chair outside the door.

"Suzie and I are going up to the parapet for a few minutes. Guard this door with your life."

"Yessir," said the grim-faced man.

Suzie held her tongue. Why did Hunter feel the need to put a guard on their door? Were they still in danger? Hunter tugged at her hand, trying to lead her up the hall, but Suzie hesitated. Should she leave Jessica alone?

"She'll be safe," said Hunter, reading her mind. "Kyle is there as an extra precaution. I'm not taking any chances with either of you, ever again."

God, that macho routine never grew old. Even traumatized emotionally, she couldn't help but feel a warmth at his protectiveness.

Suzie let him lead her down the hall—a really long hall—and up some winding stairs till they emerged on a real—kid you not—castle parapet. Suzie wandered over to the edge of the waist-high stone wall and looked out.

Oh my God. Jessica hadn't been kidding when she said they were in a real life castle. Suzie looked around her in astonishment. The huge castle, surrounded by a stone wall, encased a bailey—*is that the right term?* The land outside the wall stretched in all directions, irregular-shaped plots of green and yellow crops bisected by dirt paths. She could see thatched huts and wooden buildings scattered around. A cobbled road leading from the front of the castle went through the buildings and fields, stretching off into the distance before entering a large forest. It resembled a scene out of a fairy tale. So, did that make Hunter her prince? But it also reminded her of why she'd found herself here.

Suzie whirled around, suddenly incensed. "What the hell is going on, Hunter? Your mother told me some really messed-up story about how the world was split with magic on one side and no magic on the other. And how Damian is really some kind of dragon creature that impregnated me so he could have an heir. Now I'm in an honest-to-God castle, in a place that should only exist in history books, and apparently magic healed Jessica and me. None of this makes any sense. I want things back the way they were. I want Jared back!" she hollered, the tears finally falling.

Hunter said not a word during her tirade, just folded

her into his arms, his solid chest a hard yet comforting pillow for her to sob on. Suzie cried for several minutes while Hunter held her, his hands rubbing circles on her back, not saying a word, letting her pour out her pain. And she had a lot of pain to drain.

When she finally stopped crying and pushed him away, he handed her a handkerchief.

"Feel better?" he asked, his eyes watching her with concern.

"No," she sniffled. "I want Jared back."

"You'll get him back. I promise."

"How can you promise that?" Suzie yelled. "You don't even know where he is. He's probably so scared right now. We've never been apart before. And that pig, that fucking bastard who used me, stole him. What if he hurts him? He hurt Jessica so bad. Almost killed her, and she's just a baby still, a little girl. What's to stop him from hurting Jared too?" she whispered, her eyes haunted still by the vision of her daughter flying through the air and hitting the wall. And Jared, terrified, screaming in that monster's clutches.

"The Dragon won't hurt Jared. He's waited too long for a son. And as for finding him, that's what I do. I'm a hunter in more than just name. I've been trained since birth to track and hunt down those that need to be caught. The Dragon can run as much as he likes. I will find him. And when I do, I promise, he will never hurt you, Jared, or Jessica again."

"You swear?" Suzie asked, looking up at him with watery eyes. She wanted to believe him. Wanted to trust he'd bring her baby boy back.

"I swear. He crossed the line when he hurt you and the twins. This time, I won't be trying to capture him. As soon as I've rescued Jared, the Dragon is a walking dead man."

Suzie knew that she should be shocked at this violent side of Hunter, but instead, she felt a deep satisfaction knowing that Damian, that evil scum of the earth, would pay for what he'd done to her babies. Bloodthirsty? Fucking right! He'd hurt her babies, and for that, he needed to pay! Screw mercy. He hadn't shown her any, and she was tired of running. Tired of living in fear. If Hunter wanted to end this nightmare for her, then she was more than willing to let him.

"Can I come?" She didn't care what his mother had told her. She wanted to be there when he rescued Jared.

"No, I'll move faster on my own. And besides, you'd be much too distracting," he said with a cocky grin that warmed Suzie to the tips of her toes. He found her distracting? *Ditto*.

"Don't worry. As soon as I've got him, I'll take him to the nearest village for teleport back here."

"How long will you be gone?" How soon till she could hold her little boy again?

"Depends. The last scout report has them traveling toward the mountains. He's probably hoping to hole up in a cave up there while he plans his next move. I've got a teleport scheduled for dawn tomorrow. It'll drop me at the last village before the mountain range. I should be able to pick up his trail within the day. Then, depending on how fast he's traveling, a couple of days for me to catch up to him and take Jared back."

"I don't want Jared to see you killing him." He was too little to see something that violent. God only knew the help he'd need in dealing with the trauma from his kidnapping. He didn't need extra nightmares.

"He won't see a thing. I told you I'll make sure Jared is safe before anything else. Once Jared is back, safe with you, then I'll take care of the Dragon," he said, his eyes cold. Suzie shivered, glad she wasn't Hunter's prey. He looked so dangerous.

"Aren't you afraid?" she asked, her stomach clenched tight in fear. What if Hunter got killed instead?

"I don't fear a coward like the Dragon. Besides," Hunter said, flexing a muscle, "I've taken on much nastier things than him in my time."

And when this was all over, Suzie would have to remember to ask him about his life. Somewhere in the last hour she'd decided to go along with his mother's kooky story about magic and boundaries. It was like they said, when everything else seems impossible, then perhaps the impossible is the truth, or something to that effect.

"When were you planning to tell me about your double life? Over cocktails or dessert on our first date?"

"I wasn't sure if I'd ever tell you. For security reasons, the Realm and its secrets are closely guarded. There are many on the council, the wizards who run the Realm, and others like my father, who want to keep the Realm a secret forever."

"What about you?" she asked curiously. Just a hunch, but she thought he might feel differently.

"Me?" He laughed. "I think the world has evolved enough. People have finally stopped burning witches, and since *Harry Potter*, I think the world would welcome a real taste of magic. So while the Realm and its denizens would be a shock at first, I think, for the most part, it would be accepted if the truth ever came out. Which might be the case soon, whether the council likes it or not."

"Why?"

"The boundary separating the world is failing. There are more and more weak spots showing up every day. My job in your side of the world was to send back those who were crossing those weak spots. But the crossovers are becoming more frequent. I think it's just a matter of time before the boundary fails altogether," he said.

"What will happen then?" Like, would this be the end of days, the final Armageddon?

"No one knows for sure. Obviously, the hidden parts of the Realm will become visible to all again, and magic will abound everywhere. People who before led mundane lives may suddenly discover magical abilities. Creatures that were thought to be legend will be free to roam the land, skies, and seas again."

"Oh God, can't you just see the headlines now?" Suzie said with a ghost of a smile. "The media would have a fieldday. For once the tabloids might end up being right."

"Actually, the tabloids have been right on more occasions than you think. It's only because of myself and some select others in the world that these anomalies are hushed up."

"This is all so fucked up. Pardon my language. One day I'm a single mom hiding from an abusive ex. The next I'm in a fairytale land with my son kidnapped by a dragon. I guess my life will never be the same after this."

"When this is all over, you'll be free to go back to your life with the added bonus that you won't have to worry about the twins' father anymore."

No, Hunter was wrong. Nothing would ever be the same. "What about you?" she asked.

"What about me?" he asked, looking down at her.

"Will you be coming back too?" And it pissed her off that she felt her heart stop while she waited for his answer. She didn't need him in her life, so why did it feel as if the world would lose a lot of its flavor if he disappeared from it?

"Would you miss me if I didn't?" he asked, his eyes watching her intently.

Would she? Yes! Suzie moved closer to Hunter, her body almost touching his, his animal magnetism so much stronger now in his part of the world. His very being called out to her and made her feel weak in the knees.

"I think I'd miss you a little bit if you didn't come back. And I know I'd regret not doing this." Suzie leaned up, amazed at her brazenness, and he, smart man, leaned down. Their lips brushed. Softly. His lips sweetly touched hers.

He let out a groan, and his arms came around her and crushed her to him. He lifted her up, his lips devouring hers, an urgency in his kiss that set her instantly aflame.

Suzie felt just as frantic. She reached up and twined her fingers in his hair, opening her mouth to let his tongue dart in. He licked her inner lip before dueling with her tongue, a wet, sensual dance that lit a fire in her tummy and turned her legs to mush.

Hunter's arms wrapped even tighter around her. Good thing she had him to hold her up else she would have collapsed in a puddle at his feet. He walked over to the wall of the castle and leaned her against it. His hot mouth left her lips to trail scorching kisses down the side of her neck. Suzie arched, her body trembling with need. His hair felt so silky in her hands, and she pulled it, yanking his head back up so she could plunder his mouth, drink of his strength. A hardness pushed against her tummy, a throbbing heat that said more than words how much he wanted her.

He slid down her body, his hot lips brushing her nipples through the fabric of the gown she wore. She gasped when he opened his mouth wide and suckled one of her hard nubs through the thin material.

God, the melting heat. His mouth trailed lower, his warm breath making her shiver even through the gown. He nestled his face against the apex of her thighs, causing her to get even wetter. Her arousal, stronger than anything she'd ever felt or imagined possible, made her wild. She wanted to feel him inside of her. Claiming her. Marking her as his.

She felt his hand tugging up the skirt of the gown, the cool evening air making her thighs shiver. His hand slid up her leg, his callused palm scraping lightly against her softer skin. Rough yet gentle fingers rubbed against her kitty, tangling in her curls. Damn! She'd never had a chance to shave.

And that one thought woke her up. *What the hell am*

I doing? They were standing out in the open where anyone could come across them. Her daughter was in bed waiting for her below, and her son, her poor son, was in the hands of a madman. Suzie pushed at Hunter. He leaned back, his eyes glittering up at her.

"I can't," she almost sobbed. "I—"

Instantly, his arms came around her, and he hugged her tight. "Shh. It's okay. I'm sorry. I forgot myself. I seem to lack all control when you're around me."

He lacks control? Um hello, who started it?

"I'm sorry," Suzie whispered. "I just can't. Not without knowing if Jared is safe. It wouldn't be right."

"No, I'm the one who's sorry. You've had a traumatic day and deserve better than being mauled against a stone wall. It won't happen again."

What? "No, I want this to happen again. It's just I feel guilty about doing this while Jared is missing. Maybe once this is all over." She looked up at him hopefully. *Please let there be another time*, she thought.

He smiled at her, a sweet, warm, dare she say, loving smile. "I would be delighted to take this up where we left off when Jared is safe. More than delighted," he said with a soft kiss on her lips. "Now, time for bed. I need to get up early, and you need your sleep."

Holding her hand, he led her back to her room, and with a sweet kiss that left her trembling, he bid her good night. Suzie ignored the smirk on the guard's face, and with a last smile for Hunter, who watched, she went inside the bedroom.

Despite the dark, she could hear Jessica's even breathing, thankfully she slept. Suzie stripped off the gown she'd put on earlier, leaving on only the thin chemise, and crawled under the covers.

God, she trembled inside with fear for Jared, but she knew Hunter was right about one thing. Damian wanted his son. Jared—his pride and joy. And after trying for so long to create him, would he honestly hurt him? *No*, she had to admit. Even when he'd kidnapped him, he'd never actually physically hurt Jared, even though Jared had tried to hurt him.

But he would hurt Hunter, and that scared her. He could die, and it would be her fault. Would he still be going after the Dragon if it weren't for him getting to know her and the kids? Probably, he seemed to just be that type of guy. What if, in saving Jared, he died? Died without her ever having known his body fully. His touch. Possibly even his love.

Did she love him? Maybe. She thought she'd loved Damian once upon a time, although years of retrospect had made her realize that what she'd thought was love had, in fact, been infatuation. *Am I infatuated with Hunter?* She lusted after his body, true, but she also enjoyed being with him. Talking to him. Seeing him with her children.

But even if she did maybe love him, did he love her back? And considering the different worlds they came from, could he be content with plain old Suzie. Stretch-marked, magicless, slightly chubby Suzie. How could he be?

Suzie felt an urge to find him and ask him what he saw in her. But how would she find him? This place defined the word huge.

She could ask the guard, who'd probably just smirk again and think her a slut looking to get laid. Maybe she could pretend she had an urgent question that only Hunter could answer.

No, he needed his sleep. He'd said he'd be leaving at the crack of dawn to save her son. How dare she think of disturbing his rest to try and make herself feel better? *What a mess!*

Suzie just couldn't sleep. She tossed and turned in the bed beside Jessica. Her mind whirled and twirled in circles.

Unable to take the cloying darkness of the room, she got up and stumbled to the curtains. She needed some air. The gloom in the room hung heavily, though, and stumbling around, she hit something hard.

"Ow!" she yelped, hopping on one foot. Crap, hopefully she hadn't woken Jessica up. Suzie rubbed her bruised shin when she suddenly realized she could see a bit. She turned.

Hunter stood framed in the doorway, the dim light from the hall lighting the gloom in the room.

"Are you okay?" he whispered.

"Yeah, I couldn't sleep and whacked myself getting up."

Hunter tilted his head and indicated she follow him out to the hall. Suzie, with a quick look at the bed where Jessica still slept, followed.

Once in the hall, Hunter closed the door and turned to her.

"What are you doing here?" Suzie asked, noticing the guard had left his post in the chair.

"I sent Kyle to bed. I preferred to watch over you and Jessica myself."

"But you have to get up early."

"And? I wanted to make sure you were safe. My sister will arrive in the morning to take over bodyguard duty while I'm gone. Till then, the only person I trust you and Jessica with is me."

Suzie felt her heart melt.

"Why couldn't you sleep?" he asked softly, his blue eyes gazing down at her with tenderness.

Now facing him, Suzie felt her resolve from earlier vanish, and she looked at her bare feet, realizing suddenly that they were alone and her only attire was a thin linen chemise.

His big arms wrapped around her, and she looked up just as his mouth descended. Instant, molten heat spread through her body. She opened her mouth, inviting his tongue in. They kissed. They bit and sucked. His large hands roamed up and down her back, pressing her against him.

Suzie panted, breathless with need. When he cupped her buttocks in his hands and lifted her to press the juncture of her thighs against his hardness, she moaned against his mouth. With her back against the wall, he ground his body against hers. And Suzie pushed right back. Too many layers separated them. Suddenly, it seemed urgent that she feel his skin, taste him. She slid her hands under his shirt, spreading her hands flat on his smooth, hot flesh. He groaned against her lips then, suddenly, pulled his mouth away and pushed Suzie behind him. She staggered and grabbed his body to steady herself. *What the hell?*

"What do you want?" Hunter growled. Oh crap, someone had caught them.

"Your mother sent me to relieve you. She wishes to speak with you before your departure."

Hunter growled. Suzie just wanted to die. Oh God, to think a few minutes more and they might have been caught doing the naughty in the hall like a pair of randy teenagers.

"Give me a second with the lady."

Hunter pulled Suzie around from behind him and swept her up into his arms. Suzie got a peek of the new guard's broad back before Hunter carried her back into her room. He tucked her into the bed beside Jessica.

Suzie looked up at him, her body still aching.

Hunter gave her a wry smile. "I guess I have one more reason now to find Jared and come back quickly. Take care of Jessica while I'm gone. I'll be back as soon as I can."

With a hard kiss that left her lips tingling, he left, and Suzie huddled down in the bed frustrated but happy. He'd find Jared and bring him back. And when he did, she'd reward him. Or, should she say, reward herself.

CHAPTER 12

"Your timing leaves much to be desired, Mother," said a disgruntled Hunter, walking into his mother's sitting room.

"I know, dear," Beverly said, smiling serenely.

"You mean you did that on purpose?" Hunter barked, frustration making him short tempered.

"Well, really, Hunter. She is, after all, a guest under my roof, and you weren't exactly being discreet. Just be glad it wasn't your father who caught you."

His father. Hunter grimaced. Father would have torn a strip off his hide had he seen him with Suzie. He'd have to take better care next time. *And, yes, there will definitely be a next time.*

"Did you really want something, or was this just a ploy to get me away from Suzie? You know, I expected the commander to have a problem with my interest in her, but I have to say I never expected that from you."

"Oh, your father has a problem with everyone, dear.

As for me, it depends on your intentions. Suzie is not some light skirt that you can play with then discard. She's been hurt, badly. Not to mention the fact she has children."

"You think I don't know that!" What, like he hadn't noticed the twins? And he'd never hurt Suzie. Just the thought of someone hurting her made him want to hit something.

"Do you?" His mother got up from her seat and came to stand by him, one delicate hand on his arm. "What are your intentions, Hunter? Because I can't just stand by and watch you crush that poor girl's heart."

Hunter growled and shook off his mother's hand.

"Do you love her?" his mother persisted.

"I don't know. I do know I can't stop thinking about her. I know I want to kill the bastard who did this to her and the kids. I know I'll kill anybody who hurts her." *Or touches her*, he thought.

"So, you love her?"

"Is it love?" he asked. He couldn't help the agonized query as turned his gaze his mother. "What if I'm not capable of love? I mean, look at the commander. What if I turn out like him?"

"Your father has reasons for being the way he is. And I know you might think he doesn't care for you, but he does, deeply. He just doesn't know how to show it. He wasn't raised that way."

"So what makes you think I'll be any different?" *After all, I am my father's son, his good little soldier.*

"You already are. Can you see your father agonizing about something like this out loud? I've seen the way you look at her, Hunter. I've seen the way you are with that little girl. She adores you, and you adore her right back. How could you think that would change? Did it ever occur to you that, if you did commit, that if you lost this fear, you could be not only a great husband but also a fantastic father? You seem to forget I had a part in raising you, too. Or are you saying I had no influence in how you turned out?"

Oops. His mother looked hurt. And she did have a point. Just because his father was a cold man who showed no affection didn't mean Hunter would end up the same way. He loved spending time with Suzie's kids. Loved the smile that lit up Jessica's face every time she saw him. Could see himself teaching Jared all the things a man needs to teach a boy—like writing his name in snow when he peed, learning how to fight. Did he truly think he'd end up like his father?

"I hate it when you're right," Hunter grumbled.

"Of course you do, dear," said his mother placatingly. "Your father does too."

"I guess I do love her. How would you feel about me marrying a mundane?"

"Oh please, she's not mundane. She's a woman with great inner strength who has managed to survive on her own with two small children. I think she'd make you a marvelous wife."

"What about the commander, though?" Stupid question. He already knew the commander's answer—*No!*

"Your father has nothing to do with this. If you love her, then that's all that matters. He'll either come around, or I'll make him see reason," Beverly said fiercely.

Hunter laughed. "Mother, you always know what to say."

"Now, enough of that. You're ready for your trip?"

"Yes, my stuff is packed and sitting in the front hall. As soon as the wizard shows up, I'll leave. When's dear old sis due to arrive?" It would be nice to see his tougher-than-nails sister. It had been quite some time since they'd last seen each other.

"She'll be arriving with the wizard, actually. We were lucky. We caught her between assignments. And don't worry. I'll make sure she behaves with Suzie."

"She'd better!" Hunter growled. He loved his sister dearly, but headstrong didn't even come close to describing her. An opinionated hunter like himself, she had little time for girly pursuits and had a bawdy sense of humor. The higher powers only knew what she'd think of babysitting Suzie and Jessica. He only hoped any stories she told wouldn't be too embarrassing. She especially loved to tell the one about when she'd scared him when he was about eight by dressing up like a ghoul and coming into his room in the middle of the night. *He screamed like a girl*, she'd cackle to anyone who'd listen. In his defense, she'd looked pretty damn realistic.

"Be careful, dear," said his mother, wrapping her arms around him, and Hunter hugged her small form back.

"Careful! Ha. He'll probably scream like a girl when he finds the Dragon," came the mocking voice of his sister behind him.

"Natasha!" exclaimed their mother.

His sister scowled. "Mother, you know I like Nat better."

Hunter laughed mockingly. "Yeah, Natasha. Better be good."

A hard punch in the arm was her reply, and Hunter howled even louder. Thankfully, he'd gotten a lot bigger over the years and could now handle her sisterly love.

"Thanks for coming, Nat. I really appreciate it. Keep them safe."

"Too easy," scoffed his sister. "Now get out of here before you start getting all maudlin on me."

After giving his mother a long hug and a quick one for his sister—long hugs always got hard love taps—Hunter strode out the door. With any luck, he'd be back with Jared in a few days. Then, once he'd taken care of the Dragon, he could start wooing Suzie. Translation: taking up where he'd left off.

But first things first, he thought as he mentally dropped in hunter mode. *Time to catch myself a Dragon.*

CHAPTER 13

When Suzie woke next—yes, she'd finally fallen asleep—Jessica had disappeared. Suzie jumped up in a panic and threw on the blue dress before running out of the room, only to run smack-dab into a wall—er, someone. Suzie bounced back and stared up, and up some more, at the most striking woman she'd ever seen. Talk about an Amazon queen. This broad had to be over six feet with tightly braided blonde hair and a toned physique that would make most bodybuilders envious. This vicious-looking Valkyrie had a sword strapped to her side and tapped a black boot on the floor as she looked Suzie up and down. Just a tad intimidating.

"So, you're the mundane, are you?" said the Amazon beauty.

Jeez, apparently beauty and strength didn't equate manners. "My name is Suzie, thank you very much, and you are?" Suzie answered in a waspish tone.

A full-throated chuckle came bubbling out of the

giant blonde. "I'm Nat, Hunter's sister. Your bodyguard till he comes back. Nice to see you're not some wilting lily."

This blonde Viking is Hunter's sister? Holy crap. How the hell did Beverly, Hunter's tiny mom, create such big children? Maybe their father is part giant.

"Where's Jessica?" Suzie asked, looking up and down the hall for her, suddenly remembering her reason for rushing out.

"Having breakfast with my mother. Come, I'll take you to her."

Nat turned and strode down the hall. Suzie fell in behind her, a little intimidated by her surroundings and Hunter's larger-than-life sister.

Conversation was impossible with the pace Nat set. It was all Suzie could do not to run to catch up to her. Nat walked like a man, dressed like a man, talked like a man. *Gee, is someone fighting their feminine side?*

They arrived in the dining room with Suzie huffing a bit. She smiled when she saw Jessica sitting there eating, dolly tucked under one arm, talking animatedly with Hunter's mom, who deftly avoided the food that flew out of Jessica's mouth.

"Mommy," Jessica sprayed when she saw Suzie.

"Hello, baby," said Suzie, kissing the top of her head before taking a seat beside her.

"Gonna see a horsy!"

"You are?" said Suzie, arching a brow in Beverly's direction.

"If you don't mind, we were going to teach her to ride

a horse. We've got a very docile mare that has been the starter horse for many a child around here."

"Sure," said Suzie. Hard to believe the Realm had managed to stay so rustic. After all, come on, horses? Weren't they tall, smelly things that pooped? Ooh, tons of fun. But Jessica seemed pretty excited.

"And Nat says she's gonna show me how to 'fend myself so no bad guys hurt me."

Suzie winced. Maybe Nat could be persuaded to give her lessons, too. It would surely be better than getting the crap beaten out of her if there was a next time.

With Jessica jabbering, Suzie ate her breakfast while checking out the room around her.

Floor-to-ceiling pale wood paneling graced the elegant room, each panel carved with a flowery motif linked together with leaves and vines. High above her head hung a huge crystal chandelier with short, fat candles. The table itself could have seated about thirty people. It stretched that long. All in all, an impressive display of wealth, which made Suzie feel completely out of place. Personally, she preferred her homey, dented wooden table and mismatched chairs. Oh, and don't forget the cartoon place mats.

They finished their breakfast, and she washed off Jessica's face before they followed the freakishly tall Nat out to the stables, where a stable boy led out a very big horse.

Suzie looked up at the creature and then eyed her little daughter.

"Um, are you sure this is a good idea?" she questioned Nat nervously.

Nat just grinned and slapped the horse on the rump, who, to its credit, didn't even flinch. "Oh, old Betsy here's a peach. Little Jessie will be fine."

Suzie arched a brow. Jessie. When had her daughter acquired a nickname? Jessie, aka Jessica, grinned from ear to ear and paid avid attention to the instructions Nat gave her. Then, Nat swung Jessica up high onto the saddle and admonished her to hold on tight. Suzie closed her eyes as Nat led the horse out into the paddock near the barn.

Please don't fall, she prayed. Suzie heard a squeal and quickly opened her eyes, fearing the worst. But Jessica had only squealed in delight. Suzie watched her daughter, reins held tight in her chubby fist as the horse plodded along more slowly than a snail around the paddock area.

Suzie felt her body ease as she let out a breath she hadn't realized she'd been holding. Her little girl was riding a horse and, even better, hadn't fallen off. Kind of cool. Not that Suzie had any intention of trying herself. She wandered close to the railing and watched, smiling at her daughter's delight. A rustle beside her showed Beverly standing there, smiling at her Amazon daughter and Jessica.

"Your daughter's a natural."

"If you say so. Does everyone ride a horse around here? Don't you have any other means of transportation?" asked Suzie.

"Horses are used for long distances usually. Most people either walk or, if you're lucky enough to have a wizard, teleport."

"Teleport like in *Star Trek* right?"

Beverly gave her a puzzled look. Oops, Suzie forgot, no television. She changed the subject.

"I've been thinking about this whole boundary thing and stuff. But I still don't understand. You said the Realm was comprised of a continent and some other places, but how come they're not on any maps? I mean we've got ships crossing the oceans every day and satellites and stuff. It's impossible."

"Not impossible, dear, invisible. The spell the thirteen wove was extremely powerful. Not only is the Realm contained behind the boundary it's also invisible to all outside of it."

"But still, don't you think we'd have noticed a great big invisible island in the middle of the ocean?"

"A true spell of invisibility means objects pass through the spelled area without having noticed a thing," Beverly explained.

"If you say so." Suzie still had her doubts about it all. But curiosity nagged her. "Do you really have wizards and stuff here?"

"Oh, yes, and sorceresses, the female equivalent. Most, although not all, humans in the Realm have some kind of special ability, extra senses, shape-shifting abilities, or psychic abilities. We also have a whole host of magical creatures, too, not seen in your world since the split. Like unicorns, ogres, mermaids, pixies, goblins—"

"Goblins!" exclaimed Suzie, laughing. Well, that explained Hunter's startling leap over the fence when they'd first met.

"Yes, goblins. Although I've never heard anyone laugh when hearing their name before."

Suzie quickly told her the story of how she'd met Hunter, and soon Beverly joined in her laughter.

"Oh my," she said, her face sparkling with humor. "What a fabulous story of your first meeting. I have to say I'd given up all hope on him settling down till I met you."

Suzie suddenly felt tongue-tied. Hunter had never talked about settling down really with her. After all, they hadn't even officially gone on a date yet. Although she had let him get to second base. Bad girl!

Beverly went on as if she hadn't noticed Suzie's loss of speech. "Hunter's always been a little wild, in a disciplined way, though. His father's influence. The mischief he and his sister used to get into." She smiled fondly in memory. "I remember the time his father told him he was too young to go hunting with them. We had a wild boar in the woods causing trouble. Well, Hunter, he must have been about nine, decided to prove his father wrong. So he snuck out before the crack of dawn into the woods, determined to show us all he was a man. He tracked the beast and, when he found it, climbed a tree. Well, his sister, who was only seven, had apparently decided she'd show her father she was better than him, too. Turns out she was already in the tree Hunter climbed in. Depending on who you believe, Hunter fell out of the tree or Nat pushed him. Either way, when he fell, he happened to land on the boar, who chose that moment to charge the clearing below them. Well, you never saw such a scary or hilarious site as Hunter riding that boar right up to the castle, where the poor beast just collapsed, exhausted.

The look on his father's face was just priceless, and Little Miss Nat, who'd come running home, was just spitting mad."

"Why was she mad?" Suzie had to ask.

"Says it wasn't fair Hunter had gotten to ride the boar and she hadn't." The two women looked at each other and burst into laughter. Nat, hearing them, looked at them with a scowl, and Suzie and Nat's mom just howled louder.

"Oh my," said Beverly, wiping the tears from her eyes. "I hadn't thought of that in years. Just an example of the competitiveness between the two."

"You only have the two kids?"

"Yes," Beverly said sadly. "I would have loved to have more children, but unfortunately, my body just wasn't made for it. I tried to find some healers in the hopes of fixing the problem, but some things just can't be healed. But enough of my sad story. What about you? Will you have more children?"

Good question. "I don't know," said Suzie truthfully. "I guess if I met the right man I would. Being a mom is totally awesome, even when it hurts sometimes," she said sadly, thinking of Jared.

As if reading her mind, Beverly hugged her. "Your boy will come back to you safe and sound. You'll see. Hunter will rescue him."

"I wish I had your faith," Suzie said. Although, if she had to wager, she'd have bet on Hunter.

"I think your little girl is done with her horseback lessons. Do you mind if I take her to the gardens? She quite loved them yesterday."

"Sure," said Suzie.

Nat swung Jessica off Betsy the horse, and Jessica came running, Nat following behind.

"Mommy, did ya see me?" she asked, her face glowing.

"I sure did. You're just like a cowgirl now."

Jessica pranced up and down, yelling, "yee-haw!" Nat looked at her with an odd expression on her face.

Beverly said, "You used to be that young, too, once, my daughter, and just as loud. Although you tended to wear a lot less clothes. Naked as a wood nymph until you were almost four."

Suzie almost giggled at the statuesque Nat till she saw the crimson blush on her cheeks. Might not be a good idea to laugh at her giant bodyguard. Somehow, she didn't think Nat took teasing sitting down.

Beverly took Jessica's hand. Jessica skipped along with Beverly, who, believe it or not, skipped with her too, while Nat and Suzie followed along behind.

"Your mom is a hoot," said Suzie, watching them.

"I am assuming you mean entertaining and somewhat nutty. Then yes, she is. I take it she's been regaling you with embarrassing moments from our childhood."

"Somewhat," said Suzie, hiding a smile.

"It was tough being a girl growing up. My mother wanted me to do womanly things, but all I wanted to do was learn like the boys. It took me years to get my father to recognize that my talents were as good, and even better, than the boys. Even now, he still doesn't treat me like I'm equal to them," said Nat bitterly.

Suzie listened, surprised at Nat's candor. She wouldn't have taken her for the talkative sort.

"Why are you telling me this?" asked Suzie.

"My father is very set in his ways. Especially where his son is concerned. You'd better be careful."

"Careful of what?" Suzie asked, perplexed.

"My dear father, the commander, will never allow his son and heir to marry a mundane. No offense to you. You seem a lot more decent than a lot of the ladies I've seen him with. But our father has ideas on who Hunter should settle down with, and the mundane mother of a pair of out-of-wedlock children won't be his idea of a proper wife."

"Whoa. Who said anything about me marrying Hunter? Hell, we haven't even gone on a date yet." And who cared what Hunter's father thought? Wasn't it up to Suzie and Hunter what happened?

Nat snorted. "Oh please, my brother's interest in you is plain to anybody with eyes. I never thought I'd see the day he'd go all sappy over a woman."

"We're attracted to each other. That's it. I don't even know if I want to get married. I was involved in one bad relationship. I don't know if I'm ready to the take the chance yet on another."

"Sorry, I don't mean to preach. Personally, I don't care one way or another. I think you'd make for an interesting sister–in-law. You need a little toughening up, but your daughter is pretty nice, and that's usually a good indicator."

"Thanks." Suzie had the feeling Nat wasn't the type to give out compliments often.

"Besides, the look on the commander's face if Hunter told him he was marrying you would be so worth it!"

Ouch, that wasn't as nice.

Suzie followed Nat into a vast garden around the side of the castle and stopped dead when she saw her daughter sitting on the grass giggling as little winged creatures flew around her, dropping flower blossoms.

Wow! Real pixies. Entranced, Suzie sat down beside her daughter and listened as Beverly gave them a lesson on pixies.

ABOUT TWO DAYS travel away from home, Hunter moved quickly, already deep in the woods. His morning teleport had dropped him inside a small rustic village, the only one before the wilderness and the vast mountain range. He'd set off immediately on foot, loping into the dense forest like a shadow whispering between the trees. He'd found the Dragon's and Jared's trail within half a day of tracking, heading toward the mountains as suspected. He figured they were about a half-day or so ahead. The Dragon was moving a lot faster than expected with Jared at his side. But nowhere near as fast as Hunter could move.

Out here in the wild, Hunter was in his element. His keen senses, which he'd so missed on the other side of the boundary, emerged in full force, and as if eager to be let out after such a long absence, his special gifts seemed stronger than ever. Moving silently through the woods, he left not a sign or scent of his passage. His feet glided over the forest floor, twisting and twining automatically to avoiding the twigs and small plants that would have marked his path, a natural talent he'd honed over the years so as to not alert enemies of his passing and to fool the prey he stalked.

Nose flaring, he scented his quarry much like a dog would. The sweet living scent of the forest, like an old friend, filled his senses. His mind sorted the scents—dry bark, decaying vegetation, pine, and something else. Something that didn't belong, that stained the palette. He breathed deep. Oh, yes, the Dragon had been through here. The scent of the Dragon, which he'd smelled on Suzie and Jessica, a distinctive dry and musty reptilian scent. That odor, too faint for normal noses, wafted through the trees, which he'd brushed in his flight, and mingled with the softer, familiar sweet scent that he recognized as Jared. It was almost too easy to track their flight, the Dragon too arrogant to even hide his passage. Broken branches, bent grass, even torn clothing littered the trail, and Hunter shook his head at the sloppiness. His commander would have punished him if he'd ever been so careless. But this carelessness worked in Hunter's favor, allowing him to move quickly in pursuit.

The sun had begun dipping, signaling the arrival of late afternoon, when his nose and keen eyesight noted an anomaly. He'd arrived in a clearing where the grass had been trampled sloppily. And here's where it got interesting. Sniffing the ground, Hunter found a new smell, still Jared, but also something other. Something reptilian.

Jared had shifted. And not only shifted but had run off. Hunter could smell the Dragon, his path meandering in and out of the woods, as if searching for something—make that someone.

Hunter grinned in pride—the boy had eluded his captor. The only problem? While the Dragon had lost the boy, so had Hunter lost Jared's scent.

Impossible. Hunter never lost a scent.

Hunter walked in widening circles around the clearing, nose twitching. He found the trail where the Dragon had finally given up his search and continued on through the forest. Good news for him, but of Jared's scent he found nothing.

How can this be?

Hunter backtracked to the clearing and looked around again. Where had Jared gone? *Think*, he told himself. *Imagine being a little boy, one who has just shifted into a creature, a frightening thing to have happen alone and for the first time.* Jared knew he couldn't outrun his captor. So what did Jared do?

What would he have done in Jared's position? Hunter looked up at the trees surrounding the clearing pensively. He'd have climbed a tree.

Hunter started walking his circle again, this time paying attention to the trees in his search. About fifty meters from the clearing, he found the claw marks high up on the bark of a large maple. He sniffed. Yes, the same scent as in the clearing. Hunter craned and looked up, but the branches clustered together too densely to see anything.

"Jared," Hunter called softly. Nothing. "Jared, it's Hunter. Let me help you." Again, nothing. Now what? He pressed his face against the bark where the marks marred the wood, close enough to taste. He knew they belonged to Jared. But why didn't he answer? Had Jared tree hopped?

Hunter started walking backward to get a better look at the tree branches and to look at the trees bordering the maple when he heard a soft rustle. If it hadn't been for his keen hearing, he might have missed it.

Hunter stopped moving. What the hell should he do? The fact that Jared hadn't come out of hiding meant he was probably terrified. Couldn't really blame him. *Think like a little boy*, he reminded himself. What would his parents have done?

Remembering his own childhood, he didn't think his father's method of yelling would be the best course of action. Heck, when his father went on a rampage, everyone hid. So what would Suzie or his own mother do?

Hunter came back to the tree slowly and sat down, his back against the trunk, and he started to talk.

"I know things are kind of scary right now, Jared. I know I'd be scared if I was you. So many things have happened. I thought you might want to know that your mother and sister are fine. I brought them to my house, and my mother healed them. They're all better. They miss you an awful lot, though. I miss you, too. It's why I'm out here looking for you."

Hunter paused. Silence. Shit, maybe Jared wasn't in the tree. *Or maybe*, Hunter thought, *terror still grips him*. What if he feared his new shape? Scared that Hunter would reject or hurt him?

"Your mother can't wait for you to come back. I

promised her I'd find you. I also promised to make sure that the bad man won't hurt you anymore. No one will ever hurt you again if I can prevent it." And he meant that. "I know some weird stuff happened to you. I know you look a little different, and that's okay. One of my best friends turns into a wolf, you know, and I still like him."

Wait. Hunter held his breath as he heard a little rustle above his head and the sound of claws scrabbling on bark.

"I know you're scared. Let me help you. Trust me, Jared. I won't hurt you. Let me bring you home." Hunter held his breath and waited.

Leaves fell as the branches above him shook. Hunter looked up and saw a little dragon face peering down at him, the big, brown eyes liquid with tears.

"Mama," lisped the toothy mouth, one fat tear rolling down the dragonling's blue-scaled cheek.

"I'll take you home to her," said Hunter, his throat tight. *Poor kid!* He held up his arms, and Jared, the little weredragon, half leapt and fell into his arms.

Hunter hugged the little serpent body carefully, noting the little wings on his back.

"I'm so glad you're safe, little buddy." But how the hell would he explain to Suzie her baby was a dragonling? Maybe he could find a way to get him to shift back before they returned. Although Hunter had no idea how. All the shifters he knew hadn't come into their powers till puberty with only a few exceptions. And out here in the wilderness, he wasn't exactly likely to run into many of them. Or not any who wanted to be found.

First things first, though. He had to get Jared home and keep his promise to Suzie.

Then he'd be back to find the Dragon.

As the tall hunter carried Dragon's son away, he had to hold on to an urge to scream so as to not give away his position. But his rage, a living thing, coiled and twisted inside like a demon with claws that wanted to escape, and his breath came fast and harsh. He had to hold on strongly to his sense of self so as to not shift so close to his enemy. The moment after shifting sometimes tended to be disorienting and would have put him at a grave disadvantage, like a newborn colt that hadn't yet found its legs. So he swallowed his anger, eyes glowing, watching as the hunter strode off with his son.

The Dragon still couldn't believe his own flesh and blood had run away from him after shifting. Okay, so he'd helped him shift into dragon form. He'd gotten tired of listening to him whining and crying. He'd figured once the boy realized what he was he would come to his senses and stop asking for his mother. Wrong! Instead, the boy had panicked and taken off, and the Dragon had lost him. The Dragon had wandered off, hoping the boy would come out of hiding so he could capture him again. But no, that annoying cow had sent her suitor after him. What a surprise that had been, to know that her mundane paramour was, in fact, a Realm hunter. The Dragon had messed up. *But all is not yet lost.*

The hunter had mentioned that he'd brought

Suzanne and the girl back to the Realm. That his mother had healed them. The Dragon had heard talk in the dungeon about a powerful hunter. One who not only had a mother who healed but who'd also been sent into the mundane world to deal with the thinning-border problem. And as everyone knew, there were no coincidences in the Realm.

The Dragon smiled. He knew exactly where they were headed. Now, he only had to get there. Then, not only would he take back Jared he'd also take his daughter, too, for spite. And as for the cow that had birthed them? He'd make sure she died this time along with anyone else who stood in his way.

And the Hunter, well, it had been a while since he'd enjoyed such a tasty treat. *Yum.*

CHAPTER 14

Hunter had been gone three days. Three long, nail-biting days. And while Suzie walked around skittish as a doe, the slightest noise making her jump, Jessica was having a ball. Not only had she turned into a horse freak she'd also made friends with some of the children living in and around the castle and was having a blast discovering this new world she found herself in.

Poor Nat had to follow her like a shadow everywhere. Although Suzie had a feeling that Nat was quite enjoying herself, even if she did put on a gruff show.

Just look at the lessons she'd been giving her daughter in defense and escape, something Suzie wasn't sure she agreed with, but at least it kept Jessica from thinking too much about Jared. Jessica had picked up the concept rather quickly. Nat had taught her to stomp on a person's insole to distract them. Kick them in the shin, bite them, punch them in the jewels. All things a child could do to protect his or herself if someone larger tried to hurt them. And Suzie watched and learned along with Jessica. Too shy to ask for lessons of her own, she sucked in what the children were taught because she never wanted to feel helpless again. A mother should be able to defend her children, and she'd failed, a hard fact she'd have to live with the rest of her life. But something she had the power to change in the future.

That night, after she put Jessica to bed, Suzie went up on the parapet, her new favorite spot, leaving Kyle guarding the door while Nat trailed after her. Suzie still found it hard to accept her shadow of a bodyguard. Nat took her guard duties very seriously. About the only place she didn't follow Suzie was the bathroom. Thank God! Although she did stand right outside the door. Talk about distracting.

Suzie sighed, leaning over the wall.

"What's wrong?" asked Nat, who didn't mince words.

"I hate this waiting. Why haven't we heard anything? What if something's wrong?"

"Hunter will be back when he finds your boy."

"I know. I know. You all keep saying that. But when?" Patience had never been one of Suzie's strong points, not where the safety of her kids was concerned. Suzie wished she had gone with him. Then at least she'd be doing something instead of sitting around waiting, feeling useless.

"You have to give him time. The mountain ranges are huge. It's a walk of several days from the last village to even the foothills. If you're lucky, he'll catch them before they start heading up into them."

"This is all so strange. A few days ago, I was just a regular mom, in a regular world, where magic was something you only saw in movies. Now my ex turns out to be some half- dragon, and my kids might be too. And everywhere I look I see the impossible," said Suzie, opening her arms wide to gesture at the fairytale landscape around her.

"Apparently, not too impossible since it actually exists. It's funny. You talk about things like cars and movies, and to me, that seems impossible. I mean metal boxes on wheels that move without horses and pictures that move and talk? Who's to say what's magical and what's not?"

"I keep forgetting your side of the boundary doesn't have much contact with ours. Why is that? I mean surely there are some things in our world that you could have used to better yours. I've seen your libraries. The books are all handwritten. Talk about a lot of work when you could just get yourselves a printing press." *Or how about doing laundry by hand with scrub boards?* Suzie thought. It had made her hands sore just looking at the women with their red, chapped hands as they scrubbed and rinsed the huge loads of laundry the castle generated.

"The council made the decision a long time ago to keep the worlds as separate as possible. They're stuck in the old ways and aren't really keen on the idea of change."

"So, what, you guys are going to stay stuck in the Middle Ages forever, with women doing all kinds of backbreaking household chores while wearing ridiculous skirts?" Feminine as the skirts made Suzie feel, sometimes they could be a pain in the ass, especially when you tripped on them going up the stairs. She had bruised knees to attest to that.

"You don't need to preach to me. I'm one of the few women in the Realm who refused to stay home, get married, and birth babies like brood mares. And as for dresses, the last one my mother got me, I stuffed and used for archery practice. I think both the Realm and the council need a good shaking up, but everyone's scared of change."

"Just who, or what, is this council you all talk about?" Suzie asked.

"The council is our governing body made up of wizards, for the most part, who inherit their seat from their fathers and uncles. Although a few sorceresses have managed to fight their way onto it when no appropriate male heirs could be found. They make the policies for the Realm, the laws that all must abide by."

"So they're not even elected? But what if you have a bad bunch in charge? How do you get rid of them?"

"You don't. When one dies, another one takes their place."

Suzie shook her head in disbelief. "That's dumb. In my world, we elect people to represent our wishes. It doesn't always mean we get what we want, but if they screw up enough, we just don't elect them when the next election comes around."

"Interesting," said Nat pensively. "It would certainly make some of them more accountable if they knew they could lose their power if they didn't pursue the wishes of the people they represent. And what about the women in your world? You speak like they're more like me, not tied to the hearth or forced to marry."

"Women had to fight for their rights. We still do to a certain extent, even today. Some countries still don't accept women as equals. But in my country, women have as many rights as men. We only marry and have children if we choose to. We wear whatever the hell we feel like and can do any job a man can. You'd like it over there."

Nat, about to reply, halted as a noise came from the door leading onto the parapet. An out-of-breath Molly came out onto the walkway, one hand on her hip, hunched over, as she fought to catch her breath.

Chubby Molly running. Something had happened!

"They're back," Molly panted.

Suzie didn't ask who. She flew, Nat hard at her heels. She ran down the hall and stairs to the front hall and skidded to a stop, looking around. She heard voices from the parlor and headed in that direction when Beverly appeared in the archway to the parlor, blocking her way.

"Molly said they're back. Did he find Jared? Is he okay?" Suzie asked, heart pumping.

Beverly took her by the arm and moved her away from the doorway. Suzie's heart clenched in dread.

"What? What's wrong?" she cried. *Oh God, please let them be all right.*

"Hunter's back with your boy, but before you go charging in, you need to know. Jared shifted while he was out in the woods. He hasn't been able to shift back. I need to know you'll be strong enough to face him."

"What do you mean he's shifted?" Suzie didn't understand.

"As suspected, he's got his father's genes. He turned into a dragonling. Unusual at his age, but not completely unheard of. Before you go in there, you need to remember that, no matter what he looks like right now, inside he's still your little boy. If you do or say anything while he's in this shape, well, that could do more damage to him than his kidnapping did."

"I don't care what he looks like. He's my son," said Suzie, pricked that Beverly would even think she would ever do or say something that would make Jared doubt her love for him.

"Fine. But don't say I didn't warn you. And remember, no matter what, don't reject him. He needs you right now."

Never would I turn from him, thought Suzie. *I am his mother, no matter what he looks like.*

Suzie approached the doorway again and took a deep breath before walking in. Stupid, but Beverly's warning had made her slightly nervous about facing her own son.

She saw Hunter's broad back first. Then he turned, and Suzie gave a silent thank-you that Beverly had talked to her or she'd probably have screamed or done something equally stupid. For nestled in Hunter's arms was a little blue dragon.

Its body seemed to be about the same size as Jared's, covered in shimmery blue scales. A long tail curved down over Hunter's arm, and little claws gripped his arms tightly. But when she looked at the little dragon's eyes, so familiar, she recognized Jared. His big, brown eyes glistened with unshed tears.

Suzie approached, tears pricking her eyes, and held open her arms. "Come see me, baby," she said softly. With a flutter of little wings from his back, wings that she hadn't even noticed, he flew into her arms and buried his scaly face into her chest.

"Mama," he sobbed, his voice strange sounding and raspy.

Suzie rocked him in her arms, cooing to him softly, a flashback to a time not so long ago when he'd been a baby and colicky. She walked around with him in her arms, singing snippets and snatches of songs, holding him safe and warm as the trembling in his little limbs calmed. *Poor scared baby*.

"Hush now, baby. Mommy's here now. You're safe." Suzie's throat clogged tight with tears. How frightened her boy must have been. And so brave.

Hunter crossed the room to join them, his eyes suspiciously damp. He wrapped his arms around Suzie and Jared.

"You're safe now, Jared," Hunter said, echoing Suzie. Together they stood in a warm, three-way hug that felt so right.

Suzie felt a weird sensation in her arms. She looked down to see Jared shimmering, a kaleidoscope of light that made her eyes water. She blinked, and when she looked again, Jared was nestled in her arms, human again, his eyes closed, asleep.

Suzie looked up at Hunter, fat tears rolling down her

cheeks. "Thank you," she whispered. She had her baby back, safe and sound.

"Not a problem. He's a tough little guy. He saved me a lot of work by escaping on his own."

Thatta boy, Suzie thought with pride. "What about his father?" she asked, fearing his answer.

"Never even saw him," he said regretfully. "I leave again at first light to track him down."

"What about us?"

"What do you mean?" he asked.

"Do we stay here or go home?"

"What do you prefer? I know you're welcome to stay here as long as you need, but if you'd rather go home, that can be arranged as well." Hunter watched her face intently, as if her answer was important.

"I don't know. How long will you be gone?" If she left, would he come back to them?

"I don't know how long it will take. Could be days, a week. I figure two at the most. It all depends on how fast the Dragon is moving and how quickly I find him again."

Suzie felt torn. Should she stay and wait for him? Or go home and try to get her life and the children's back to normal?

"Why don't you sleep on it?" he said. "Now, come on, let's get Jared to bed. It's been an eventful couple of days for him."

Hunter took Jared from her arms, cradling him against his chest as if he belonged there. Suzie followed him upstairs, and together, they tucked Jared in beside his sister.

As they stood there, side by side, looking down at her

sleeping children, Suzie had an urge to tell him to stay. To forget about hunting Damian down. But she knew Hunter would refuse. And a part of her knew he had to do it else they would live in fear the rest of their lives.

Hunter hugged her, his lips brushing the top of her head.

"I should go and get some sleep so I can leave early," he said.

Suzie felt a moment of panic. She didn't want him to leave yet. So many things had been left unsaid. What if he never came back?

But she stayed silent as he left. Fear kept her rooted while her heart screamed at her not to let him go.

Too late.

Suzie wandered around the candlelit room, content at having her son back but restless.

What the hell is wrong with me? She should be happy now, but instead, she felt dread. Hunter would be leaving again tomorrow. She might never see him again because she knew she couldn't stay here. *This isn't my world. It's Hunter's. He belongs here.* But if she returned to her life, would Hunter follow when he'd completed his quest? Or was this her last chance to be with him?

And God, she wanted to be with him. Even if it was only once, she wanted, no, needed this. She didn't want to spend the rest of her life wondering.

She had to find him.

Easing out the door quietly, Suzie did a double-take when she saw Nat sitting in the chair.

"What are you doing here?" Suzie asked.

"He's on the walkway. Go."

"How—" Suzie started.

"Oh please. The way the two of you make calf eyes at each other is disgusting. Go on. I'll watch the children."

"Thanks," said Suzie over her shoulder as she hurried up the hall and steps.

She emerged into the cool night air and felt a moment of panic when she didn't see him.

Arms wrapped around her from behind, and she let out a half-scream, which Hunter cut off with his mouth coming down hard over hers. Suzie turned in his embrace and clung to him, her lips opening under his, allowing his tongue to slide in and dance with hers. His hands slid down her back and cupped her buttocks, pressing her against him firmly, the proof of his arousal hard against her stomach. She moaned against his mouth as a flash of heat zigged its way through her body, making her melt bonelessly against him. She wrapped her arms around his solid torso, hugging him tight, her knees too weak to support her.

It felt so right to be held by him. Kissed by him. Under his ravishing mouth, she felt her body growing even hotter, igniting a fire that only his body could put out.

He pulled back from her, and Suzie moaned in protest. The night air on the parapets was cold against her wet lips. She opened her eyes and blinked at him dazedly.

"I want you, Suzie. But not here."

Oh, thought Suzie, head dropping. Once again, she'd forgotten herself. She'd never been an exhibitionist before, but when he touched her, she forgot everything around her. Hell, his kisses were so powerful she almost forgot her name. She willed her body to calm down. But the fire he'd ignited smoldered inside and refused to go out.

Suddenly, her feet were swept out from underneath her as Hunter swung her up into his arms. She looked up at him, startled.

He chuckled. "I didn't say we had to stop. I just think we need to retire somewhere more discreet."

"But the children. . ." Yeah, how could she have forgotten? Nice mother.

"Will be fine," he finished. "Nat is watching them, and she knows where we'll be if you're needed. I want you, Suzie, or have you changed your mind? It's your choice."

Up to her? The children were asleep and well guarded. The choice? Simple. Suzie kissed him, putting as much of herself as she could into the kiss. He groaned and tightened his arms around her.

Hunter pulled his head back again. "Behave, or we'll never make it to my room," he growled. Suzie ducked her head into his chest with a smile. It was nice to know he felt as wild around her as she did around him.

His leggy stride had them down the stairs and in the hall where Nat sat positioned farther up. He opened the door closest to the stairs with one hand—good thing she had her arms wrapped around his neck—and entered a very masculine room. One she didn't have a chance to really look at for, as soon as the door shut behind them, his hot mouth devoured hers again.

His kiss had urgency to it, an untamed wildness that

had her just as frantic. He let her body slide down his, inch by tantalizing inch, and she could feel his hardness pressed against her belly. Suzie slid her hands down his back, stroking the firm muscles under his shirt before tugging it out of his breeches. She wanted to feel his skin like she'd dreamed so often of doing. She wanted to do other naughtier things too, like lick it to see if his skin tasted as good as it looked. Sliding her hands up under the fabric, she shuddered at the feel of his smooth, oh-so-hot flesh. She raked her nails lightly down his back to the top of his trousers. He responded by grinding his hips hard against her.

With her lips swollen from his touch, his mouth left hers and trailed a path of fire down the side of her neck. Suzie drew her head back to give him better access but had to grip him tightly around the waist as her knees buckled at the sweet sensation.

Once again, he swept her up, this time to deposit her on the bed. Suzie looked up at him with passion-slitted eyes and reached out to him. He leaned over her and kissed her. But Suzie couldn't take anymore. Her hands tugged at his breeches. He chuckled against her lips and stood up to take them off.

God, glorious didn't even come close to describing him.

Well acquainted with the view of his muscled torso, she was pleased to see that his lower half appeared just as attractive. Muscled thighs and sandy-colored curls made his jutting manhood seem larger than possible. Hopefully, it would fit.

His eyes grew smoky with desire as she gazed upon

him, and she saw his cock jerk like a beast raring to go. He leaned down and started tugging the skirt of her dress up, slowly revealing her legs. He crawled between them and kissed his way slowly up her legs. He tickled the backs of her knees with his tongue while Suzie writhed on the bed.

Oh the sweet torture.

Suzie cried out. "Please." And with that one cry, he stopped his teasing and pulled her skirt up, baring the crux of her thighs to his view.

He braced his arms on either side of her and leaned down for a kiss before pushing his hardness against her, nudging her, as if asking permission. She thrust her hips up in reply and sighed when he slid his member slowly inside her wetness. Suzie arched up, hands grabbing his buttocks to slide him deep inside, her patience finally at an end. He groaned as she clenched tight around him, savoring his thickness and length.

Then he started to pump, slowly at first. Driving the head of his shaft deep then holding it there for a few seconds before pulling out. In. Out. Slowly, he pumped her. Each plunge brought her closer and closer till, finally, Suzie reached a peak she'd never climbed before and crested. With a scream, she convulsed around him, her mind and body exploding in a maelstrom of pleasure that had her quivering.

And that was the end of Hunter. With a hoarse shout, she felt him shudder, his seed spilling deep inside. Then he collapsed on her, breathing hard, as if he'd run a marathon.

Suzie giggled.

"What's so funny?" he asked, lifting his head and opening one bleary eye.

"I've never seen you so out of breath. I should have known all those muscles were just pretty instead of practical."

The look on his face? Priceless, and Suzie giggled harder.

But she should have known he'd pay her back.

"I'll show you pretty," he said with a mischievous grin. "First, let's clean up. Ever since I met you, I've had this naughty fantasy involving you and my large tub."

Ooh, that sounded promising, Suzie thought with a shudder. But when he started to undress her, Suzie suddenly went rigid.

"What's wrong?" he asked.

How to explain she didn't want him to see her nude? A moment ago, lost in the moment, she'd forgotten that her body wasn't an unblemished canvas. If he saw her completely, in the light, stretch marks, loose tummy and all, would his desire shrivel?

"Can we turn out the light?" she asked hesitantly.

"Why?" he asked, confused. "I want to see every inch of you."

Suzie blushed. He was going to make her spell it out. "Pregnancy left its mark on me, and, well, to put it bluntly, it's not pretty."

Hunter chuckled. "Suzie, all women get those marks. It's nothing to be ashamed of. Would you turn from me because I have scars from battle?"

"Well, no, but it's different," she insisted.

"Really?" he said, turning around. "See that white

scar up on my shoulder? I got that in a fight with an ogre. And this one," he said, lifting his leg onto the bed, "on my calf here, from a goblin."

"But your scars make you sexy," she said. "My stretch marks and stuff are just ugly." Heck, if she couldn't stand to look at them in the mirror, how could she expect him to?

"Let me prove to you that I love your body as it is."

Suzie looked into his eyes, and she wanted to believe, wanted to so badly. Wasn't it best if she found out now? Hiding her body from him now, only to have him reject her later, might hurt more. Well, it would hurt now if he did, but Suzie hadn't completely given her heart over yet. Had she?

Slowly, she nodded yes.

She closed her eyes and only trembled slightly when he undid the buttons down the front of her gown. He tugged down on her dress, and she lifted her hips so he could ease it off her, leaving her in only her chemise. He slid the straps of her chemise down her arms, and she helped him slide it off, as well, eyes clenched tight, holding her breath. The cooler air in the room and his silence made her skin goose bump.

Suzie almost jumped when she felt a light caress on her stomach. Her eyes fluttered open. He bent over her tummy, intent blue eyes watching her face. When he saw her looking, he dipped and, again, lightly kissed the stretch marks that ran across her rounded tummy. Suzie sighed. With the tip of his tongue, he traced them.

"Do you know what I see when I look at you?" he asked, his low voice making her shiver.

Suzie didn't answer, just watched him as his tongue circled around her belly button, making her breath hitch and halting her thoughts.

"When I look at you, I see a woman who is a mother. A beautiful woman who bears the proud signs of having birthed two healthy and beautiful children."

Suzie felt her eyes get wet.

His head moved up her body, his breath lightly fanning her breasts, making her nipples pucker. He brought a hand up and cupped the heaviness of her breast and brought his mouth down to it so he could kiss lightly around her areola.

"Here, I see a woman who fed her children the most precious of ambrosias. Who gave of herself instead of relying on a bottle," he said seriously. Then his lips quirked in a grin. "Not to mention beautiful breasts for me to play with!"

Suzie screeched at him and rolled away then giggled. *God, he is so irresistible.*

Hunter crawled on the bed, mock-growling at her. "Come back here, wench. I have been dying to play with those since I've met you. You have an incredible bosom, big and soft the way I like it. Who needs tiny, perky ones? I like a big handful that I can take in my mouth and squeeze in my hands. Perfect breasts, just like yours."

Suzie laughed and felt, wonders of all wonders, beautiful. How could she not with evidence of his desire in eyes and in his already swollen shaft?

"You're bad." She laughed. Laughter in the bedroom, what an odd concept. She'd never known lovemaking could be playful.

"You have no idea," Hunter said solemnly, but the twinkle in his eye gave him away. "But I intend to show you. Now come, wench. I've waited long enough to see you wet," he said, waggling a brow at her. "I'll not wait any longer."

Suzie jumped off the bed, ran into the bathroom, and stopped dead. *Wow! Now that's a tub*, she thought, eyeing the mini swimming pool sunken into the floor. Large enough for several people with benches running around the inside of it. Hmm, she could definitely think of some things she'd like to do to him here too!

Hunter came up behind her, his hard body pressing up against her backside. Suzie bent over, her rounded bottom thrust up, and wiggled against him as she turned on the tap. His hands shot out and grabbed her around the hips, and he rubbed himself against her. The hardness of his shaft poked at her bottom.

"By the higher powers, Suzie, stop that, or we'll never make it in the water."

Suzie wiggled again then straightened and moved away from him. She stepped into the tub and went to the far side to sit down. Hunter watched her, his shaft jutting out like the prow head of a ship from his body.

She crooked her finger at him, beckoning him closer. Where had this wanton side come from? He climbed into the rapidly rising water and knelt in front of her. The water covered most of his body—unfortunately—but it did nothing to hide the smile in his eyes and on his lips.

Without taking his eyes from hers, he reached back and shut off the water. Suzie watched him, body tightening in anticipation. His hands came up, and he cupped both of her breasts, fondling them almost reverently. He leaned forward and brushed his mouth across both of them, his slight bristle creating a pleasant friction against her delicate skin. Suzie shivered. He smiled wide.

He opened his mouth and lightly touched her already erect nipples with the tip of his tongue. Suzie closed her eyes and let her head fall back. Oh God. She wanted to grab his head and push her breast into his mouth, but he had other plans, and she wanted to see what they were. He licked her hard nub, first the left then the right. His slippery tongue made her squirm on the seat.

She almost came again when he finally closed his mouth around it, sucking in a large mouthful of her round globe, tugging it hard and grazing it with his teeth. A jolt of pleasure zinged right down to her groin and made her cry out. Suzie couldn't help it. She grabbed his hair and ground his face harder into her chest. She felt a vibration as he chuckled around his mouthful. He stopped sucking the one side, only to repeat the torture on the other.

Suzie was incoherent. She could hear someone making sighing and little breathy sounds, surely not her. She lay back, unable to stop moaning at the feel of his mouth and tongue laving, sucking, biting her tender flesh. When he stopped, she opened her eyes a slit—*please don't stop*, she thought. Then she felt his hands cupping her buttocks and floating her up, bringing her level with his mouth. Surely, he wouldn't...

He did. His tongue lapped at her, and Suzie screamed as a tiny orgasm ripped through her. No one had ever done that to her before, and it was amazing. No, beyond amazing, utterly fan-freaking-tastic! He spread her with his tongue, flicking her clit with his tongue before delving deep inside of her. Suzie thrashed in his grip.

"Please. Please. Please." She gasped.

When she thought she'd die on the spot, he finally lifted her up out of the tub, but they didn't go far. He held her up effortlessly and leaned her back up against the wall. Suzie wrapped her legs around his waist as he plunged himself inside of her. Hands gripping her ass, he pumped her. His unbelievable strength kept them upright while he plowed her. Already close to the brink, it didn't take much pumping before she died and went to heaven.

Suzie screamed as her body clenched and convulsed around his throbbing shaft. It was like the orgasm that never ended, and with each stroke, she felt her body ripple.

With a bellow, he drove into her pliant flesh one last time, his body rigid, as he found his pleasure inside of her.

Suzie lolled against his body like a rag doll. None of her muscles wanted to work and were gripped in a pleasant lassitude that she never wanted to end.

He stumbled back to the tub, which was thankfully still warm, and sat down in it with her on his lap. She opened her eyes when she felt a cloth sliding over her skin. He bathed her, washing her body with a tenderness she'd never known, not even at her mother's hands.

"Are you okay?" he murmured.

"I might never be able to move again, but other than that, I feel great."

"Don't take this wrong, but I've been with a lot of women, and I have to say, it's never been that good."

No way, Suzie thought. He had to be putting her on. She'd barely done anything, so how could she be the best?

Some of her thoughts must have shown in her face for he said, "You don't believe me. You think it's some kind of line. I can promise you, I never lie. Can you honestly tell me that you ever felt that way before?"

Well, actually, no, she hadn't. Sure, she and Damian had been together, but he'd never made her come like that. Never made her feel as if the whole world exploded in her body. She'd always assumed that the problem was with her. That she expected too much. *Turns out Damian just wasn't as good a lover as he thought he was. Ha!*

"I guess I'll just keep having to prove it to you," he said with a cocky, self-assured grin, lifting her dripping from from the tub.

Mmm, those muscles definitely were good for a lot of things. She could understand now why so many women liked to swoon in the romance novels she read from time to time. Being carried around like a delicate damsel was definitely arousing.

After wrapping a towel around them, he carried her back to the bedroom and fell with her on the bed. Suzie giggled as he attacked her with the towel and rubbed her dry. Once dry—and her hair fluffy—she grabbed the towel from him and returned the favor. But her brisk rubbing of his body turned soft as she became entranced by the sight of all his bare skin. Soon, she'd lost the towel and, instead, skimmed her hands over the ridges of his body, exploring him like an archeologist on a new dig. But her hands weren't enough. She needed to taste him.

She straddled his stomach and looked at him. He grinned and placed his hands behind his head.

Time for her to play.

Suzie started with his chest. Laving it with her tongue. Swirling her tongue around his pecs and then nipping his flat nipples. She felt him tremble. She slid down his body, but something hard blocked her way.

How was it possible for him to be ready again so quickly? Suzie climbed off of him and parted his legs so she could kneel between them. She looked at his jutting manhood, amazed that it had even fit. She reached a tentative hand out and touched it.

She gave a small cry when it jerked at her touch. She looked up at him and saw him watching her, but he wasn't smiling anymore. His eyes smoldered again, and she could see his muscles corded tight as he tried to feign nonchalance.

This time, when she grabbed him, she held him firmly. He felt so hot in her hand, and he pulsed, she could feel it thumping in her palm. She slid her hand up to the tip and down. He sighed.

She leaned down, and still working her hand up and down, she licked the tip. He bucked, and she smiled, the satisfied smile of a cat who'd gotten into the cream. She licked him again, all around the tip and down to the base of his shaft. That got her a tortured moan.

Then, she did something she'd never tried before. She slid him into her mouth, not too deep—he was quite big—but enough that he let out a hoarse shout.

"Suzie," he moaned, his hands reaching down to twine in her hair. "If you don't stop that, you're going to do me in."

But Suzie wasn't quite done. She sucked him, feeling that strange pulse on her lips and tongue. Just knowing she drove him wild had made her wet again. She didn't torture him for long. It was simply too arousing. Leaning up, she straddled him and lowered herself on him.

Oh God, he felt even bigger inside her like this. She rocked on him, the motion sending jolts of pleasure right through her. She felt his hands grab her hips, and he thrust up into her. He helped her find a rhythm that soon had her panting and sweaty, her boobs jiggling, as she came closer and closer...

He came first this time, and she could feel him inside her as he did so. His shaft pulsed hard, which, in turn, made her shiver and orgasm around him.

Suzie collapsed on him. Oh God, that was it. She'd definitely never move again.

Hunter chuckled.

"What's so funny?" she asked, still trying to catch her breath. If he made one remark about her boobs bouncing around, she'd smack him.

"I can't believe you got my sword to go so quickly again. That's a record even for me. I mean two, okay, but three? I should have needed a rest, maybe some food. You are amazing."

"Oh." Suzie glowed at the backward comments. Then she lifted her head. "Wait, did I hear you call it your sword?"

Hunter grinned. "Hey, I figure anything on my body

that's got a mind of its own deserves a name. What should I have named him instead?"

Suzie grinned. "How about Excalibur? Or, hey, how about the ram?"

Hunter mock-growled at her. "Are you mocking me, woman?" He dove on her, fingers stretched, and found every ticklish spot she had. Suzie howled and squirmed under his torturous fingers. But she got him back when she licked a finger and stuck it in his ear.

He recoiled with a look of shock. "Enough, you win," he said, chuckling.

"Wet willies always win," said Suzie, happier than she'd ever been in her life.

Hunter laughed and rolled her so she was snuggled at his side in his arms.

"Promise me you'll be here when I get back," he said, suddenly serious.

"I promise," Suzie replied. She'd worry about her jobs, their things, the house later. Right here, right now, being in his arms felt so right. And if he wanted her to stay, then stay she would. She didn't think she could give him up. Somehow, somewhere along the line, she'd fallen in love. And while he hadn't said the actual words, his actions spoke volumes about his feelings for her.

Spooned against his body, her cheek resting on his chest, lips curved in a smile, she fell asleep to the sound of his heart beating and the feel of his hand stroking her hip.

Watching her sleep curled against him, Hunter smiled. He finally understood what his mother had tried to tell him all those years ago. He'd found love, or maybe love had found him. And having found it, he was never going to let it go.

First, he'd take care of the Dragon. Quickly. Then he'd come back and ask Suzie to be his wife. Now that he'd found the one, he saw no reason to wait. An eagerness filled him at the thought of starting a new life with her and the twins. Smiling, he hugged her tighter and, for the first time ever, fell asleep with a woman.

CHAPTER 15

*H*unter was gone again. They'd spent the rest of the night in his bed, spooning naked. He'd carried her back to her bed before dawn, tucked her in with the children, and kissed her softly.

"I'll be back as soon as I can. Wait for me," he'd whispered.

And then, he'd left. But Suzie glowed. Hunter cared for her, and while they hadn't said the words *I love you*, she had a feeling it was only a matter of time.

Suzie felt too wired to sleep, her body sore in that pleasant way that happens only after a night of hot loving. She snuck off and had a bath before the children woke up. The musky scent of their lovemaking stuck to her skin, and while she would have loved to bask in it, she didn't want the children asking why mommy stunk. She hummed as she bathed, running the cloth over her body and remembering his tongue and hands doing the same much more intimately the night before. Just the thought aroused her again and made her nipples tighten. Apparently, her body hadn't had enough yet. And she couldn't wait till he came back to indulge some more.

She ran some cold water to cool down her body and libido then got out and dried herself off. Dressed in a new gown that Beverly had thoughtfully lent her, she went into the room to see if the children were awake. She made it just in time.

Jessica woke first, sitting up in bed, her hair all tousled, yawning. She hadn't yet noticed the bed's other occupant, but her movement disturbed Jared, who was still asleep beside her. He grunted in his sleep and rolled over.

A piercing shriek came out of Jessica's mouth. "Jari!"

Jessica dove on her twin, hugging him awake. Jared, to his credit, didn't scream back but hugged his sister just as enthusiastically. But Suzie screamed as the door came flying open, hitting the wall hard, and Nat dove into the room, sword in hand. A blonde warrior princess in action.

"Where is he?" Nat asked, eyes scanning the room, looking for enemies.

Suzie laughed. "Jessica was a little excited at seeing her brother back."

Nat relaxed and grinned at the kids as she slid her sword back in its scabbard.

Jessica looked over at Nat, her beaming face, a rainbow of happiness. "Nat, loo, it my brodder. Jari, dat Nat. She Hunta's sista. She show me how fight."

Jared looked at Nat with interest. "Thow me too?" he asked. "I wanna fight da bad man."

"Sure thing, little fellow. How about we have some lessons after breakfast? Get dressed, and I'll wait for you out in the hall so we can go down together."

Two tousled heads nodded eagerly, and Nat went out the door, shutting it behind her.

Suzie had started toward the twins when she heard a thump at the door. Who could be knocking? Nat had just left.

The door opened, and Suzie opened her mouth to ask Nat what she'd forgotten. But it wasn't Nat.

Suzie screamed. "No!" Immediately, the twins echoed and hugged each other in fright. Her heart plunged down to her toes, and she could have sworn she heard her knees knocking. How had he found them?

Damian sneered. "Surprised to see me, Suzanne? I admit, your hunter boyfriend took me by surprise, but he's not here now, is he? But I am," Damian said ominously. "I've come to take my boy back, and this time, I think I'll take the girl, too."

"Never," said Suzie, moving to stand in front of the children. "Go away, Damian. You lost. We've got a guard coming for us in a few minutes and more all over the castle. You'll never take them. Leave while you still can."

"Oh, if you mean that blonde giant, she's out in the hall, bleeding. Someone forgot her training and didn't think to check before leaving the room." Damian made a tsking sound as he shook his head. "I'm surprised. I expected better from the commander's daughter. Needless to say, she won't be coming to your rescue. No one will. That's the beauty of stone walls. Sound doesn't carry."

"You're not taking them, Damian. Kids, hurry, the bathroom, now." For once, the kids didn't argue, just bolted off the bed into the washroom, and Suzie dashed after them, turning to slam the door shut. But Damian moved fast—faster than a regular human could. His fingers caught the edge of the door and curled around it. Suzie couldn't fully shut it. She leaned against the door, but her smaller weight was no match for Damian, who slowly inched it open. Then Suzie remembered one of Jessica's defense lessons.

Suzie leaned over and bit Damian's fingers. Hard. *Eew!* She felt the crunch of flesh and bone between her teeth and a spurt of blood, which made her gag, and let go.

Damian screamed, and his fingers were gone. Quickly, Suzie slammed the door shut and bolted it. Unfortunately, this would give them only a small respite. The door lock was only a flimsy affair meant for privacy and not keeping out big, bad men.

Suzie looked around desperately, her eyes scanning the bathroom for a weapon, something, anything, she could use to fight him off. She knew Damian wouldn't give up.

Bang! The door shuddered in its frame. Suzie leaned against it, stomach clenching in terror. *Oh God, help us.*

The twins were huddled against the far wall under the window, eyes wide with fright, lips trembling as they choked back sobs. *This is so Goddamn unfair.* They were supposed to be safe here. Hunter had saved Jared. This wasn't supposed to happen.

The door shook again and again as Damian threw his weight against it. The splintering sound of wood giving way made Suzie's throat tight as it choked with tears of frustration and fear.

She needed a plan. But she wasn't a hunter or a warrior, just a suburban mom, whose only idea of violence previously had been beating the eggs and whipping some cream. They didn't teach protecting your family from psychopaths in her parenting books. So what could she do? She needed to get the children to safety. Maybe, if she distracted Damian, the children could get out of the room and run for help. But how?

Suddenly, the banging stopped. Suzie held her breath, listening. Had Damian left? Suzie knew better than to open the door and check. He was probably waiting for her to do that. Hey, she'd seen enough suspense movies to know the bad guys didn't just leave. She could picture him, crouched like some dark predator beside the door, waiting for her to be stupid and open it so he could pounce on her and steal her babies.

But Suzie didn't know what else to do. Her plan to escape to the bathroom had become a trap of its own. The only way out, other than the door, was the window. She looked up at the window. While big enough to wiggle through, it didn't lead to a balcony but went straight down, and it was too high for the children to reach and cry for help. She didn't dare leave the door for fear that Damian would burst in with one mad-bull rush.

Jared, watching her, looked up at the window too. "I get help," Jared said.

"No baby, the window's too high." And Suzie didn't want him to fall to his death.

"I fly."

What did he mean he could fly? Wait, he could, but only when in dragon form. "Can you turn into a dragon again?" Suzie asked, a spark of hope in her voice. Beverly had said it was a rare thing at his age. But having done it once, maybe he could he do it again.

"I tink tho," he said, scrunching up his face.

Jessica watched Jared as he clenched his little fists and held his breath, his little face going red with the strain.

"Jari, what you do?" Jessica asked. "You loo funny."

"I be a dwagon," he said, opening his eyes.

Jessica giggled. "A dwagon, dat silly."

Suzie almost laughed at her look, but the situation had gone beyond dire. The silence out the door had been replaced with a slithering sound, as if something heavy dragged along the floor. Had Damian shifted? If he had a tail like Jared's, would it make that sound when he moved? Oh God, please let her wake up from this nightmare.

"I no thilly," said Jared indignantly, unaware of their newest problem. "I was a dwagon. Ask Hunta. He thee me. Mommy too."

Jessica looked at Suzie as if expecting her to refute this claim.

"I know it sounds crazy, Jessica, but when your brother came back last night, he was a dragon."

"Me too den!" exclaimed Jessica, closing her eyes. Unlike her brother, she didn't turn red in the face or clench anything. On the contrary, she got a peaceful look on her face, lips slightly parted as if about to sigh. She began to hum, and as she hummed, her body became enveloped in a shimmery light so bright that Suzie had to close her eyes. When she opened them again, Jessica had disappeared. Instead, a little pink—yes, pink—dragon sat there. Suzie looked at her in shock. Where had her baby girl learned to do that?

"It easy," Jessica said to her brother. "Cwose your eyes and hold my hand," she said, reaching out to take Jared's hand.

Jared looked in slackojawed amazement at his sister. He held her hand and closed his eyes. Calming himself, aping his twin, he started to shimmer.

Here we go again, thought Suzie, shutting her eyes tight.

Opening them, she now saw two dragons sitting on the floor, pink Jessica and blue Jared. What do you know? Even dragon colors were sexist.

"We get help, Mommy," said Jessica, fluttering her little wings. Suzie swallowed in pride, tears shimmering in her eyes. Here they were, in the midst of danger, and her little girl was cool as a cucumber and taking charge. How quickly they were growing up. How unfair that they had to.

Jessica's pink dragon body fluttered up to the window. Using her hands—er, claws—she opened the window wide enough to fly out.

"Come, Jari," she ordered, poking her head back in.

Jared looked at Suzie. "I wuv you, Mommy. We come back and thave you." Then he flew out the window too, his flight a little wobblier than his sister's. Looked like Jessica was a natural at being a dragon. A thought to ponder for another day, if she ever woke to another day, that was.

Suzie sagged against the door. At least now, whatever happened, hopefully the children would be safe. All they needed to do was find some people. But Suzie had doubts about her own well-being. Unfortunately, her situation hadn't changed. She still remained trapped in the bathroom with a very pissed-off dragon on the other side.

She felt something lean against the door at her back, and a smell wafted through the cracks, a dry, leathery smell that tickled her nose unpleasantly.

"Suzanne," hissed a rough voice. "Open the door, Suzanne. I'm getting very angry. And I'm also getting very hungry."

Holy freaking psycho. Thankfully, the children were gone because Suzie almost wet her drawers in fear. Eat her? He wanted to eat her! *Help. Please. Anyone.*

The door rattled again. Suzie closed her eyes and prayed.

"Hail Mary, full of grace, the Lord is with..."

Harsh, barking laughter sounded. "Your god isn't listening. And even if he were, he'd be too late. I'm going to count to three, Suzanne. Open the door like a good girl, and maybe, just maybe, I won't kill you. Don't open it, and you will feed me while the children watch," he said in a whisper that sent shivers up Suzie's spine.

One bright spot. He didn't know the children were gone. She needed to buy time.

"One."

Oh shit. What am I going to do?
"Two."
Why the hell isn't anyone coming to help me?
"Three."

Dammit, Suzie wished she'd taken lessons from Nat. She heard him pull away from the door, stepping back, she imagined, to rush it. Inspired, Suzie counted to five then flung open the door as a large, black creature came rushing through, only to hit the far wall with its momentum.

Ha! Take that. Not waiting to see what happened, Suzie dashed out the door and flew on swift feet to the bedroom door. She had the handle in hand when sharp claws dug into her shoulder.

"Aaah!" she screamed at the fiery pain as Damian dug his talons in.

"Where are the children, Suzanne?" he asked, turning her cruelly by digging his claws deeper into her.

Suzie gasped at her first glance of her ex-lover. Facing her stood a man-sized lizard, something from a horror movie, and she knew how those ended. Ebony in color, scales covering him all over like plate armor. Only his eyes looked human. Oh, and did she mention he had big fucking teeth? Gulp. The better to eat her with.

"Answer me," he raged, shaking her like a rag doll. "Where are the children?"

"Gone," Suzie said triumphantly, even as tears ran down her cheeks from the slicing pain. "They're safe now. Do what you want. You'll never get them back."

"Bitch!"

Suzie felt herself flying through the air, too quickly to

scream, before crashing into the wall. She didn't even have time to shake the stars from her eyes when he picked her up again and shook her.

"Where are they, you annoying cow? Get them back here now, or I swear I will—"

"What?" Suzie spat. Where she had found the courage to talk back, she didn't know but dearly hoped it would stay with her a little while longer. The excruciating pain throbbed through her, a ball of fire eating her shoulder from the inside out. But even amid the pain and terror, she mustered up all the strength she'd never realized she had. Damian and his threats were becoming tiresome, and if she were going to die, then by God, she'd do it fighting. "What will you do, Damian? Kill me? Eat me? Do it. I don't care. The children are gone. And you won't be getting them back."

Damian, although his name Realm Dragon now seemed more appropriate, screamed in rage, a primordial sound that echoed around the room. He threw her again, and Suzie hit the wall with a jarring thud, but she managed somehow to keep her feet. And finally, a break. She landed right by the door, which he'd left open.

Out she flew as if she had little wings on her feet. A quick glance down and she saw, with horror, Nat's limp body. Up the hall she ran, though, not stopping.

A scream sounded behind her, and unable to resist, kind of like Lot's wife, she had to look back.

A live Nat had managed to roll on her side, sword in hand, and stab Damian in the leg. Unfortunately, though, Damian had two legs, and he kicked her with his good one hard in the head, putting Nat down for the count again.

Damn! Suzie kept running, up the stairs, onto the parapet and clear blue skies. *Stupid!* She wasn't a dragon like the kids. She couldn't bloody fly. Suzie looked around wildly, but the walkway gaped back empty with only one way back in.

Maybe Damian had given up.

Not so lucky. Laughter bubbled up from the stairway leading down.

"Oh, Suzanne," came his taunting voice. "I know you're up there with nowhere to go. And I'm coming, Suzanne. Oh yes, I'm coming, and I'm really, really h-u-n-g-r-y," he said, stretching the last word as he came into sight.

Suzie backed away, hands held out in front of her, eyes wide in terror.

Nowhere to go. No one to save her. Just her and a monster.

Where was a fainting spell when you needed one?

"Stop, Damian," she tried, pleading again. "You've lost. Just leave now while you still can."

"Never. I will not give up till I have my children back and you are dead."

Damian lunged at Suzie, and though she tried to dart out of his way, his long reach snagged her arms and pinned them at her sides. He smiled at her, a grotesque parody of a grin with very large, pointed teeth. "Say goodbye, Suzanne," Damian said, lifting her up and holding her over the side of the parapet.

Suzie looked down and felt her head spin with

vertigo. The ground lay so far below, hard paving stones and not a trampoline in sight. This last incongruous thought made her want to giggle. Not a good idea. Damian shook her over this abyss of air, and Suzie did a very girly thing. She screamed. Really bloody loud.

CHAPTER 16

*H*unter teleported back to the castle in a foul mood. The idiot wizard they'd sent over had teleported them to the wrong place, a village north of the area he needed. Apparently, he'd never seen the teleport location for the village Hunter wanted. So back they came to the castle, where he now needed to wait till a wizard who knew their location could arrive, a delay Hunter could have done without. His being vibrated with eagerness to go after the Dragon and take care of him once and for all, but he found himself even more anxious to have this done and over with. Could it have to do with a certain curvy mother that he missed already? Even after the glorious night they'd spent, he still craved her like a man dying of thirst in the desert. He wanted to sink in her glorious depths and soak her up. He might be besotted, but he loved it! And he'd punch the first idiot who dared make fun of him.

Screams sounded from outside along with the word, "Dragons!"

Shit! Hunter spun and ran out the front door, drawing his sword as he went. How had the Dragon found them? No matter. He'd take care of him. Hunter skidded to a stop in the courtyard and looked up where a crowd of castle folk was pointing. Soaring through the sky were two tiny dragons—one pink, the other blue.

Oh no, the twins. What the hell had happened? Suzie would be frantic if the twins had taken off on her.

"It's okay," Hunter said, his loud voice cutting through the din. "They're friendly!" What a relief. And here he'd thought the real Dragon had shown up. Even he wouldn't dare strike at the heart of the commander's home. That would be plain stupid. There were guards all around, not to mention Nat and himself. Good thing he'd been here, though, or the castle guard might have hurt the twins.

The screaming died down as the people watched the dragonlings coast lower and lower. The blue one, definitely Jared now that he could see him up close, landed in a tumbling roll at Hunter's feet, clouds of dust making the little weredragon cough. The pink one, with a dainty flutter, hit the ground with just a slight wobble. His sweet angel—a natural.

"Jessica and Jared, what are you doing fly around like that? I'll bet your mother is worried sick," Hunter admonished them.

"Hunta!" panted the pink dragonling. "Help Mommy!"

"Da bad man ith here!" lisped the blue one, eyes rolling in terror.

Hunter felt an icy hand grip his heart and squeeze hard. Suzie was in danger! The Dragon had found them.

Hunter ran, his powerful legs pumping up the stairs, his mind running along with them a mile a minute, caught in a dreadful nightmare loop. Suzie bleeding and ripped to shreds. Suzie dead. No! Never! He wouldn't be too late this time. He couldn't.

He hit the hall her room was on and almost froze when he saw his sister's limp form lying on the floor in the hall.

"Nat," he bellowed, and to his relief, his sister stirred on the floor. Her blonde head, matted with blood, lifted, and he gasped when he saw wet, red rivulets of blood painting the left side of her face. Someone had done a job on her. That would piss her off. His sister hated losing.

"Are you all right?" he asked, reaching her and kneeling beside her.

"I'll be fine," Nat winced. "Save Suzie. Up on the walkway. Dragon followed."

"The twins are downstairs. Can you make it?" Hunter's concern over his sister warred with his need to save Suzie.

"Go," she said, getting to her knees. "Save her. My fault."

Hunter didn't hesitate any longer. Up the stairs he ran to the castle parapet, emerging into the bright light and blinking. When his sight adjusted, his breath left him in a whoosh, and if it hadn't been for his training, he might have lost all control then and there.

The Dragon stood at the edge of the parapet, dangling Suzie over the side, her shoulder bleeding where the Dragon had scored her with its claws.

Hunter whistled to get his attention. "Oh, Dragon," he taunted. "Don't you want to play with someone a little more your size? Or are you only capable of beating up on women and children?"

The Dragon turned his head sideways and snarled at Hunter, but he kept dangling Suzie, who turned wide, pleading eyes at him.

"Come on, Dragon," Hunter cajoled. "Put the woman down, and let's do it. Man to dragon. Let's see who's tougher." Igniting words, but then dragons were well known for their arrogance and superiority complex. Which, according to stories, usually led to their downfall. *Here's to hoping the stories are right.*

"Do you think you can trick me, Hunter? I've seen you with my little brood mare. I know you care for the fat slut." The Dragon chuckled, and Hunter held his breath as Suzie swayed in the Dragon's grip. "I'm surprised you'd even think about touching something I'd tasted first. Tell me, how do you like her little whimpers when you take her? She's a bit passive in bed for my tastes, but then, what can you expect from peasant stock? I didn't choose her for her courtesan skills, but she has excellent child-bearing hips."

"You bastard," hissed Hunter, his anger a simmering pot about to boil over. He needed to calm down before his rage completely clouded his judgment. He needed to find a way to make the Dragon let her go. But how?

"Enough talk, Dragon. Put Suzie down, and let's take care of this once and for all."

"Oh, I intend to take care of you, but first, let's put out the trash, shall we?" said the Dragon with a toothy smile.

Hunter watched in horror as the Dragon opened his claws and let Suzie fall to what would be a quick, but certain, death. Her eyes widened in shock as she started to fall, and she opened her mouth as if to speak, but all too quickly, she dropped out of sight. The woman he loved killed because he'd failed her.

Hunter saw red, his anguish and need for revenge overcoming his training. He charged, slashing his sword at the Dragon, who pulled away from the wall and danced out of reach. The bastard, even with his bulky size, was lighter on his feet than expected.

"You'll have to do better than that, boy, if you intend to hurt me," taunted the Dragon.

"Oh, I will," growled Hunter, dropping into his fighting stance. He breathed deep, trying to calm his mind and block the sight of Suzie's face as she fell. She might have died, but he would avenge her. Finally, his training kicked in. Hunter felt his body relax and his mind enter that still place inside of him, the quiet zone where only he and his opponent existed. He held his sword loosely in his right hand and watched the Dragon, eyes of the hunter alert to his every body movement, waiting for an opening. Only one of them would walk away from this encounter, and Hunter intended to be that person.

The Dragon lunged forward, claws extended, going for Hunter's soft underbelly, but Hunter twirled and came up behind the Dragon and managed to slice the scaly hide, a shallow but bloody wound that dripped dark blood. Ha, first blood went to Hunter and his Realm-forged, enchanted blade. Hunter smiled coldly.

That pissed the Dragon off. He snarled and rushed Hunter but, at the last second, feinted and sent his tail swinging instead, sweeping Hunter's feet out from under him. Landing hard, Hunter immediately rolled. Good thing because sharp claws came down where his face had been a split second before.

Hunter sprang to his feet and paced around the big, black beast. "I'm going to kill you for what you did," promised Hunter. Oh yes, the monster would pay for killing Suzie, and Hunter intended to make sure it hurt.

"Oh, please." The Dragon laughed, pacing around Hunter, the two engaged in a warrior's dance that spanned the ages. "I have not waited this long to die at the hands of one man. You would need an army much bigger than just you to kill me."

"Now who's deluded?" taunted Hunter. "You seem to forget you're only a half-blood. Or did you forget your mother was human? You're not a real dragon, only a poor excuse for one."

The Dragon screamed, a high-pitched sound full of rage, but unfortunately, he didn't rush Hunter as he'd hoped. No matter. Time to go on the offensive. Hunter stalked toward the Dragon, who watched Hunter's sword avidly. Hunter started swinging the blade back and forth.

The hypnotic effect had the Dragon distracted, so when Hunter swung it close, the Dragon lifted an arm to block it as expected, but Hunter did the unexpected. He flipped the sword to his other hand—oh yes, he was ambidextrous—and swung at the Dragon's now unprotected side. The sword sank deep, and the Dragon bellowed in pain. Hunter pulled the sword out, dark blood bubbling from the wound. Hunter brought the sword back to strike a killing blow, but the Dragon, sensing his imminent defeat, stopped fighting and, instead, untucked his large wings. Flapping them, the Dragon started rising above the parapet, the bastard deciding to ditch the battle and escape.

Like hell, thought Hunter. He dropped his sword and, with a running leap, wrapped his arms around the Dragon's scaly, lower legs.

The Dragon sagged in the air and screamed again. Hunter smiled grimly and held on tight. The Dragon flapped harder and recovered altitude with Hunter going along for the ride. Hunter looked down at the ant-sized people in the courtyard. To his surprise, he couldn't see Suzie's crumpled form on the ground. Had she somehow survived? He scanned the crowd on the ground but had no time to really see anything, as, suddenly, the Dragon swooped down, heading toward the outer bailey wall. *Crap*. Hunter could see what the Dragon planned. Smack Hunter like a bug off the wall in the hopes of making him fall. Like hell. Hunter tightened his grip. No way would he let go. He had a mission to finish.

Inch by inch, he moved his hands up the Dragon's

legs, hiking his body higher up. Damn stinky bastard. The wound Hunter had given him made his scales slick and stink of sulfur. Hunter wished he'd just hurry up and die.

He needed to go back and see if Suzie, by some miracle, had survived the fall.

CHAPTER 17

Suzie felt herself plummeting, too frightened to even pray, the look of horror on Hunter's face etched in her mind. She hoped being smashed to bits wouldn't hurt, and she closed her eyes tight.

But instead of hitting the hard, cobbled stone of the courtyard, she slowed and floated lightly till she landed on the ground on her butt.

Opening her eyes, fearfully, because, after all, maybe she'd died and turned into a ghost, she let out a relieved breathe when she saw the anxious faces of Beverly and other strangers crowded around her, including a wizard in dark blue robes.

"Oh thank the higher powers!" exclaimed Beverly, clutching a hand to her heart.

"What happened?" asked Suzie. Yeah, like how the hell had she gone from certain squishy death, you know the type that needed the parts scooped up and reassembled like a puzzle, to not a mark or bruise? Well, except for the ones the Dragon had given her beforehand.

"Finnius, the wizard over there in the blue robes, had just arrived when we saw the Dragon drop you from the parapet. Thankfully, he's a quick thinker and a magic caster. He managed to slow your descent, or things would have ended very badly."

Badly was an understatement. But wait, this wasn't over yet. She'd left the Dragon up there with Hunter. *Oh no!*

Suzie sprang to her feet and looked up in time to see Hunter launch himself and grab the legs of the Dragon, who pumped huge wings as he tried to fly off. Holy shit! What next? Fire breathing?

"Someone has to help him," Suzie cried, running across the courtyard, trying to follow his flight, Beverly scurrying after. *Where the hell are all the soldiers and stuff? Why is Hunter fighting him alone?*

"We can't," Beverly panted, trying to keep up. "If the archers shoot, they might miss and kill Hunter by accident. I'm afraid he's on his own," said his mother sadly.

Suzie and Beverly stood watching at the edge of the courtyard as the Dragon flew, dipping down toward the outer bailey wall. Suzie's heart thumped like a frightened rabbit's, and her mouth went dry as she watched the Dragon try to get in a position to smash Hunter off the side of the outer wall. But Hunter had a few tricks up his sleeve and started inching his way up the Dragon's body so that the Dragon couldn't slam him off without hurting himself too. Yay Hunter!

With a piercing shriek, the Dragon flapped his great

wings and went over the wall, out of sight. Suzie waited impatiently, foot tapping, for the soldiers to open the castle's gate, but by the time they did and she rushed out, the Dragon appeared just a distant speck in the sky with an extra pair of dangling legs.

Suzie sank to the ground in shock, tears running down her cheeks. Hunter was gone.

She felt little arms encircle her in a warm hug, and she buried her face in between the twins, hugging them tight. While she'd been busy, they'd managed to shift back to their human forms.

"Mommy, you hurt," said Jared, pulling back, looking at her shoulder.

Suzie looked down and saw the red fluid seeping out, her now ragged gown soaked in her blood, and said, "Why, yes I am." She wondered why it didn't hurt then fainted.

CHAPTER 18

The Dragon, after hours of flight across forests and villages, had begun to tire. A good thing because Hunter now drew on his last reserves of strength. As the Dragon's wings slowed ponderously and they lost altitude, Hunter prepared for their journey's end.

Hunter would have loved to kill the Dragon while they flew, but considering their altitude, well, that would have been certain suicide for him. He'd known, however, that the Dragon couldn't fly forever, so when the ground started approaching, their impromptu flight over, Hunter readied himself. The Dragon made for an empty field, and Hunter, waiting for this moment, let go and dropped to the ground in a tuck and roll.

The Dragon still floated down when he attacked Hunter, but his slash was slow, and Hunter parried it easily. Thank the higher powers he still had the long knife in his boot. He'd dropped his sword back at the castle. While they were both tired, and Hunters arms burned, their determination meant they circled each other, looking for an opening.

"Come on, you overgrown lizard," taunted Hunter. The fatigue from their flight had sapped the energy from his body. He needed to end this quickly while he still had the strength.

"I am going to enjoy eating you, Hunter. And then, once I'm done with you, I'm going back and taking the children. Maybe I'll eat the girl child, too. Children are sooo tasty."

"Never!" cried Hunter, feinting to his left, hoping to draw the Dragon in, but he'd apparently predicted that move, and instead, Hunter felt a stinging burn across his arm as the Dragon raked him with his claws.

Ow! Hunter pushed the pain down, a trick he'd learned long ago. Time enough to lick his wounds once the battle had been won. Hunter prowled around his foe, ready for when the Dragon rushed him. The damn flight, though, had left him weaker than expected. He sidestepped the rush, but the Dragon's tail whipped him hard across the shins and down he went, flat on his back. The Dragon immediately jumped on top. Hunter had predicted that, though. He thrust his dagger up just as the Dragon landed, and he smiled grimly at the wide-eyed look of incredulity on the Dragon's face. Unfortunately, the Dragon wasn't done. Even though Hunter had given him a killing blow, it wasn't an instant one, and the Dragon slammed both hands—er paws with claws—into Hunter's shoulders. The wounds, deep punctures, began bleeding copiously.

"If I die, Hunter, you die with me," gasped the

Dragon before a blankness stole over his eyes and the breath left his body in one last, fetid whoosh.

Alas, he also collapsed on top of Hunter. Hunter brought his hands up to shove him off. However, the Dragon, a dead weight on top of his body, resisted his feeble attempts to extricate himself. Hunter, gravely injured and losing precious amounts of blood, lacked the strength.

Hunter fought against the blackness, feeling the light-headedness signaling too much blood loss. He couldn't pass out. He had to...

Hunter's head fell to the side, and he knew no more.

CHAPTER 19

When Suzie awoke again, she found herself in a new room, this one done in shades of turquoise, and alone. She sat up without a twinge and looked at her shoulder. Someone had washed and dressed her in a clean, linen chemise, and her shoulder, while showing three faint white scars from Damian's claws, had been healed. Made her wonder just how much magic could heal—just injuries, or did it cure disease too? Wouldn't that put the researchers earning big bucks back home in a snit? Sorry, no need to find a cure for cancer anymore, we've magicked it away. Here's your pink slip. Lovely, making jokes to herself when at this very moment Hunter could be dead. Speaking of which, was Nat okay? She'd been injured too.

Suzie got up out of bed and shrugged on the gown she found on a chair. She'd have to thank whoever kept loaning her the gowns. Dressed, she had to wonder, where was everybody? Had Nat recovered? Where were the twins? Had they received news of Hunter yet?

A knock sounded.

"Come in," Suzie called, turning to see who it was.

The lanky form of the butler, Benson, appeared in the doorway. "The commander wishes to see you," he said, bobbing his bald head at her. Kind of looked like a bobblehead when he did that. Suzie wondered if he practiced that bob because he seemed to do it a lot. Maybe he'd learned it at butler school. Suzie bit her lip so as to not giggle at the image of a bunch of bald men learning to bob their heads just right. *Not nice*, she chastised herself.

So the commander wanted to see her. Interesting. Suzie hadn't yet met Hunter's father. An oversight or intentional on his part? Perhaps he had news of Hunter.

"Is Hunter back?" Suzie thought to ask because, after all, in the movies, the butlers always knew everything that was going on.

"I do not know, milady."

"How's Nat?" she asked. Last time she'd seen Nat, her face had been a bloody mess.

"Recovering. My mistress is tending her."

Benson didn't seem to be the chatty type. It was like pulling teeth getting anything out of him. "Where are the twins?" Suzie found herself surprised they hadn't come to find her yet.

"I believe they are having a snack. If milady would please follow me, the commander does not like to be kept waiting."

Well, too freaking bad. Suzie had to pee, and her mouth felt as if something had crawled in it and died.

THE HUNTER

"A moment please while I freshen up," Suzie said to the startled butler before going into the bathroom. She took a little longer than necessary. She wanted to be clear headed before she finally met the man who scared so many and who apparently disliked her simply because of her place of birth. How juvenile. And besides, what was the worst the man could do? Forbid her from dating Hunter? That wasn't up to him.

What if he had bad news about Hunter? No, surely Beverly or Nat would have told her themselves. She needed to quit stalling and get some answers. Suzie went back in the room, where the impatient butler twitched, and followed him through the mazelike castle till they stood in front of a large, carved wooden door.

The butler rapped sharply on the door then scurried away—the man really defined creepy—leaving Suzie alone. Someone barked, "Enter." Taking a deep breath and squaring her shoulders, Suzie opened the door and walked in. Time to meet Hunter's dad.

The commander was a fierce-looking man. A harder, fleshier version of Hunter sat behind his heavy wooden desk with his fingers steepled and stared at her with arctic blue eyes. Suzie shivered at the coldness that radiated from him. *Wow, definitely not the friendly sort.*

"You wished to see me, sir," Suzie said politely.

"Yes, I decided I needed to meet for myself the person responsible for my son's lack of judgment and behavior. I have to say I was expecting someone a little more spectacular-looking."

Suzie gasped in outrage. She couldn't have been more shocked if he'd slapped her. "I'm sorry I don't meet your expectations, sir. I didn't realize this was a test of looks." It wasn't as if he was a prize, himself. The commander had definitely let himself go. That is, if he hadn't always looked like that to start with.

The commander—no way could this rigid man be called a father—grunted. "Well, at least you have a little backbone. Pity you didn't have one three years ago. We might have avoided this mess. No matter. Have a seat, you and I need to have a talk." The commander motioned to the straight-back chair in front of his desk, and Suzie sat on it gingerly, hands clasped in her lap to control their trembling. She had half a mind to just get up and walk out. Somehow, she knew this conversation was going to be unpleasant. Heck, it already was.

"I assume you have news of Hunter? Is he alive?" she asked, unable to wait. She needed to know, and he seemed to be taking his time getting started.

"They haven't been spotted since they flew off this morning. My son is a fighter, though. He'll take care of this unfortunate problem, but that's not why I called you in here."

The commander stood and wandered over to a beverage cart, where he poured out two glasses of something, one of which he handed to her. Then he sat back down, twirling the glass in his big hands.

Suzie didn't want to speak first again, so she took a sip from the glass, surprised to find it was some kind of sweet juice. Thank goodness because she had a poor stomach for liquor.

For some reason, the commander looked pleased. What, had he been expecting her to throw the drink in his face? Eying the glass, she suddenly had to control the temptation to do so.

"I won't beat around the bush. I know you're involved with my son. You may even think he cares for you, but I'm afraid that a relationship between you is impossible."

Wow, talk about straight to the point. "Why?" she asked. Not that she really cared about his answer. Whether or not she and Hunter ended up together was their decision, not his father's.

"You don't belong here. Hunter does. I've been letting him sow his oats, but I've got other plans for him. Plans that don't include him marrying a woman with two children out of wedlock who is mundane to boot."

Ouch. Talk about brutal honesty. "Isn't that Hunter's decision?"

"Hunter is my son. He will do as he's told."

Somehow Suzie didn't think Hunter would agree with that. "Hunter's a grown man. I'm sure he can decide for himself."

"I don't think I've made myself clear enough. Hunter is going to marry a young lady of breeding from the Realm. He is my heir and, as such, will do his duty by the family. I will not have my family name and honor besmirched by a mundane woman of loose morals."

That pissed Suzie off. She did not consider herself easy. Hell, she'd gone three years without even dating. *So why the hell am I letting this ass insult me? Screw that.* "I can't believe you're Hunter's father. How on earth such a kind and gentle man could have come from you is a mystery. You're rude and hateful, and I'm not listening to any more of this. Whether or not Hunter and

I stay involved is no one's business but our own. Good-bye."

Suzie stood up in a show of defiance and swayed, her head suddenly fuzzy. *What the hell?* Her vision blurred, and her knees buckled, sitting her back down hard in the chair. She tried to focus on the commander's face—there were three floating in front of her—and saw him smiling coldly. *Brr, is it me, or is it getting chilly in here?*

"You don't have a say. This is my house, and I've decided you're not welcome in it. I've laced your drink with a narcotic to put you to sleep. When you wake, you and your misbegotten progeny will be back in your world. You should thank me for that. I could have just had you all killed. But I'm not an evil man. I will, however, do what's needed to protect this family. With you out of the picture, Hunter will come to his senses."

The bastard had drugged her! "Hunter will find me. He won't let you do this," Suzie said with a thick tongue. And oh boy, would Hunter be pissed.

"It's already done. Good-bye." The commander threw that back at her, like a slap, and Suzie recoiled from the venom in his eyes.

Suzie tried to speak, but her mouth wouldn't work. It felt as if it had been stuffed with cotton balls, and try as she might, she couldn't keep her eyes open. Suzie felt herself falling forward, and then her mind went blank.

CHAPTER 20

*S*uzie woke in her bed with a throbbing head. Wait a second, her bed, her room. How had she gotten here? Suddenly, she remembered her meeting with the commander. The bastard had drugged her. Boy would Hunter be mad when he found out.

Oh no, the children!

Suzie rolled off the bed and fell to her knees on the carpet, fighting a wave of dizziness. Head hanging, she paced her breathing. In, out. Slowly, the spinning feeling receded and she managed to stand up. On trembling legs, she left her bedroom and staggered into the twins' room.

Thank God! Both children were asleep in their beds. Suzie dropped to her knees between the beds and shook them, one at a time.

Little brown eyes blinked open in tandem.

"Mommy," said Jessica sluggishly.

"We home," said Jared thickly.

"Yes, babies. We're home. How are you feeling?"

The twins quickly shrugged off their stupor and felt fine. Apparently, the drug used on them hadn't been as strong. The last thing they remembered was having a snack that Benson brought them and then waking up in their beds. Suzie really wanted to have a talk with that scuzzbag Benson, a talk involving her closed fist. He'd drugged her babies! What if he'd miscalculated the dose? He could have killed them. Just another thing to tell Hunter when he came back to them.

Suzie fought off the urge to crawl back to bed and sleep. Instead, she kept moving about her home, tidying things that didn't need tidying, trying to keep her hands busy. Pity it didn't work on her mind.

She had mixed feelings about coming home. Relief—thank God they were all safe and healthy. Sad—she missed the new friends she'd made in Beverly and gruff Nat. Anxious—had Hunter succeeded? And pissed! How dare Hunter's father drug them and ship them back like some unwanted piece of garbage. No matter. Hunter would deal with his dad when he came back. She'd just bide her time.

The children, considering their ordeal, adjusted back to normal life quickly. They squabbled, they played, they destroyed the house one room at a time. Oh yes, her never-ending job of maid and referee, also known as motherhood, returned. She also started her new web design project, anything to keep her mind off what might be happening back in the Realm.

And while Suzie worked, cleaned, and pondered, she found herself, on more than one occasion, peeking out the window. Listening for the sound of his Harley. Looking to see if he'd leapt over the fence. Anything.

But the house next door stayed silent. Maybe he'd failed and died, a horrible thought she couldn't shake. Or maybe, said her pessimistic side, he'd decided against coming back and she should just consider herself another notch on his bedpost. Worst of all, maybe his father had told the truth and Hunter had caved into the plan to marry someone proper.

Her children had no doubts when it came to Hunter, though.

"Mommy, why you loo' so sad?" asked Jessie. Had she mentioned her daughter now insisted on being called by her new nickname. *Thanks, Nat.*

"I'm not sad."

"You mith Hunta," said Jared sagely. "He'll come back. He wuvth uth."

"Yes, Mommy, Hunta come back soon. He wuvs you."

Suzie didn't answer. Funny, the children seemed so sure of his affections. Suzie, though, only had doubts. Lying in bed at night, she couldn't stop her thoughts from running around in circles. Had he found Damian yet? Succeeded? Did he miss her? Why didn't he come back or at least contact them? Had the man she'd fallen in love with been a myth?

One lonely week went by. Then two, the max he'd said it would take him. On the third week, Suzie started throwing up.

Hugging the porcelain god of the bathroom, she cried. No fair. She couldn't be pregnant. They'd been together only the one night. But fate, like Murphy, had an evil sense of humor.

Suzie drove into town with the children who, for once, were subdued. Could it be the red-rimmed eyes she hid behind sunglasses? She'd literally cried a river since she'd realized Hunter wasn't coming back.

Suzie bought the dreaded home pregnancy test at the pharmacy and brought it home, smuggled in its bag like a piece of contraband. She waited till the children were in bed then sat down and peed on the stick. Any woman who's peed on the stick knows how that feels—the anxiety, the dread, the prayers. And let's not forget staring at the little stick, waiting, even if the box says it may take up to three minutes. She didn't have to wait long. It instantly lit up like a Christmas tree. Double cross. Pregnant.

Suzie sank down on the floor beside the tub and cried. And cried then cried some more. Arms hugged around her knees, she lay on the bathroom floor in the fetal position. *What the hell am I going to do?* She couldn't have an abortion. She couldn't kill this sign of love, even if it might have been a one-sided love. But how would she manage? Her snide inner voice said, *Contact him. Tell him about the baby. He'll come back.*

Problem was she didn't want him back because of her pregnancy. She wanted him to come back because he wanted her. Because he loved her.

Stupid, maybe, but Suzie refused to accept any less. And besides, it didn't matter. She had no way to contact him.

Suzie cried again. Something she'd been doing an awful lot. Mostly after the kids went to bed. But sometimes all it took was looking at his house and off she'd go. Good thing she never wore mascara or she'd have permanent raccoon eyes by now.

The kids walked on eggshells around her. They stopped making big messes. Miracle of all miracles, they even started cleaning up after themselves. And they hugged her. A lot. It seemed like every time they went by, they had to hug her or touch her. The worst part? She didn't know if they were doing it to reassure themselves or her. Nice mother.

Another week went by. It had been almost a month now since their return. Life had returned to normal, or as normal as it could get with her throwing up in the morning, and afternoon, and sometimes even at night. Morning sickness was a bitch, especially when you had the twenty-four-hour kind. Suzie gave serious thought to buying stock in soda crackers, the only food she seemed to be able to eat.

The puking, she'd survive. The loneliness, however, proved to be much harder to keep at bay. Hard to keep her spirits up when the only thing she talked openly to was her new porcelain friend. She had decided one thing, though, in between hugging her new best friend—no more relationships. Caring about someone led to hurting, and Suzie was done with pain. She'd leave it to the sadomasochists. From now on, it would be just her and the twins, and, in eight months, baby.

Just over a month after her return, she dropped the kids off in the morning at a play group she'd signed them up for. They needed a change of scenery, and her stomach still wasn't behaving well enough for her to go out for long periods of time to socialize them. She came back home and decided that the overgrown jungle known as her yard really needed a mow. She wrestled for a while with the dreaded red machine but finally got the mower started—by herself, yay—and was cutting the lawn when something finally happened next door.

A panel van pulled into Hunter's driveway next door, the logo Magical Emporium splashed across its side. *What the hell?*

Suzie's heart sped up. No, she refused to get excited. Probably just someone coming to pack up his stuff. But no, Hunter got out of the van, his body moving stiffly. He paused when he saw her then, as if reaching a decision, crossed the lawn to her, his face a blank canvas. Suzie tried to control her own facial expressions, but it was hard with her heart pumping madly while fighting an urge to run and throw her arms around him.

"Hello, Suzie," he said, stopping in front of her, not a sign of warmth in him.

Suzie said nothing, tongue-tied in front of this cool-acting stranger.

He frowned at her lack of response. "How have you been? How are the kids?"

"Fine." Suzie wanted to kick herself. What had happened to the speech she'd prepared in her head in anticipation of this dreaded—wished for—moment?

"So that's the way it's going to be, is it?" he said with a harsh bark of laughter. "I really misjudged you, didn't I?"

"What the hell are talking about?" Suzie said, annoyed at his cool attitude and cryptic comment. "I'd say it's the opposite. I misjudged you. How could you do this to me? To the kids?"

"What I did to you? I almost died out in the woods after killing the Dragon. I was lucky some woodsmen found me, or I would have bled to death. As it was, I was out of it for over a week, and when I was finally strong enough to travel, I came back home to find out that you'd packed up the children and left."

"I left? I didn't have a choice." Suzie screamed at him while part of her wanted to cry. Hunter had almost died?

"What do you mean you didn't have a choice?" Hunter raked a hand through his hair, wincing as if the simple motion hurt. "Listen, I think we need to talk. Why don't we have dinner tonight, just you and me? I need to go back to the office. I just came by because I had to see you. To make sure you and the twins were all right." He said the last part almost reluctantly.

"I can't leave the children."

"I didn't figure you would, which is why I brought Nat back with me. Will you trust her to mind them while we talk? We could wait till after they go to bed if it will make it easier?"

Suzie nodded. He was right. They needed to talk. And if the kids were in bed, then Nat would have no problems.

"I'll come back around seven thirty then. It is good to see you, by the way. I've missed you."

Suzie didn't answer, her throat too tight, and she turned before he could see the tears glistening like dew drops on her lashes. Dammit! She'd cried enough over him already. She wasn't going to cry anymore.

She powered up the red beast again and didn't hear him leave. She finished mowing the lawn, tears running down her cheeks. Why couldn't love ever be simple?

Suzie didn't tell the kids Hunter had returned. She had to know what he wanted, what his plans were first. After all, why get their hopes up if he only planned to leave again?

She put the kids to bed and dressed simply in a skirt and blouse. Eyeing her makeup, she ended up putting on a light coat, enough to camouflage the red eyes and hollows around them. Well, she'd finally get her answers tonight, whether she liked them or not.

She went downstairs just before seven thirty, opened the front door, and sat on the step, waiting. Her stomach felt full of butterflies, fluttering and dancing inside. Her hands were clammy, and she kept wiping them on her skirt.

What would she say to him? What would he say to her? Just seeing him had brought back a host of feelings and memories. She didn't even know what she wanted anymore.

Hearing the murmur of voices, she looked up to see Nat walking across the lawn with Hunter.

Suzie stood up, smoothing down her skirt. "Hey, Nat," she said.

"Hi," said Nat coldly.

What the hell was Nat pissed about? Shouldn't Suzie

be pissed at her instead since Nat had let her father drug her and the kids?

"The kids are already asleep. The remote's on the living room table. There's juice and pop in the fridge, chips, and cookies on the counter. Do you have Hunter's cell number in case you need me to come home?"

"Actually, we're having dinner at my place," Hunter said. "I thought it would be easier to have our talk without an audience."

Alone? Suzie hid her panic at his words. She swallowed her misgivings and nodded. She still didn't know if she'd end up screaming at him or crying. Either would have been embarrassing in public.

"All right." Nat went into the house and shut the door. Hunter looked at her and started walking. Suzie followed him in silence across the lawn to his place. God, this felt so awkward.

He opened his front door and ushered her inside. Suzie looked around with interest. She'd never seen the inside of his place before, but she could tell from one glance a man lived there.

The living room was all male with a black leather couch and matching chair. Chrome end tables flanked the couch, and all faced a large, flat screen TV. *Wanna bet he has the sports package?*

He took her through the living room to the kitchen with its black melamine cabinets and more glass and chrome for the table and chairs, which he'd set for two. Two lit candles flickered in the darkness, making the room seem cozy and romantic.

He seated her, still in silence, and then went over to the oven, where he pulled out an aluminum dish.

Suzie jumped when he finally broke the silence. "I'm not good at cooking, so I bought a ready-made lasagna with garlic bread at the deli. Hope that's okay?" he said, still not looking at her while he prepared two plates.

"That's fine." Suzie wanted to scream at him. She didn't care about the food. She wanted answers.

But he took his sweet time and didn't sit down till he'd served them both. He opened a bottle of red wine and started to pour. Suzie waved him away from her glass.

"Sorry, could I have water please? My stomach's been a little touchy lately." That was putting it mildly! She only hoped she made it through dinner without puking on him.

He put the bottle away and went to the fridge and got her a bottle of water.

Finally, he seated himself across from her and looked at her, his blue eyes so beautiful and, dare she even say, sad-looking? They stared at each other for what seemed like an eternity while their food got cold.

"Why did you leave?" he finally asked.

"I wasn't given a choice. Didn't your father tell you?" Suzie replied. Oh please, like he didn't know what his daddy had done.

"What do you mean you didn't have a choice? My father said as soon as you woke up from being healed, you demanded he send you and the children back right then and there. That and I quote, 'You couldn't handle the magic and the monsters anymore and that it was better if you just made a clean break.' Sounds to me like your choice was pretty clear."

"Really?" said Suzie sarcastically. "Well, see, that's funny. The way I remember it, your father ordered me down to his office. Told me I wasn't good enough for you and that he already had plans for you to marry some proper Realm lady. Then he slipped me a narcotic in a drink, drugged the children too, and when I woke up, we were back home. But let me guess, Daddy dear forgot to mention that part, didn't he?" Suzie said bitterly.

Hunter's brow's knitted together in a frown. "He wouldn't dare. He knew how I felt about you."

"Oh, he did dare. Please, don't insult my intelligence by telling me you believed that cock-and-bull story he gave you. Did you really think I would leave after everything that had happened between us? Did you really think I could be cold enough to go without even knowing if you lived or died?" she shouted. How dare he insinuate she'd lie about something like this? He should count his blessings she wasn't a violent person, or she'd have slapped him. As it was, her hands were balled into tight fists in her lap.

"That bastard," Hunter swore, jumping out of his chair and pacing the small kitchen. "You never told him I scared you, did you? Or that you couldn't handle the fact I was more than human?"

"What? Of course not. I lov—" Suzie stopped herself. Oops. She needed to watch her mouth. "I never had a problem with what you were once I found out. Hell, my kids are bloody dragons. I don't love them any less. As for scaring me, the only thing that scared me was the thought of never seeing you again."

"Dammit! I can't believe he lied to me." Hunter's face grew tight with anger and anguish. How awful it must be to know his own father, someone he trusted, had lied to him and hurt him. Gee, kind of like her own mother. The two should get together.

But Suzie wasn't about to let him off the hook that easily. Hunter was a grown man who knew his father well enough to know how ruthless he could be. And even in the short time they'd known each other, he should have known her better than that.

Still annoyed and showing it in her tone, she said, "I can't believe you thought that load of crock was the truth. Did you really think I'd let you make love to me if I thought you were some kind of monster that frightened me? Did I ever look away from you in disgust or push you away any of the three times we made love?"

Hunter hung his head as if in shame and sat back down in his chair. "I understand why you were so pissed now this morning. I had no idea. When I came back, still hurting from my injuries, and my father told me what had happened, it never occurred to me it wasn't the truth. I mean he's my father. Why the hell would be lie to me?"

"Because he didn't want you getting hooked up with a mundane slut with two evil kids."

"He didn't say that?" said Hunter, brows arched in astonishment.

"Not those exact words, but yeah. He didn't think I was good enough for you or the family. So he made an executive decision to take care of the problem. He figured

THE HUNTER

if I was gone, you'd come to your senses and marry the girl he had picked out for you."

"What? I told him years ago, I'd marry when I was damn good and ready and that the choice would be mine. After all, I'm the one who has to live with that decision the rest of my life. I'm sorry," Hunter said, shaking his head. "I should have known he was lying. I knew his hatred of the mundanes ran deep, but I never thought he'd do something evil like this. And I certainly had no idea of his plans. Can you ever forgive me?"

"You, I forgive. Him, no. But what happened to you? Why did it take so long for you to come back? I thought you didn't care about me anymore."

"First off," he said, sliding off his chair to his knees beside her, "I never stopped caring for you. Hell, this might seem like a crummy time to say it, but I love you."

Suzie felt tears pricking her eyes. He loved her? "But why did you leave me for so long?" she said in a lost-little-girl voice, fat tears rolling down her cheeks. "I was so afraid and lonely."

"After I flew off with the Dragon, it was hours before he finally landed and we fought. He's dead, by the way. He won't be coming back to hurt you or the children. But he hurt me, bad. I thought I was a goner, but some woodsmen came by and took me to their hut in the woods. They treated me best they could. Still, it was almost a week before I was coherent enough to tell them who I was. Then it was almost another week before help arrived. When I did finally get home, I was still sick. The wounds had gotten infected. My mother spent days healing me. When I finally recovered, my father gave me his version of events. I spent a week moping around, depressed and cursing you. Then Nat asked me why the hell didn't I come back and confront you. Lay the demons to rest, so to speak."

"Oh my God. I never realized," gasped Suzie, still crying. "I've seen the way your mother can heal. I guess it never occurred to me it might be a rare talent in your world. All this time I've been sitting here thinking you didn't care. Or that your father had managed to convince you to marry some proper little lady."

"Never!" he said vehemently, his eyes earnest. "The only person I want to marry and spend my life with is you and the twins."

Sweet words, but, "Your father will never agree."

"To hell with my father!"

Suzie felt like dancing, even as the tears kept rolling down her cheeks—damn hormones! He loved her. He hadn't left her or abandoned her. It was a scheme by his father to separate them. Talk about a Romeo and Juliette story. Except here they had a chance at a happy ending now that the truth had come out.

Speaking of which, Suzie knew it was time to tell him her news. He deserved to know. She only hoped it didn't scare him off. Sure, he'd talked about starting a family, but that had been just talk. She being pregnant, that was a whole different kettle of fish. She'd opened her mouth to tell him, bracing herself mentally for his reaction, when she heard voices out front.

"It can't be," muttered Hunter, getting up and trying to peer through the archway to his front bay window.

"Is that your dad I hear?" asked Suzie as the voices

got louder. Oh yeah, she'd recognize that harsh tone anywhere. And the softer one, could it be Beverly? *What's going on?*

"Sounds like my mom, too. Come on," he said, grabbing her hand and pulling her up. "Let's go find out what's going on. I have a few things I'd like to say to the commander."

As did she, thought Suzie. She hoped only that the yelling didn't wake up the kids.

CHAPTER 21

*H*unter held Suzie's hand firmly in his as he walked to the front door of his house. No way was he ever letting her go again. He felt like such as ass for believing his father's ridiculous lie. He should have the word gullible printed across his forehead. But when he'd come back so weak and half delirious, he'd felt such a blow when she hadn't been there to greet him. And he still had a hard time believing his father had the nerve to drug Suzie and the twins and cart them off with no one being aware of it. How had he hidden it from his mother? She usually knew everything that was going on, and Hunter knew she'd never have allowed it. Or had his mother been part of the plan? Did she also harbor a hidden dislike of Suzie? Well, they were here now, and by the higher powers, he was determined to get some straight answers.

Hunter flung open the door and stared dumbstruck at his parents on his front lawn yelling at each other.

Hunter had never, ever, ever seen his mother yell at his father. She'd always been the soft-spoken one, the mediator, and here she bristled, standing toe to toe with the commander, her petite frame looking somehow tall and menacing. Enough that his father cringed before her.

Leaning against the Magical Emporium van in the driveway was Bob, an amused grin on his face as he avidly watched the yelling match.

Hunter decided to ignore his brawling parents for a second and, still holding Suzie's hand, walked over to Bob.

"What the hell are my parents doing here?"

Bob grinned wider. "Well, first, the commander came through the portal. Said you'd come back here without authorization and he was coming to take you back. Seemed real pissed about it. Then next thing you know, your mother shows up, and she starts yelling at him. Your mother is one tough lady, Hunter. I've never seen anybody stand up to the commander like she is." Bob's face shone with admiration. "She told him she was coming along with him because this was his fault, and by the higher powers, he was going to fix it. He kept telling her to stay out of it, that he had things under control and it was for the better. They fought the whole way over, and, well, as you can see, they're still going at it."

Hunter groaned and rubbed his face. Good news, sounded like his mom wasn't part of the commander's plan. Bad news, he had to get in the middle of this spat and referee. *Exactly how does one go about telling their parents to stop acting like children?*

More voices joined the fray as Nat came out on Suzie's front porch, a crying twin on each hip.

"What the hell is going on? All this screaming woke the twins up. Mother? Father? What are they doing here?" Nat asked while bouncing the kids on her hips.

"Oh no," exclaimed Suzie, letting go of his hand and hurrying across the lawns to see the twins. Hunter rolled his eyes heavenward, praying quickly for patience, then followed her.

The kids quieted as soon as they saw their mother and reached out arms to her. Suzie wasn't as strong as Nat, though, and staggered under their combined weight. Hunter came up behind her though and helped her hold them, sliding his arms around the twins so they could hug Suzie.

The kids beamed through their tears when they saw him.

"Hunta! You back," said Jessica, holding out her arms to him. Hunter, with a smile, scooped her up and hugged her tight. He'd missed her sweet little smiles.

"Of course I am, little angel. How could I ever leave my favorite girl?"

Jessica giggled in his arms. Jared, holding on to Suzie, though, scowled at him. "You made my mommy thad."

"I'm sorry about that, Jared. I never meant to hurt her. I have apologized, though, and I promise to do my best to never make her sad again."

That seemed to make Jared happy, for he stopped scowling and snuggled in Suzie's arms.

But Hunter remained angry. How dare they wake the

kids with their argument and scare them? Time to put a stop to it.

"Hey, baby girl, can you go to Nat for a minute? I'm gonna make my mother and father stop yelling. Is that okay?"

Jessica nodded and allowed Nat to take her from Hunter's arms.

Nat looked at him and mouthed, "What the hell is going on?"

"The commander did something bad to Suzie and the twins, and I think Mother found out."

Nat's face went slack jawed with surprise, and she turned questioning eyes to Suzie, who just shrugged.

Hunter strode across the lawn till he stood a couple of feet away from his mud-slinging parents.

"Enough," Hunter bellowed, his tone eerily like his father's on the training fields back home.

Instant silence.

"I hope you're both proud of yourselves. You managed to wake and frighten two small children, not to mention make an absolute spectacle of yourselves." He turned to his mother. "You know, Mother, I expect this kind of behavior from the commander, but you?" Hunter let his anger and disgust show in his tone and look. "Come on. It's obviously time for a family meeting, and I don't think the front lawn, in front of the neighbors, is the best place to do it."

Hunter turned on his heel and started walking. Tempted to look back to see if they were following, he restrained himself. It wouldn't do to show weakness and ruin his speech. That was the first time he'd ever spoken to his parents like that, and he felt a little nervous about it. Although, really, what could the commander do? Send him to his room?

Hunter walked right up to Suzie and Nat holding the kids and motioned for them to go into the house.

"I think I should put the kids back to bed," said Suzie.

"Good idea," said Hunter. "I'll make sure my parents behave. 'Night guys." Hunter leaned in to give Jessica a big kiss, which made her giggle, and a manly pat on the back to Jared, who finally smiled back at him.

"I'll help," said Nat. She followed Suzie upstairs while Hunter stayed in the front hall, waiting for his parents.

Through the door came Hunter's parents who appeared subdued for the moment, however, Hunter could see his mother still bristled, and his father had a sullen look on his face. Hunter shook his head at them. How many years of repressed anger had his mother been holding in to lose it like that? And his father must have been feeling pretty guilty to take it without completely blowing his stack.

Hunter motioned them to the couch and stood staring at them, arms crossed. When his father would have opened his mouth to speak, Hunter shook his head. Oh no, this discussion would wait till Suzie and Nat came back. They both had a right to hear what was coming.

The women came back down and flanked Hunter, facing his parents.

"Now," said Hunter. "First, some ground rules before we start this family meeting."

His father just couldn't keep his mouth shut. "She's not family," he said, pointing at Suzie.

"She will be, and this affects her, which brings me to rule number one. No mistreating Suzie. Start insulting her, and this conversation is over." His mother and Nat nodded while his father just sat there glowering.

"Rule number two, no yelling. There are two small, frightened children upstairs. So keep it down. Try and act like adults. And finally, rule number three. I want the truth, the absolute truth. You start lying, and this conversation ends."

"Why do you keep directing these rules at me?" The commander snapped most belligerently.

"Because you're the reason we're having this meeting, Father," said Hunter, putting a hard emphasis on the "father" part.

"I am not going to just sit here and be accused." Hunter's father made to stand up, but Beverly put a hand on his arm.

"Sit down," she said firmly, blue eyes flashing. "It's time you listened for once. I, for one, would like to know what's going on. And not just your version, either."

"Thank you, Mother. Now, first off, Father..." Hunter, again, emphasized the "father." "You told me some tale about how Suzie demanded to leave because she couldn't handle me being who I was. Said she was scared of me. Thing is I didn't quite believe it, and even though you advised me against it, I came back to talk to her, to understand, because the Suzie I know would never have said or done that. Do you want to guess what she told me?"

Beverly turned and gave her husband a hard look. "Yes, Adrian. Tell us."

The commander squirmed on the couch like a little boy with his hand caught in the cookie jar. "Well, I might have embellished the facts a bit."

Suzie laughed harshly. "How do you embellish the fact that you drugged me and the kids and shipped us back without a say-so in the matter?"

"Adrian, you didn't!" exclaimed Beverly.

Nat just gasped.

The commander colored under their scrutiny and squirmed even more. "Okay, so I drugged them. It was still the right thing to do. They didn't belong in the Realm. And I had higher aspirations for Hunter than some chit with baggage."

"How dare you call my children baggage!" said Suzie in a low hiss.

Hunter put his hand on her arm to restrain her, although he felt just as incensed. But he still wanted some answers, so he choked back his anger and, instead, enveloped himself in an icy calm. He wanted to make things very clear to his father. "First off, Suzie is not some chit. She's a wonderful woman, whom I have come to love. And her children are a joy, not a burden, and I would be proud if they decided to accept me as their father. And finally, you had no right to make that kind of decision on my behalf. I told you before, and I will now tell you again, I will decide who I marry, not you."

"Adrian, what is wrong with you?" said Beverly sadly. "Don't you remember what we went through to be together? You know as well as I do that, had I not told my father I wanted you, he would have married me off to some other lord. How could you treat our son like that considering how you made us fight to be together?"

"I—um." The commander didn't look so commanding anymore with his family glaring at him. "I just wanted to do what was best for the family."

"What's best is letting our children choose their own paths and destinies so that they can find happiness and not be stuck in some loveless marriage. I, for one, think Hunter has made a marvelous choice. Suzie is a lovely, caring person with beautiful children. I think she would be a great asset to our family."

"But she's mundane!" exclaimed the commander. And there lay the crux of the problem. At least in his father's mind.

"And so are you!" Beverly shot right back. "Just because your parents weren't doesn't make you any better than her. Don't forget I know they had to buy your commission. And guess what? I still loved you in spite of it, and look, our children inherited the gifts you did not. I can't believe you, of all people, would hold that against her."

Hunter reeled, stunned at the revelation. He'd always assumed his father had the same extra senses he and Nat had inherited. The man always seemed larger than life, and tougher than everyone else, it was hard to believe his father had no extra powers.

Beverly turned so her back faced her husband, whose face sagged under the recriminations of his family.

"I just wanted to do the right thing," mumbled the commander. "I don't see what the big deal is."

"The big deal is you drugged not only Suzie but also children. Innocent little children. How did you know that the drugs wouldn't harm them? How dare you put them in that kind of danger." Beverly's eyes flashed in anger.

"Benson said he'd used it before. He said he knew what to do."

Hunter's eyes narrowed dangerously. But his mother's narrowed even more.

"The giving of drugs of any kind is no light matter. One miscalculation and there could have been dire consequences. Shame on you both for putting those children's lives in danger. Benson will find himself fired when I get back. And he can forget a letter of recommendation, as well," Beverly said venomously.

"I'd prefer to hit him," said Hunter. Yup, a couple of good, hard smacks in the face and Benson would think twice before ever trying something like that again.

"Get in line," said Nat gruffly. "And I owe you an apology, Suzie, for my behavior earlier. I, like an idiot, believed my father's stupid lie."

"It's all right," said Suzie. "It's always hard when someone you trust lies to you." Hunter felt his heart clench at the sadness in Suzie's eyes. It made him want to punch something again.

"But now, what about Father?" said Hunter, eyeing his father with disdain. "It's all well and good we can fire Benson, but then again, he was only following orders."

"I'm your father," blustered the commander. "You have to forgive me."

"Actually, I don't," said Hunter. "As far as I'm

concerned, you are no longer welcome in my home or my life. Get out. The sight of you right now sickens me."

"You can't do that," said his incredulous father.

"I can and I will. Maybe later, I'll be able to put aside what you've done, but right now, all I want to do is hurt you. So get out."

The commander looked at Beverly, who shrugged her shoulders. "You brought this on yourself. Count yourself lucky that I'm still coming home with you. As it is, you can move your things to another room. I need some time to think about what you've done, and I don't want you near me while I do it."

The commander shuffled out of the room, turning beseeching eyes at his daughter, who turned her head. He left the house not the same man who had come in, his arrogant tyranny vanquished with the revelations of his actions and condemnation of his family. A wake-up call that had been coming for years.

"Hunter," said Suzie. "Are you sure you want to do this? He is, after all, your father."

"Eventually maybe I'll forgive him, but not too quickly. He needs to understand that he can't decide everything. We're his family, not his soldiers, and he needs to learn what it means to be a father instead of a commander."

"Well spoken, my son," said his mother with pride. "So, what are you plans now?"

Hunter drew Suzie into the circle of his arm. "First, I convince the twins to let me marry their mother."

"Hey," Suzie laughed, looking up at him. "Don't I get a say?"

"No. I love you and don't ever intend to let you go. So you'll have to get used to me being around."

"Well, I think I can manage that," Suzie said, smiling up at him happily.

Hunter hugged her tight and stared into her eyes, drowning in the sweetness and love mirrored in there. To think he'd almost lost her.

"Oh by the higher powers," groaned Nat. "Go get a room. You two are so besotted it makes me sick. Go on, get out of here. Mother and I will watch the twins."

Hunter didn't need any more encouragement. With a quick good-bye to his mother and sister, he just about ran out of Suzie's house and dragged her next door to his.

They fell into his house, out of breath and laughing.

Suzie looked up at him with bright, shining eyes, and Hunter couldn't resist. He captured her sweet lips with his own, groaning when she opened them to slide a tentative tongue against his mouth. She tasted so sweet, and it was all he could not to rip off her clothes and take her pressed up against the wall. Something in the urgency of his kiss must have frightened her, for she pulled away from him and clasped her hands together nervously. What could be wrong? He'd told he loved her, that he wanted to marry her. Oh shit. He hadn't actually asked, had he? Sure, he'd boasted in front of his mother and Nat of never letting her go, but really, he should ask. Didn't all women have some kind of dream about romantic proposals? Heck, he'd seen enough of them in movies on this side of the boundary to know what was expected.

Hunter dropped to one knee in front of her and looked up at her, trying to show all the love he felt for her in his eyes. To his chagrin, though, she lowered her lashes and hid her eyes from him.

Something was definitely wrong. Fix it quick. Stupid him. When he'd come back to confront her, it had never occurred to him to bring her a ring. Could that be the problem? Women seemed to set great store by the size of the rock. He'd promise her a big one, a huge one that would have everyone envious.

Hunter cleared his throat. "Um, I know this might not be the romantic evening you'd pictured when I proposed to you." By the higher powers, he sucked at this. He'd never had a need for flowery words before, and now that he needed them, he felt tongue-tied like a boy asking a girl out on her first date.

"Hunter, wait." Suzie fluttered her hands at him.

"No, let me finish," he said, worried at the vibes her body was giving off. "I am not the most romantic of men, although, since meeting you, I wish I were."

"Oh, Hunter," she sighed. "I don't expect you to change on me. I love you just the way you are."

She loved him! Hunter felt like crowing. After all, it was the first time she'd said it out loud to him. Hold on, though, if she loved him, then why did she seem so nervous?

"Anyway," he said, continuing with his impromptu speech. "Since I've met you, I can't stop thinking about you. I think about waking up with you every day. Eating breakfast, lunch, and dinner with you. I want to hear every detail about your life, good and bad." Oh man, that sounded so lame, like something out of a B-movie, of which he'd watched too many.

"Oh God, you so don't want to hear about my boring life. But, Hunter, there's something I have to—"

Hunter cut her off, determined to say his piece. He hurried now. "I love you, Suzie, and want to be with you the rest of my life. It would be my greatest honor if you'd agree to be my wife. I wasn't really expecting to propose today, so I don't have a ring yet, but I promise you, I'll get you a ring, a big one," he added as she shook her head at him with a soft smile.

"Oh, Hunter," Suzie said, reaching out a hand to stroke his hair. "I would love to marry you, and I don't care about the ring, but first I need to tell you something."

What? he wanted to yell. What could she have to tell him that had her looking so nervous and green?

"Hunter, I'm—" Suzie never finished what she going to say. Instead, she ran to the kitchen and, with hands braced on his kitchen counter, proceeded to throw up in his sink.

To say he was stunned was an understatement. He'd never made a woman sick before. Was it something he'd done or said? Something she ate? He approached her, and he rubbed a large hand across her back, trying to soothe her as she stood there gagging and wracked with sobs.

Suzie ran the water then rinsed her mouth and face before turning a pale face to Hunter.

"What's wrong?" he asked. Maybe he should get his mother. If Suzie was sick, she could fix her.

"Before I agree to marry you, you need to know something." Suzie paused, as if gathering her courage, and

Hunter resisted an urge to shake her and tell her to hurry it up.

Suzie took a deep breath and said in a rush, "You need to know I'm pregnant."

Hunter felt his jaw drop. No, seriously it did, low enough to hit the floor. Suzie was pregnant. That meant he was going to be a daddy! As that piece of information filtered through his thick brain, he finally understood her stricken look. She thought he might change his mind. That the baby would scare him away. Like hell! But how to show her?

"Yippeee!" he yelled, picking her up and swinging her around exuberantly. Oops, bad idea. He saw her face turn green again and moved just in time to lean her over the sink when she heaved.

Hunter calmed his inner jubilation and wrapped his arms tight around her.

Suzie clung to him. "I wanted to tell you earlier, but then your mom and dad showed up, and things got all intense. And then you proposed, but I didn't want to accept unless you knew the truth. I'm so sorry. I should have told you right away," Suzie blabbered quickly. Hunter couldn't believe it. She still seemed afraid.

He tilted her chin up and looked into her eyes, those beautiful brown eyes. "Suzie, you didn't have a chance to tell me sooner. It's all right. And it doesn't change anything. I love you. I want you to be my wife. Being pregnant already just means we're one kid closer to the half-dozen I want."

Suzie gasped then giggled. "You're bad, six kids." She

chortled in his arms, and Hunter hugged her, so glad the stricken look was gone from her face.

"Are you sure it's okay?" she whispered. "I mean, it's kind of sudden, and with everything that's happened..."

Hunter would have silenced her with a kiss, but truth tell, a small part of him was a little afraid she'd be sick on him again. So instead, he hugged her tight, letting his hands roam across her back then lower, cupping her buttocks.

Suzie pulled back. "I don't suppose you have some mouthwash? I've got a case of it at home since I started getting sick."

"Have you been getting sick a lot?" he asked with concern. He'd have to ask his mother if that was normal and if there was anything they could do to help control it. No wonder she'd been so scared and distant when he first showed up. Pregnant and alone. Now he felt like an even bigger jerk for believing his dad.

"The nausea is pretty much all the time, but it should go away after the first trimester."

So much for him to learn about. His first child. He wanted to celebrate—naked. But first, mouthwash. He led her to the bathroom and let her clean herself up. While she did that, he ran up to his room and lit some candles and thanked Owen, or whoever else had tidied up his room and changed the sheets. He ran back down and leaned nonchalantly on the wall when she came out looking pale but no longer green.

Hunter smiled and opened his arms. Suzie dove into them and leaned her head against his chest. He scooped her up into his arms, such a yummy armful, and carried her upstairs. He laid her carefully on his bed, and it was as if the lights went out again. Her face got a shadowed look.

"Are you going to be sick again?" he asked, ready to scoop her up and whip her into the bathroom.

"No, but I understand if you don't want to make love to me right now."

Hunh? "Why wouldn't I want to?" She looked so scrumptious lying there, and her breath smelled minty fresh now. So what gave?

"Well, with me being pregnant and all."

Hunter sighed. "Suzie, please explain. Why would your being pregnant change my wanting to make love to you?"

Suzie shrugged and got a lost look on her face. Hunter wanted to smack himself as he suddenly clued in.

"Let me guess," he said, crawling onto the bed so he straddled her. "Damian stopped touching you once you got pregnant."

Suzie just nodded.

"Suzie, you'd have to be dead or seriously injured for me to not want to touch you. I know there's no medical reason not to make love. And I, for one, look forward to rediscovering every inch of your gorgeous body. No only that, but I promise you, even when you start showing and your belly gets big enough to cast a shadow, I will still find you the most beautiful woman ever."

Suzie's smile erupted like a rainbow after a storm. It lit up her face and made a promise of treasures at its end. Hunter felt his whole body tighten. Now, to prove to her he meant what he said.

He undressed her quickly, tossing her clothes onto the floor. He then peeled off his shirt and shucked off his pants till he stood there as nude as she was.

"Look at me, Suzie."

She looked up at him, uncertainty painted on her face. Her gasp when she saw the evidence of his arousal made him chuckle.

"Does this look like I don't want you?" he said.

She smiled then gasped again. "What happened to your shoulders?"

Oh yeah, he'd forgotten his new scars, courtesy of the Dragon. The healing from his mother hadn't been enough to erase the knotted white streaks of his last battle.

"A farewell gift from your ex."

"I'm so sorry. Do they hurt?" she asked softly, sitting up on her haunches and leaning forward to trace them with her fingers.

"They're still a little stiff, but a bit of stretching and exercise should take care of that."

Suzie leaned in closer and traced the jagged streaks with her tongue and lips, as if her kiss could erase them. They didn't disappear, but Hunter felt a whole lot better, make that a whole lot randier.

He wrapped his arms tightly around her and tumbled her back on the bed.

"You can play with those later," he growled against her. "I want to touch you like I've been dreaming of doing for the last month."

He almost breathed a sigh of relief when she giggled, a happy sound that made his heart swell. Okay, so he was going soft, but only where Suzie was concerned. He'd still punch the living daylights out of anybody who dared remark on it.

He slid down her body till he could see her beautiful breasts. Pregnancy agreed with them. They were even more bountiful than before, and he worshiped them reverently with his hands and lips, enjoying her little sighs and moans of pleasure as he played with them.

It had been so long, though, and he could feel himself already so close. The tantalizing feel of her body squirming under his made him so hard.

He nudged her opening and felt a glimmer of satisfaction when he realized how wet and ready she already was for him. Leaning up on his forearms, he thrust into her, looking her in the face as he did so, her eyes watching him dreamily as he slowly teased her.

"Please," she whispered.

And that simple word was his undoing. He pumped faster, eyes locked on hers, enjoying the feel of her body as it met his thrust for thrust. When he reached the edge of the abyss, she was right there with him, screaming as her body melted and convulsed around his, a whirlwind of pleasurable sensations that left them both winded.

Collapsed beside her, he cradled her in his arms. She nestled against him and said softly, "I love you, Hunter."

"Not as much as I love you," he murmured back. Gone were the doubts and fears that had plagued him. He'd found his one true love. The one who made him feel complete, happy, and made him want to be a better man. The hunter had finally been caught in love's net, but he had no intention of trying to break free. Truth be told, there was no place he'd rather be than wrapped in her arms and love.

And in the morning, after an almost sleepless night spent lovemaking, he still had a smile when two little imps dove onto the bed—at the crack of dawn—and said, "Hunta, why you and mommy naked?"

Suzie, thankfully, had an answer for that one. "When a man and a woman love each other, sometimes they like to snuggle."

"Naked," whispered Jessica. It was utterly emasculating, and just to be clear, he'd kill any man who accused him of blushing. Hunters don't blush, much.

EPILOGUE

Hunter stood on the back deck barbecuing while playing Frisbee at the same time with the twins. Sound impossible? Not with an ambidextrous husband it wasn't. Pretty handy in the bedroom sometimes too—sigh...

Jessie and Jared giggled as they whipped Frisbees at Hunter, who caught them one-handed while flipping the burgers. *Show off*, Suzie thought, grinning at the sight. The kids sure had thrived the last few months having a father around. Oh yes, Hunter had officially adopted them, to their glee, and they proudly called him Daddy. And he loved it! The first time the kids had called him by his new name, she'd thought he was going to cry. According to him, it had just been dust in his eye. Yeah, right.

They'd gotten married months ago at city hall with just the kids, his mother and sister, and his coworkers from the agency. A simple ceremony to Beverly's dismay.

She'd complained, "Now how will I get my white wedding?" looking pointedly at Nat who, to her credit, had only stuck out her tongue in reply. Suzie had dressed in a simple white empire summer dress, and Hunter had been devastatingly handsome in a three-piece suit. Nat—who actually wore a dress for the occasion—had been her maid of honor and Bob, Hunter's best man. They'd feasted at a restaurant before taking off to Niagara on their honeymoon, leaving the kids with their new grandma. Their wedding night still made her shiver. God, that man had talent!

Smiling in remembrance, Suzie lumbered out the backdoor, her eight-months-pregnant belly a ponderous but welcome weight. Only four more weeks to go before they'd get to meet baby Jason. Who needed an ultrasound for the gender when you had a mother-in-law who could just lay her hands on you?

Even the commander had softened when he heard the news. According to Beverly, he'd been strutting around crowing about the fact he was going to be a grandfather. Even better, he and Hunter were finally talking again. It was stilted and painful to watch, but at least they were both trying. The commander had even taken Suzie aside to apologize for his treatment of her—Suzie had checked the weather forecast right after to see if hell had frozen over. But it hadn't, and pigs weren't flying, yet. Just went to show that sometimes miracles could happen.

Hunter had been livid when he found out she'd forgiven him and invited him to be there when the baby was born. But his anger had been an easy thing to fix. A little striptease and he suddenly ended up on the same page as her. Amazing man. The bigger she got with his child, the sexier he found her. He seemed to always be grabbing her ass, rubbing her big belly, or nuzzling her enlarged boobs—when the kids weren't looking, of course. She might have felt like an elephant, but according to him, she looked like a glowing goddess, and he kept proving it to her. Over and over again. Boy, did she love him.

Only one baby in there this time, thank God, although Hunter had been disappointed. He still dreamed of half a dozen kids. Suzie had half a mind to give them to him. He'd turned into an awesome father, and his new job as head of the department of Realm Incursions meant he didn't go out in the field anymore. Bob had left for the Realm, a promotion that had his jolly belly shaking with glee. And, of course, Hunter still had his private eye business, which had been picking up lately. He was just too good at finding things. He'd even had to hire an assistant investigator, his sister.

Yes, Nat had moved from the Realm into Hunter's old house next door. Suzie had been ecstatic as she and her gruff sister-in-law had become the best of friends. Nat had not only taken a job helping Hunter with his detective work but had also taken over Hunter's old position of hunter and tracker with the agency. The kids loved having their Aunt Nat nearby—she was currently teaching them hand-to-hand combat, using Hunter as her dummy. Poor man. Although she found it hard to feel sorry for him, seeing as he grinned and cheered every time the kids bruised him.

Even wilder than the commander apologizing, Nat

had a boyfriend. A giant of a man with a hot body who was an up-and-coming UFC fighter. Nat had said with a wink that he made her almost feel dainty and girlie. And nope, hell hadn't frozen over when she'd said it. He'd won her heart after beating her in an arm-wrestling match. It was love at first sight—er, pin.

Suzie eased her weight into her sling back chair on the deck with a sigh of relief. Yes, life was good, and it just kept getting better and better. Feeling the baby kick, she rubbed her belly with a smile. Strong little sucker, just like his daddy.

Suddenly, the air around her went still, an expectant hush that she could almost feel, that tingling electrical feel before something momentous happened. Suzie gasped as a multi-colored flash lit up the sky and radiated outward, going through her body like a shockwave. Hunter, in the middle of flipping a burger, actually staggered, and a flying Frisbee not only hit him in the head he also dropped the burger! A clumsy first.

The weird phenomenon disappeared as quickly as it hit, but the residual effect did not. The air now hummed lowly, and her yard seemed brighter. A whole new dimension seemed to have been added to the world, and everything felt more alive and vivid.

The kids squealed in the yard, and when they looked at Suzie, she could see them shimmer like they had back in the Realm before they shifted into dragonlings.

Uh-oh!

"What the hell was that?" exclaimed Suzie, first to recover the ability to speak.

Hunter looked around him, dumbfounded. "The boundary came down! Magic is loose in the world again."

"How can you tell?" asked Suzie as junior in her tummy gave a few energetic kicks.

"I can feel it." Hunter laughed. "I bet the commander and the council are wetting their pants right now."

Suzie's brow knitted in a frown. "What does that mean to us and the rest of the world, though?" How would this change their lives?

"Magical things are about to happen, my love. The world is about to get a whole lot more interesting."

And it did. Especially later that night in bed when Hunter, whose special senses were now awake again, showed her some new techniques that had her screaming in all the right ways.

The world, and their lives, would never be the same again.

The other books in The Realm

THE END

Even more books at EveLanglais.com

www.ingramcontent.com/pod-product-compliance
Lightning Source LLC
LaVergne TN
LVHW041623060526
838200LV00040B/1407